TIC

'I could suck it,' she said, cupping his balls in one hand, her other on his penis. 'I'd kneel for you and take you in my mouth. I'd roll your balls over my tongue and kiss your anus. I'd suck until you came and play with the sperm in my mouth or lick it from your hand –'

'Ciriel,' he said warningly and removed her hand from his penis.

'Think of my lips, soft and warm on your beautiful cock,' she continued. 'Think of my mouth running with your sperm. Or you could do it inside me, deep in my vagina.'

'Ciriel, I have warned you,' Comus said sharply. 'Stop tormenting me or I'll not only slap your bottom to a ruddy pink but leave you tied for the night with a measure of oil of pimento in your rectum. Do you recall how it burns?'

'Yes, Mentor,' Ciriel answered, 'but not so much as it does when your penis is coated with it and in my bottom.'

By the same author:

THE RAKE
MAIDEN

TIGER, TIGER

Aishling Morgan

*Dedicated to Dr Richard Hetherington,
without whose work Suza could never
have been created.*

This book is a work of fiction.
In real life, make sure you practise safe sex.

First published in 1999 by
Nexus
Thames Wharf Studios
Rainville Road
London W6 9HA

Typeset by TW Typesetting, Plymouth, Devon

Printed and bound by
Cox & Wyman Ltd, Reading, Berks

ISBN 0 352 33455 X

Contents

1

Inception

Tian-Sha laid down her stylus and set her eyes to the oval of the window. Beyond lay the night of Suza; warm, still and rich with myriad scents and sounds. Each was known to her, creating a familiar and concordant melody of sensations. On a common night this would have been no more than the accustomed background to her thoughts, to be noticed only if disturbed by some unfamiliar element. Now it had her nose twitching and set the hairs on her spine rising and falling in a slow rhythm.

Once more she took up her stylus. Applying it to the parchment in front of her, she formed the elaborate shape of an orthodox capital, only to stop once more. She rose abruptly, then stepped to the window, leaving a ragged ellipse of dampness on the seat of her chair. Outside a brilliant moon illuminated Suza, casting dark shadows among the tumbled confusion of roof, garden, dome and spire. The dominant hot sienna tone of day was now reduced to a dull tan, with the brilliant highlights of malachite, scarlet, lapis and gold faded to pale tones. Terrace after terrace fell away below her, ending in the distant wall beyond which low hills showed as dun outlines against the night sky.

Her nose wrinkled and her ears came forward as she focused on the scents of the city. The heady zests of orange, lime and jasmine formed the strongest notes, undercut by earth, dung and human scents. Of these there were many thousand, each distinct, each a pattern unique to one of Suza's inhabitants. Despite being invisible to her, the scents of the suan guards on the far parapets were evident, their porcine tang mixed with leather, bronze polish and tusk oil. Each, she knew, would be bored, restless and more than willing to fulfil the needs that were now building rapidly inside her.

A low purr rose from deep in her throat at the thought – their snouts pushing on to her neck, mouth and breasts – their thick fingers pawing at her buttocks, stroking the fur of her belly, pulling at her tail – their cocks twisting into her vagina; rough, urgent, male . . .

With a single lithe movement she rose to the sill of the window, bracing herself in its tall oval, a shape to mirror the marking of dark fur that ringed her sex. The hair on her spine was now fully erect, a low ridge of russet and black fur. As she drew deeply at the hot night air her claws unsheathed and her mouth opened to a smile that revealed sharp fangs and a small, pointed tongue. Running a single claw up from the soft, pale down of her belly, she teased herself, touching the shallow dimple of her navel, tracing the low, hard swell of her stomach. Finding the lowest and smallest pair of breasts, she touched each nipple in turn, bringing them to erection and then moving higher until all six stood proud and firm from the pale ginger pelt of her chest.

With each breath her excitement rose, but she held herself back, allowing her need for sex to rise to a burning urgency as she scanned the city. The guards, she knew, would be good as a start, rough and brisk, eager only for the rapid satisfaction of their corkscrew cocks in the damp embrace of her vagina. Once she had taken five or six she would be ready for something less abrupt, a true-man who could be used as she pleased or a felian who would mate her with a lust that best reflected her own.

She sheathed a claw and put a finger to her vulva, finding it moist and swollen, the vagina gaping and sensitive, the clitoris a hard bud, too tender to bear her own touch. Her mouth opened, emitting a high, vibrant call of pure need. Forgetting all restraint, she tore away the loinwrap of light silk that was her sole garment and leapt from the window, landing neatly on the roof some three times her own height below.

Within moments she had crossed the maze of tile, stone and garden that separated her chambers from the wall and was among the suanthropes. Surprise and aggression quickly turned to pleasure as they realised who she was and why she was there. Soon six pig-cocks stood proud from their owner's belly armour as the guards watched their Warden mount up between her open thighs.

Her claws raked his bronze-clad back and her hips met his thrust for thrust in the frenzy of their copulation. With one hand he gripped the hair of her head, the other pulling at her tail to bring her lust to ever more manic heights. Within moments the couple climaxed to a crescendo of Tian-Sha's hissing and the Warden's frantic squeals, then separated, leaving the first guard to take his place. Each one she accepted, until all seven had taken their fill and her vagina was running with the same thick, sticky sperm that matted the hair of her inner thighs, belly and the tuck of her buttocks. Only then did she rise again, purring deep in her throat and leaving a sticky pool on the warm stone of the parapet. To the sound of ribald boasts and demands for more from the suans, she stole back into the shadows of the city, now intent on less hasty and more refined prey.

Her head was thick with the smell of suan sperm and her own sex, making it hard to pick individual scents from the air. A deep stone trough at the edge of a roof garden provided water, and with a few economical

3

motions of fingers and tongue she had cleaned her fur. Calmer than before, but still with a deep need for the satisfaction of cock inside her, she climbed to a high roof and stood looking across the city, her nose wrinkling for the subtleties of scent that would allow her to choose a suitable mate.

Suza now reared above her, a great crag of rock and masonry, foliage and the bright shapes of those windows still lit. Above it all stood the citadel, twin towers of stone rising high into the night sky with their connecting bridges showing as black arcs. For an instant a smile crossed her lips, only to return to the set of sexual tension as she became aware of a new and intriguing scent.

This held the musk of the male true-man, less heavy than the suan smell, lacking the bite of the felian. There was leather with it, but only as a minor undertone, while a *melange* of spices, herbs and distillates combined in a flare of scent that could come from only one person. With her mouth open and her fur once more prickling along the length of her back, she made for the source of the scent.

Comus pushed through the lich-gate, his eyes intent on the path illuminated by the flickering orange light of his torch. Between that and the moonlight, the tombyard was broken into a patchwork of shadows in a thousand shades of silver, orange and black. Struggling to adjust his eyes, he moved forward.

Among the tombs and statues of the yard were clumps of ebony ashwort, each carefully tended. Tonight, with the full moon soaking the ground, the herb would yield the strongest and purest essence; each drop sufficient to spice the grease yield of a good sized duck. Alternatively, doubly distilled and made into a black paste with charred bone, the extract provided a virulent poison.

Noting the characteristic statue of a long-dead Lord of Suza, he moved to the right, only to halt abruptly. Ahead was a figure, tall and lithe, the red fur, pointed ears and tail revealing the nature of a tigranthrope, while the soft curve of hip and the half-lit shapes of six firm, high breasts showed undoubted femininity. Comus' initial alarm died as he recognised the features of Tian-Sha, calligrapher of architects. Desire and a faint unease replaced it as he realised that there was only one reason why she would be in the tombyard in the dead time of the night.

'Tian-Sha,' he greeted her, 'you do me honour, but perhaps in my rooms, after a flask of muscat and a little essence of cathridine . . .'

'No, now.'

Tian-Sha took three fast steps forward, then stopped to stand at the side of a squat tomb, deathly still, her slit eyes reflecting a brilliant green in the light of Comus' torch. Her fur showed burning red, brighter even than the reality, the black stripes rich and glossy in contrast, the paler down of her breasts and belly catching orange highlights.

She stepped forward, her tail twitching to one side, then the other. Comus watched, entranced by her salacious elegance as she pulled herself on to the marble slab that surmounted the tomb. She faced him on all fours, her eyes burning into his, then spun abruptly to display the rounded muscularity of her bottom with her tail swishing gently from side to side above it. Comus could feel his cock stiffening and the scent of her sex was rich in his nostrils. He moved forward, his fingers working at the pegs of his trousers and his eyes held fast to the mesmeric sight of her tail moving back and forth over the stripy globes of her bottom.

Suddenly she rolled, her thighs spreading to reveal the wet flesh of her sex, the centre of an oval target of black fur in the ginger-white down of her belly. Overcome by

5

lust, Comus dropped the torch and hastily pulled himself on to the tomb. He mounted her, putting his cock straight to her sex. She hissed as it slid into the warm, wet embrace of her vagina, her arms coming hard around his back even as his chest met the soft fur of her high-thrust breasts. Her thighs clamped hard around his body, locking him into her as he began to work his cock inside her vagina.

His lust was running high, the feel of her fur and the musk of her body driving him to a frenzied pumping that was mirrored by her jerking thighs. Their lips met, her sharp tongue touching his, then a fang bruising his lip as her claws tore through the linen of his shirt and sank into his back. Comus cried out, half in pain, half in ecstasy. Tian-Sha paid no heed, but only jammed his body tighter against her own with a powerful contraction of her thighs.

Comus tried to slow the pace of his thrusts, only to have her jam him hard into herself, overriding his will with the same ease that he might have dictated the pace of copulation with an ordinary wench. With Tian-Sha there was no such choice, and his body was quickly being jerked into hers like a doll, his erect cock ramming home inside her with ever greater energy as her mouth worked against his and her claws raked his back. Before really knowing it he was coming, his cock jerking inside her, once, twice and then a last time with a spasm of agonising ecstasy as her teeth locked in the flesh of his shoulder. He screamed, his sperm still flooding into her as her legs continued to force his cock in and out of her vagina.

Her movements became frantic, her clawing de-mented, the bucking of her hips a manic frenzy that set her buttocks slapping against the cold marble of the tomb. For a moment Comus felt sure that he would die in the heat of her climax, and then she threw her head back and screamed, high and long into the night air, the call echoing among the tombs and the buildings beyond until it finally died to leave a silence broken only by their breathing.

Comus dismounted, pulling his cock from Tian-Sha's now inert body and raising himself to his knees. His body was wet with sweat and blood, his shirt torn to a sodden scrap of linen, his legs and buttocks bruised from the sheer force of her passion. Unable to find words to express the pain and ecstasy of his experience, he could only stare as Tian-Sha raised herself and came forward, then kissed him on the lips with as much tenderness as any true-woman had shown him after an act of love. He responded, allowing his mouth to open under hers and their tongues to meet in a long gentle kiss. The ferocity of her first passion seemed entirely gone, and he reached out a tentative hand to find her breasts. Cupping one, he felt her begin to purr, a deep, rhythmic throbbing at the back of her throat. Growing bolder, he squeezed the fullness of her breast and allowed a thumb to graze her nipple. She pulled closer and he felt a hand cup his scrotal sac, the claws tickling and moving his testicle with a tenderness extraordinary in one so powerful.

Trying to ignore the biting pain in his back, he settled down to make love to her, slowly and carefully in the way of true-humans, indulging each other's bodies to the full. As she coaxed his penis back to erection he explored her breasts, feeling the shape of all six and bringing the nipples to erection one after another. Each pair were two full mounds of flesh grown with soft down, the highest pair largest, the two lower each smaller in proportion. As his fingers worked patterns on her chest her kisses became fiercer and the energy with which she worked his balls and penis grew.

Finding himself ready, he moved into a squat and drew her body towards his own. Her arms went around his neck as his hands filled with her tight, muscular

7

buttocks. Lifting her bottom, he mounted her on his penis and she gave a long, sibilant hiss as the length of it slid up her vagina. She came forward, smothering his face in the downy flesh of her chest and starting to bounce on his cock.

Comus found a hard nipple with his teeth and began to suckle her as he cradled her bottom under one arm and took hold of her tail. Her purring grew louder as he tugged at the root of her tail and dug his nails into her bottom and she began to ride faster, bouncing energetically on his erection. In no hurry to come, he began to explore her bottom, touching the furry groove where her tail met the crease of her bottom. Her cheeks felt firm, the fur thick and smooth, then thicker still and changing to a dense fluff down close to her sex. A brief naked patch marked her anus, which he touched gently, pushing his finger at the tight ring but holding short of penetration at her warning growl.

'Make me do it, but not that way. Pull my tail,' she hissed.

He complied, putting both hands to her tail and giving a sharp tug. She hissed and pulled herself sharply against him, altering the set of her hips to bring her clitoris into intimate contact with his pubic hair. He tugged again and she began to buck, hissing and yowling as she brought herself slowly towards her peak. As her muscles tensed in his lap and her vagina locked hard on his penis he gave her tail a hard wrench. A scream rewarded his efforts and Tian-Sha came in his lap, bucking and writhing against him until he could take no more and ejaculated deep inside her for the second time.

Exhausted, Comus slumped back on to the cool marble of the tomb. His back burned with pain and he could feel the damp of blood in several places, while his cock felt bruised and drained. Tian-Sha dismounted with an easy grace that showed none of his tiredness.

Then, folding her legs beneath her, she began to lick her fur.

Filled with a sudden strong feeling of being an intruder, Comus jumped down from the tomb. He gave a courteous farewell, but Tian-Sha made no response. As he made his way off across the moonlit tombyard, he looked back only once, finding the tigranthrope silhouetted against the sky, one elegant leg raised high as she tongued herself clean.

High above, in the main chamber of the male citadel tower, Pallus the Lord of Suza lay stretched on a pallet, his breathing slow and shallow, his expression one of deep weariness. Despite the patterns of grey and white among the black of his fur and the deep lines of his face, he retained a rare elegance and nobility. Intelligence still shone from his eyes, along with a fierce will to live. Yet it was plain that he was dying, and although the distant scents and sounds that drifted in through the window brought a smile to his lips, it was as much of regret as of pleasure.

In a malachite-roofed dome adjoining the citadel, an act of love was approaching its climax. Ilarion, second of the male citadel of Suza, sat at ease on a couch, his patrician face set in an expression of languid pleasure, his robe of deep-blue velvet raised to his midriff. Between his open knees knelt Zara, a true-girl whose mouth and tongue were busy with his genitals. Her position left the broad hemispheres of her bottom spread wide, with the soft swell and wet centre of her sex on full show. What clothes she wore, a short kirtle of saffron silk and large, loose culottes, were pulled up and down respectively to bare her glorious curves. Occasionally Ilarion would give her an instruction, or stroke her opulent bottom with the lash of the long goad he held in one elegant hand. Eight scarlet lines across the alabaster skin of her buttocks showed the consequences of an earlier stage of their love-play.

'A little lower, Zara, my pleasure,' he directed. 'Yes, wonderful. Now take the testicles into your mouth.'

She obeyed, placing three fingers beneath his scrotum and flipping the mass gently into her mouth. Ilarion gave a quiet groan of satisfaction as she once more began to suck, rolling his balls across her tongue as her fingernails tickled the sensitive flesh between the root of his genitals and his anus.

'Exquisite,' he remarked, 'continue in that manner, but ring my foreskin with your free hand.'

Zara moved her fingers from where she had been busy with one of her nipples and circled his cock. He was fully erect, the foreskin pulled down into a taut, fleshy mass which she began to rub. Ilarion groaned again as she started to masturbate him and she felt him tense in the first motion of orgasm.

The faint jingle of the beaded jet and amber curtain that shut off the apartment signalled the arrival of a newcomer, a tall, spare man of appearance strikingly similar to Ilarion. Zara hesitated only briefly and made no move to hide the intimate details of her open bottom and thighs, instead raising herself a fraction to exaggerate the flare of her hips from her tight waist and to better display the beauty of her richly furred sex and tightly puckered anus.

'Xerinus, brother,' Ilarion greeted the man. 'Give me a moment to allow Zara the full expression of her skills.'

Xerinus nodded and stepped back, watching politely as Zara performed her task, his interest born as much of technical criticism as of lust. Releasing Ilarion's balls from her mouth, she quickly substituted his cock. Ilarion swallowed as a spittle-wet finger penetrated his anus and her hand squeezed his testicles even as her mouth closed firmly on his shaft. With a sudden gasp he came, ejaculating deep into her throat as she

10

manipulated his organ. After swallowing she cleaned him with a few carefully placed dabs of her tongue and then stood, allowing her kirtle to half cover her welted bottom but not troubling to hide her heavy breasts.

'Shiraz of Alaban, my pleasure,' Ilarion ordered, 'and five cups, the etched silver.'

Zara bowed her head and left the room, kicking her silken culottes free of her feet as she went.

'She is skilled at her art,' Xerinus remarked as he watched the sweet movement of Zara's bottom as she left.

'Exceptionally so, for her age,' Ilarion replied. 'If she has a fault it is that she is inclined to be perfunctory, and not allow her own passion to come to the front until her male is spent.'

'Some would see that as a virtue,' Xerinus answered. 'Myself included. You are right to enjoy her mouth, yet my own particular pleasure is to come between her breasts, which are of a size and shape rare even among true-girls. Others can suck and lick, none have breasts like Zara.'

'A pleasure indeed! But here are Urzon and Lomas.'

Two more entered the room, both suanthropes with the tusks and heavy bodies characteristic of the genotype. As with the two true-men, both wore deep blue to indicate their rank as councillors, only instead of simple robes these were elaborate garments of several pieces. Each took a goblet of wine from the returning Zara, greeting her with gruff snorts and eyeing her naked breasts with undisguised relish. Of the two, Urzon stood taller and the ridge of hair that ran backwards from his scalp showed only a trace of grey among ruddy brown. Lomas was broad, his great belly stretching out the fabric of his tunic, while his hair was pure white.

Zara gave each a respectful bob that made her breasts wobble and draw fresh noises of admiration, then she

11

offered her tray to the two true-men. Each took a goblet as greetings were exchanged and then the curtain rustled once again.

A sixth figure entered the room, close to the height of Urzon but with a natural grace in place of the suanthrope's ungainly bulk. Red fur banded with black and paling to his front marked him as a tigranthrope, while there was little to show his age. He nodded to the others and took a goblet before curling himself on to a couch in a fluid motion.

'Khian-Shu,' Ilarion greeted the newcomer, 'and so we are complete. To work then. What news of the Lord?'

'Lord Pallus is fading,' Khian-Shu replied. 'With all his strength he can have no more than days left to him.'

'Then it is certain,' Ilarion answered. 'We must decide, it seems, upon a new Lord.'

'Can there be a choice?' Urzon demanded.

'There is always a choice,' Xerinus put in.

'Not now,' Lomas grunted. 'Who but Otomos is a hero to the full populace? Who but Otomos has the power to hold the Lordship?'

'None, it is true,' Ilarion admitted, 'but has he the experience? Has he the skill at diplomacy?'

'To the former,' Lomas answered, 'we will advise him. To the latter – he has no time for such niceties, preferring to crush his opponents, as he did at Arajan ford.'

'What of you, Khian-Shu?' Ilarion asked. 'You lead the soldiery and are Otomos' chief. Surely you have a prior right to stand for the Lordship.'

'My position is this,' Khian-Shu stated carefully. 'I realise that after thirty-four years of Lord Pallus' Lordship neither true-man nor suan cliques will want the Lordship to be held by another felian. Yet should Otomos become Lord then three seats of the council will be held by suans. Thus he may count on my vote as long

12

as one or other of you surrenders his seat in favour of a felian candidate. Besides, his Uhlans already call him Lord, and others, not only suans.'

For a long moment there was silence, then Lomas spoke.

'For over twenty years I have been third male in Suza. I will surrender my place in order to see my son take the Lordship. What of you, Ilarion, Xerinus?'

'I have reservations, as you know,' Ilarion replied. 'Yet I can conceive no other suitable candidate. If Khian-Shu does not seek election then Otomos must have my vote. The Lord Pallus I believe is also prepared to support him.'

'Reluctantly, but yes,' Khian-Shu replied.

'My vote also must go to Otomos then,' Xerinus announced, 'and I trust that our wise council will rein his aggression. On another key, I cannot imagine that the Lady Alla-Sha will enjoy the news. She shuns Otomos even when in her heat of season.'

'Rein his aggression!' Urzon retorted. 'With Otomos as Lord we will swallow our neighbours and build an empire from sea to sea! As to the Lady Alla-Sha, she may either learn to accept him as mate or vacate her position as first of the female citadel!'

'The Lady may well step down,' Khian-Shu put in, 'but only in favour of a strong successor, and certainly not a suan.'

'Otomos will want Pomina as mate,' Urzon stated, 'and besides, what true-girl could accommodate his phallus? What felian could endure his lovemaking?'

'Pomina lacks the potency to be Lady,' Khian-Shu retorted.

'What of it? With Otomos as Lord . . .'

'Friends, friends,' Ilarion broke in, 'that is a problem for the council of the female citadel and not for us. However, perchance Zara can enlighten us as to how the pattern lies in the female citadel?'

13

'The Lady Alla-Sha prefers that Khian-Shu succeed, Master,' Zara answered softly. 'Her vote would stand his way.'

'Naturally,' Lomas remarked, 'but it carries no weight with six against it.'

'Yet she recognises the difficulties involved,' Zara went on. 'Should Otomos succeed I do not know her decision.'

'Councillor Rufina would dearly love to be Lady,' Xerinus remarked.

'Rufina!' Urzon exclaimed. 'I would give half of what I own to see that haughty she-devil impaled on Otomos' cock!'

'She would never allow such a thing,' Zara answered.

'Quite so,' Ilarion said thoughtfully. 'We are agreed then? Upon the death of Lord Pallus the Lordship will be offered to Otomos without dissent?'

All agreed with varying enthusiasm and the discussion turned to other matters while Zara continued to serve wine and provide the spectacle of her superb breasts and neatly whipped bottom. At length the two suanthropes rose to leave, followed by Khian-Shu.

Xerinus bowed politely to the departing tigranthrope and then turned back to his brother. For a space he waited, listening to the footsteps of the departing councillors and admiring the swell of Zara's breasts. The girl returned a coy smile and cupped the heavy globes in her hands, offering them for the preference that Xerinus had stated earlier.

'How kind, my pleasure,' Xerinus addressed her, 'but do you not have other appointments tonight?'

'Not that are urgent, Master,' Zara answered.

'No, no,' Xerinus responded, 'you must keep your schedule. Visit me tomorrow; perhaps a glass before sundown.'

'With pleasure, Master.'

Zara bobbed her head to Ilarion and Xerinus in turn

14

and went to retrieve her culottes. Both men watched with unconcealed pleasure as she wriggled her full buttocks into the thin silk. Still struggling to fully cover her ample bottom, she made a hurried exit through the curtain.

'An exquisite girl,' Xerinus remarked.

'Undoubtedly,' Ilarion agreed, 'so why did you not take advantage of her offer?'

'Because I suspect that her next appointment is not related to her art but is with the Lady Alla-Sha,' Xerinus answered.

'Indeed, and she will report that the male council is to support Otomos for the Lordship without dissent. But what of it? The Lady would have learnt soon enough.'

'True, but I feel that you share my doubts about the suitability of Otomos.'

'Otomos is a gross brute and his Lordship will bring us largely strife, but perhaps also greater wealth and power.'

'Not so. Since Arajan ford our strength is perhaps three times that of any other city. No one can stand, but with Otomos as Lord I foresee as many as seven cities in league against us and we can only succumb.'

'Unlikely; there are too many old feuds to be overcome. Anyhow, Otomos has a hero's status among the populace, and he has the council's support. Who could challenge him?'

'Someone must. We need a diplomatist, not a warrior.'

'But who?'

'Overtly, none.'

'And covertly?'

'Comus.'

'The essencier?'

'The same.'

'Why?'

'He is intelligent, refined, well known and generally liked. Also devious, cunning and subtle.'

'Good qualities in a Lord, but he is also something of a narcissist, and said to practise sodomy.'

'The populace see vanity as normal in a Lord, desirable even. As to the sodomy, that is a problem for the women he chooses to mount.'

'He is also your son, is he not?'

'Possibly, although several might claim otherwise, including the Lord himself, which gives an added strength to the suggestion.'

'True, yet how do you propose he mounts his challenge?'

'Not easily, yet if he is worthy of the Lordship he will succeed. If he is not he will fail, which is as it should be.'

'I cannot say I share your philosophy, yet you may assure him that if he mounts a realistic challenge he may be assured of two votes on the council.'

Far below across the moonlit roofscape of Suza, Tian-Sha sat mounted on a fat young suanthrope, his penis twisting in and out of her vagina as she rode him. She had caught him relieving himself in a roof garden, and the first he had known of her presence was the soft pad of her hand closing on his exposed genitals.

After the initial shock he had gleefully accepted his fate and allowed her to lay him down on the soft sward, coax his penis to erection with her claws and mount him. Now his grunts of pleasure were turning to the squeals of approaching climax as she moved on him and his fingers fumbled clumsily at her bouncing breasts. Twice she peaked herself before his sperm flooded into her with a sudden gush – and then she was gone, vanishing among a cluster of chimneys as silently and as suddenly as she had arrived.

* * *

As Ilarion and Xerinus supposed, Zara had fled directly to the Lady Alla-Sha with news of Otomos' acceptance as Lord Presumptive. Entering the bedchamber at the heart of the female citadel, she found the Lady stretched out on a couch with a vial of essence of lime at her side. Seeing Zara, she extended a languid arm to adjust the loose loinwrap of heavy black silk that was her only garment.

Despite her years, her body showed few signs of age. Pure white fur covered her sleek curves, broken only at the pink of her nipples and vulva. Her face showed a calm intelligence, now marred by sadness as her mate lay dying in the adjoining tower of the citadel of Suza.

'So,' she addressed Zara as the girl approached, 'is it to be my beautiful Khian-Shu or the grotesque Otomos?'

'Otomos, my Lady,' Zara replied.

'As I feared,' Alla-Sha sighed.

'It is generally supposed that you will step down, my Lady,' Zara continued.

'Step down?' Alla-Sha retorted with an immediate flush of temper that faded as suddenly as it had risen. 'Perhaps, rather than endure being mated by Otomos. Who though would take my place? Rufina is a termagant, Pomina a giggling girl . . .'

The remarks were directed not at Zara but to the warm night beyond the window of the tower. Bobbing her head, the girl moved away to leave the lady Alla-Sha with her thoughts.

Leaving the citadel, Zara made for her room. The slaps of her bare feet on the worn flags of corridors and stairs sounded loud in her ears as she went. Repeatedly she found herself glancing back over her shoulder, only to walk directly into a tall true-girl at a junction.

'Mistress . . . my pardon,' she stammered as she recognised the second female of Suza, Rufina.

'Zara, my pleasure,' Rufina purred, placing a taloned

17

finger under the girl's chin and tilting it upwards. 'I had hoped to chance upon you.'

Zara looked up into Rufina's eyes, finding cold power that sent a tremor of apprehension the length of her spine. Although the form of her body ran pure to her mother's genes, as it always did, Rufina's build owed more than a little to her father, Lord Pallus. She stood a full head taller than Zara and her body was slender and taut, feminine but not luxuriant. Her jet black hair also came from her father and was twisted into tight coils, adding to her natural severity and making a striking contrast to Zara's tumble of brown curls. A clinging sheath of leather covered her body from neck to thighs while a cloak of deep-blue velvet showed her council rank. At her waist hung a long whip of oiled cane that ended in a braided leather snake's tongue.

For a long moment she held Zara's gaze and then abruptly tilted the girl's chin up still further. Zara could feel her lower lip trembling and found herself suddenly conscious of the mild throb of the whip marks that decorated her bottom.

'So,' Rufina addressed her, 'what of the male council?'

'Otomos is Lord Presumptive, Mistress.'

'That vile pigman! I had hoped for better! Was there no dissent?'

'No, Mistress.'

Rufina hissed and made a sudden movement of her hand, taking Zara by the throat.

'Mistress . . .'

'Silence!'

Zara felt the tall woman's grip tighten. Her body was lifted, held by the throat until she was on the balls of her feet. She found herself shaking hard as a hand began to explore her, sharp nails tracing a slow line down over her breasts to the curve of her belly.

'Do you know how I detest the obstruction of my

18

needs, little one?' Rufina whispered as her eyes bored into Zara's.

Zara nodded weakly in response. Abruptly, Rufina took one of Zara's full buttocks in her hand and squeezed.

'You have been whipped?' Rufina demanded.

'Lightly, Mistress,' Zara replied.

'Too lightly, I suspect, if it was by that effete harlequin, Ilarion. Do you have further appointments?'

'No, Mistress.'

'Then you are mine for the night. Come.'

Zara was dropped and followed without protest as Rufina strode away. Knowing full well that the councillor's anger and spite was about to be taken out on her body, she found herself shaking. Her apprehension increased as they followed the corridors and stairs of Suza, walking in the flickering red of torchlight or the pale silver of the moon. Never once did Rufina turn, but walked ahead with the absolute certainty that Zara would follow. They climbed, ascending level after level until Rufina stopped at the entrance to a dark stairwell. Zara gave a frightened glance at the blackness within the archway, to which Rufina responded with a cruel smile.

The stairs curved down, a tight spiral of cool, smooth stone that Zara followed with her heart hammering in her chest. Another arch opened at the bottom, through which she stepped. A trickle of fluid ran down the inside of her thigh, warm against the suddenly chill air.

A light-well admitted pale radiance from far above, showing an iron ring that hung by a silk rope from a boss at the centre of the ceiling. Dark shadows hid other details of the chamber: rough-hewn stone and shapes that brought her images of tightly bound limbs and the pain of whips and hot unguents. She heard Rufina enter behind her and a hand caught her shoulder, spinning her round.

She stood trembling at the centre of the chamber while Rufina lit a torch, increasing the light and adding an orange tone, both of which served to enhance details of the chamber that Zara would have preferred to remain in gloom. To the fore was a grotesque homuncule of beaten bronze, its naked body worked to enhance the repulsive details of its salacious face, bloated belly and a set of grotesque genitals out of all proportion to the squat body. It was in a seated pose, the belly and balls splayed out on its crossed legs. The penis reared from the centre of its lap, forming a thick, blunt spike that rose some two spans above its pointed head.

Realising the function of the awful thing, Zara swallowed hard and then gasped as Rufina's hand locked in the front of her kirtle and tore it down, exposing her breasts. Even as the torn silk fluttered to the floor around her ankles Rufina had taken a heavy globe in hand and squeezed, digging her long nails into the soft flesh. Zara choked at the pain, but sighed as the palm of Rufina's hand brushed the stiff bud of her nipple. With a faint noise of contempt Rufina stood back, releasing Zara's breast.

The girl was quickly stripped; her culottes pulled down and off to leave her naked. Her torn kirtle was then twisted around her wrists and knotted to the iron ring, leaving her helpless. Loosening the silk rope from its cleat, Rufina adjusted it to leave Zara hanging from the ring by her hands with only her toes in contact with the floor.

Twisting the rope back on to the cleat, Rufina moved to the brazen homuncule and pushed it to a point directly beneath the ceiling boss, leaving Zara no option but to part her thighs around it. The girl's eyes were round, her mouth wide in horrified anticipation as she felt the cold, smooth bronze against her calves. Rufina moved back to the cleat and, with her mouth set in a malicious grin, started to lower her victim on to the waiting phallus.

As her body sank slowly down, Zara felt the cold bronze of the homuncule's massive penis touch her thighs, then the bulge of her sex. The instinct to writhe away was strong, but matched by the need to know the feeling of having the huge, cold phallus within her. The head was at her vulva, pushing the lips apart, nudging at the wet hole, stretching her open, sliding within . . .

Rufina laughed as Zara's vagina filled with cold, hard metal. Only when the peak of the homuncule's pointed head was lodged between the girl's buttocks did Rufina again cleat the rope off, leaving Zara in an obscene squat with two spans of thick, hard penis in her vagina and a blunt metal stub pressed against her anus.

With her severe mouth set in a light smile, Rufina circled her victim, pacing slowly on long, elegant legs and pausing occasionally to flick the girl's skin with her whip. The expression on the homuncule's face now appeared more lecherous than ever, with the upraised eyes seeming to peer at the juncture of its cock and the vagina of the helpless girl in whom it was thrust.

Rufina completed her circuit to stand a little behind and to one side of Zara. Lifting her whip, she touched the adder-tongue to Zara's quivering bottom, teasing the soft flesh of the crease. Zara found herself biting her lip at the touch, the feel of the whip raising her to an agony of expectation as a slow pattern was traced over her earlier welts and on the most sensitive areas of her skin.

Then it happened: a sudden whistling and the bite of the whip laying a line of hot pain clear across her fat cheeks. She gasped at the impact, then again as her body jerked involuntarily against the phallus inside her. Again Rufina struck, bringing the lash down on the soft slope of Zara's upper bottom to make her howl and gag on her tongue. Then, as the second whip mark flared from white to red Zara began to mewl, a soft, plaintive noise that spoke as much of need as pain.

'Keep your whining to yourself!' Rufina snapped.

'I . . . I can't help myself, Mistress!' Zara stammered.

'You pathetic little slattern. How do you manage to serve when you squeal at the first touch of a whip?'

'I . . .'

Zara's answer was cut off by a fresh scream as the whip cut hard across the plump tuck of her buttocks. The fourth stroke landed before the girl could recover from the third, then the fifth and sixth, leaving Zara screeching, thrashing in her bonds and bouncing on the thick shaft of the homuncule's cock in a lewd and involuntary response to her torture.

Rufina stopped abruptly, allowing Zara's panic to subside until the girl hung there whimpering in her bonds. Fingering the whip she admired her captive. Zara's buttocks were heaving to a slow rhythm, their plump, pink surfaces marred by the six angry welts, each laid full across both cheeks. The crease was open and as Rufina watched a bead of sweat ran down the middle to disappear under the curve that hid the girl's anus. Rufina gave a soft chuckle and once more began a circuit of the chamber. Zara's head was hung down to her chest, her eyes shut but her mouth wide with her breath issuing from it in ragged pants. Her face was streaked with sweat and tears, her brown hair plastered over her forehead and down her back. The whole of her body was slick with sweat, wet and glistening in the ruddy light, enhancing the fat curves of her breasts and the swell of her belly. The hair of her pubis was matted to the skin. Her vagina was agape on the bronze phallus, the lips spread wide and the clitoris a bead of glossy white at the centre of her sodden vulva. The tension in her thighs was evident as she struggled to hold herself up, to prevent the tip of the homuncule's head from forcing her anus open. Again Rufina laughed and, completing her circuit, she sank to her haunches to admire her captive's straining bottom-hole.

'Let the head tip into your anus, my pleasure,' she instructed.

'No, Mistress . . .'

'Do it!'

Zara whimpered as she allowed her bottom to settle on top of the homuncule's head. The point touched her anus, spread the sweat-slick hole, entering her to splay her ring into a cone around the hard bronze. Rufina watched the sphincter stretch, smiling to herself as Zara accepted the penetration of her bottom.

'Stay still, exactly still,' she instructed as she stood to her full height.

A miserable sob signalled Zara's acceptance of the order. With two quick motions, Rufina pulled the pins from her hair. As she shook her head it billowed out in a black halo, then settled to lie rich and thick across her shoulders and down over her chest and back. Once again she lifted the whip high above Zara's naked bottom and once again she brought it whistling down on the unprotected skin.

Zara yelped but held her position, not daring to lift her anus free of the intruding knob of bronze. The whipping went on, Rufina's poise melting away with each stroke. A rapid manipulation of catches freed her breasts, revealing the nipples at full erection. A quick tug lifted her dress to her hips, exposing her sex, and as she lashed her victim she began to masturbate. Eighteen fresh welts of vivid scarlet decorated Zara's heavy buttocks when Rufina could control herself no more and dropped the whip to leave her victim writhing on the homuncule's penis.

Thrusting out her hips and spreading her vulva apart with two fingers, she began to rub hard, all the while with her eyes locked on Zara's soiled, beaten body. She screamed as she came, a drawn out yell of bestial ecstasy that died slowly to a sigh of fulfilment.

Zara, meanwhile, had began a slow, surreptitious movement on the homuncule's cock, moving her body up and down to gain friction within her vagina and repeatedly splay her anus.

'You are a hopeless wanton,' Rufina commented as she watched. 'Do it then, make yourself come.'

The beaten girl stopped, seemed to hesitate and then once more began to move herself, working slowly up and down on the bronze prongs within her orifices. Rufina adjusted her dress and sat to cover her breasts, always watching as Zara's efforts became increasingly unrestrained and increasingly lewd. Twice the captive girl began to pant and mewl, but both times her climax failed. Only when the girl suddenly slumped down in apparent exhaustion did Rufina speak.

'Come, you little slattern,' she sneered. 'Or do you need help?'

'Yes, but gently, I beg you, Mistress.'

Rufina laughed and took two quick steps to Zara's front. Placing a sharp fingernail against the helpless girl's straining clitoris, she began to tickle. Zara's movements immediately became more pronounced, more urgent. As she bounced on the cock and her anus filled and emptied again and again she began to cry out, then to scream, finally reaching her climax with a serious of ear-splitting screeches as her clitoris grazed again and again on her tormentor's fingernail.

As Zara's screams rang out across the night of Suza, Tian-Sha paused to listen and sniff the air. At the scent of Rufina – true-girl musk with an edge of leather and azure balm – the tigranthrope's claws appeared and then unsheathed fully at the recognition of Zara's sweeter musk and the implication of their being so combined. For a moment she eyed the nearby cluster of gables among which the light-well emerged, only to turn back with a shake of her head.

24

She stood on a high ledge below the male tower of the citadel, looking down to a block of stables that housed the great riding Baluchitheria. Their huge, shaggy shapes could be made out beyond the grills of the stable doors and their reek hung strong in the air. Tian-Sha's nose wrinkled as she sought to distinguish specific scents from among the overriding waft of hot mammal. Somewhere in the stables, she knew, would be Hoat, the sole ursanthrope of Suza and a favourite mate. Not only did his mass and power make him one of the few males upon whom she could release the full force of her mating frenzy, but his slow responses and equable temperament made for long, satisfying bouts of lovemaking. Also his sheer size made most females of Suza avoid him, resulting in a permanent head of sexual tension.

Detecting his scent in the furthest of the stalls, she dropped from the ledge. Landing three times her own height below, she stalked quickly along the length of the stable block, ignoring the uneasy snorts of the Baluchitheria as they became aware of her predatory scent. Pushing open the inset portal of the furthest stall, she found her target.

Hoat stood, the vast hoof of a Baluchitherium clasped in one hand, the other holding a vial of horn oil. Hearing the door open he turned, spoke a single calming word to the frightened beast and came towards Tian-Sha. As he lifted his leather apron her eyes locked on the thick, dark mass of his penis. As they came together her hand closed on its shaft.

Even as Tian-Sha took the enormous bear's penis in her hand, Urzon was pushing into the hall of the barracks that housed the Uhlan cavalry. The great room was thronged with suanthropes; Uhlans in, or half-in, their uniforms of brown leather and bronze, females naked or half-out of elaborate confections of silk and gauze.

25

Many were coupling, others drinking or exchanging coarse remarks and taking bets on the stamina of those in congress. A ragged cheer and several offers from females greeted Urzon, who responded with a gruff snort and made straight for the stair that led to the private chambers of Otomos, Captain of Uhlans.

The barracks stood back from the wall of Suza, a massive hall surrounded by long, low dormitory buildings and flanked by three great towers, the largest of which housed the Captain. Reaching the stairhead, Urzon gave one satisfied glance out over the moonlit city and rapped on the massive door. A gruff bellow answered him and he pushed inside, finding the Captain sprawled on a couch with a great tankard of some dark liquid clutched in one hand.

For all his height and mass Urzon was dwarfed by Otomos. The giant suanthrope was monstrous even by the standards of his genotype. A colossal body supported a head large in proportion. Heavy jaws protruded, producing a jutting snout that clearly showed the effect of his porcine genes and from which great tusks jutted up and down, their bands of gold filigree doing nothing to reduce their ferocious appearance. Other features mirrored this: his heavily lidded eyes, the thick crest of ruddy hair that ran from his forehead and down along his spine to form an impressive ridge-back, a thick neck and a body rolling with solid muscles and bulging with reams of fat. Heavy armour and elaborate clothing in the dark red of his rank concealed much of his body, yet did little to soften the overall impression of raw power.

'So?' Otomos demanded, the belligerence in his tone waning only marginally at the sight of the councillor.

'You have unanimous support,' Urzon answered him.

'What, even from the brothers?'

'Yes. Khian-Shu assures his support on condition that your father retires. Ilarion and Xerinus could propose no alternative and so give you support. Yet both oppose your programme of conquest.'

'Old fools, but it is no matter. Khian-Shu is certain to choose a successor to my father from among the felian soldiery, probably Ares of the arbalestiers. So we will command the council. Good, now for celebration. I'm off to find your brat Pomina slap her arse 'til she's ready for three span of pig's cock!'

As Otomos began his search for Pomina in the labyrinth that was Suza, Tian-Sha had reached what she knew would be the pinnacle of her night's heat. Even while on her knees in the stable block with her tail clasped in Hoat's hand and over half of his mighty penis inside her she had scented aroused male tigranthrope in the still air.

Urging Hoat to a quick orgasm, she had taken her leave of the ursanthrope and scaled the wall above the stables with her need mounting fast within her. The scent she recognised as that of Khian-Shu, fifth male of Suza and the dominant felian save for the dying Lord Pallus. That his scent was mingled with the musk of another female only added to her urgency.

Leaping recklessly from wall to wall and roof to roof, she made quick progress, arriving beneath the tall oblong of his window with his scent swirling in her head. Catching the sill, she pulled herself up and sank into a squat in the stone frame.

Khian-Shu lay on his couch, his muscular body sprawled at ease, naked with his erect penis rearing from the nest of pale fur at his groin. Between his legs knelt a small, svelte acyonthrope, her yellow and black fur raised along her back and her nipples stiff with excitement.

One glance at Tian-Sha was enough for the smaller female. With a hiss of frustration she clambered from the bed and fled. Khian-Shu gave a look that mingled annoyance with expectation, to which Tian-Sha lowered her head even as she stepped forward and reached for the male's rigid penis.

The target of Otomos' lust was amusing herself with two friends in a caldarium some way across the city. Although clearly a suanthrope, Pomina showed none of the grossness that characterised Otomos. Where he was a great mass of hard muscle and rolled fat, she was compact, pert, and with what fat she had well distributed to enhance the femininity of her body. Her skin was milk-pale and smooth, with no trace of the coarse body-hair that so often marred her genotype. Among her features, full lips, an upturned nose and huge, lustrous eyes showed her origins. A round dozen porky little breasts decorated her chest, each a plump handful of flesh and tipped with a big, rose-pink nipple.

Each of these was now erect and slick with scented oil as she and her companions played. To her left was Tamina, her half-sister, of similar build but larger and fleshier. On her other side was Ciriel, a true-girl with slighter hips and much smaller breasts than was typical of the city. The air was hot and thick with steam, while a round-bellied cauldron of oil sat warming on a low fire. Each girl held a long-handled ladle, which she would occasionally dip into the cauldron to take up the apple-scented oil and pour it on another's body.

Pomina giggled as the warm oil ran down her breasts. Her pleasure was approaching the point where she would want to climax. The plump, hairless mound of her sex was swollen and ready, the large clitoris protruding from between the lips like the head of a tiny cock. Her thighs were open, making her excitement plain to her companions, who themselves were in no less aroused a state.

Smiling at Ciriel, Pomina took her friend's hand and

began to guide it firmly towards her vulva. Ciriel responded, her tongue flicking out briefly to moisten her lips in happy anticipation of Pomina's sex. Tamina shifted her plump buttocks round to watch, only to jump sharply back at the crash of the outer door of the caldarium. A grunt sounded, an expression of unbridled lust that was quickly followed by the clash of metal on stone.

'Otomos?' Ciriel questioned, her lower lip trembling as she quickly pulled her hand back from Pomina's sex.

Her question was quickly answered. Even as he kicked away the last of his clothing, the giant suanthrope tore aside the drape that held in the steam of the caldarium and stepped within. Formidable enough clothed, the naked Otomos was simply terrifying. His skin was greyish pink, rough and sparsely grown with coarse red hairs. In places it folded, forming plates and creases to provide a natural armour. Great muscles rolled beneath it, while his belly, hips and buttocks were packed taut with wadded fat. A massive set of genitals hung from his groin, protected by a thick flap of belly skin but now showing as the enormous phallus slowly engorged with blood. The testicles depended in their thick, heavily wrinkled bag, each as large as a grown man's fist and squirming as the scrotum softened in response to his rising lust. The penis, at first a thick coil of dirt-coloured flesh, was growing, thickening and lengthening as its owner feasted his eyes on the naked girls.

Pomina gave a high-pitched squeal of alarm and expectation, which Tamina echoed while Ciriel screamed and scampered into a corner. Ignoring both the hopeful Tamina and the terrified Ciriel, Otomos reached out with one great arm and grabbed Pomina by the scruff of her neck. With no apparent effort he hefted the suan girl into the air and held her with her legs kicking and her plump bottom turned half towards him. Bracing his massive legs on the floor, he began to spank her, rapidly turning her buttocks a rich pink as her squeals rang out around the chamber.

Ciriel watched Pomina spanked with round-eyed wonder. Tamina, bolder, sat with her chubby thighs open and a hand caressing her sex. Otomos grunted as he worked on Pomina's bottom, his cock unwinding ever more as her watched her body writhe under his well-directed slaps. Twice the slippery apple oil proved too much for his grip and she fell to the floor, only to be snatched up once more and have her spanking resumed with renewed vigour. Her squealing became frantic as the colour of her buttock skin rose from pink to a fiery red and then an angry crimson. Her breasts swung and jiggled beneath her chest, all twelve dancing to the rhythm of her beating. Between her legs her vagina was running juice to drip and splash on the damp floor.

Finally Otomos' cock was ready, a rigid pillar of twisting flesh, seemingly far too large for the body of the wriggling girl in his grip. With a well-timed flourish he flipped Pomina into the air and caught her by the hips, applying the straining tip of his member to her vulva as she fought for breath and her hands grabbed at his shoulders.

'My Lord, my Lord, slowly,' she gasped as his massive hands locked in the smarting flesh of her buttocks. 'You know my cunt twists the other . . . ah!'

Her eyes became quite round as her inside twisted to accommodate the spiral of his cock.

'I know, that's why I like you best!' Otomos crowed.

Pomina's breath came out in one long gasp as he lifted her off his cock and the thread of her vagina once more returned to its normal, left-handed twist. Then she was filled again and cried out at the wrenching sensation that seemed to twist her entire sex around. As Otomos began to ride Pomina on his cock, a long squeal of ecstasy signalled that the sight of her sister being entered had proved too much for Tamina.

Otomos grinned and paused to watched the plump suanthrope in the throes of her climax, then returned to the task of mating with Pomina. Holding her easily under her bottom, he bounced her on his penis, choosing his own rhythm and grunting in time to her ever more desperate squeals as the tube of her vagina twisted back and forth around his cock. Despite her small size her sex took the full length of his cock with each thrust, while her jutting clitoris met the coarse skin and matted hair of his belly flap each time. Her legs kicked with the same vigour they had during her spanking, while her breasts shook and jostled together, each nipple a swollen bud of bright pink flesh.

With his eyes locked on to her heaving body he increased his pace and the power of his thrusts. Her squealing rose in pitch and volume, turning to a demented piping as her clitoris slapped again and again against his hide. Her entire body seemed full of cock, the huge thing stretching out her vagina, twisting and twisting her inside as she was ridden towards his climax. It burst, a great gush of sperm exploding inside her and bursting out around the mouth of her vagina even as her poor, bruised clitoris jammed one more time against him and her own climax hit her, sending her into rapt, mindless spasms of joy.

On a rooftop no more than a bow shot away Tian-Sha sat listening to Pomina's crazed squealing with a faint smile on her bloodstained lips. She could still feel the heat of her season in her loins and breasts, but she was satiated for the night and now performed a leisurely toilet with her tongue and claws. In the apple-rich steam that issued from the distant caldarium chimney she could catch the scents of those within: Otomos, a pungent tang stronger than any other; Pomina, a softer, sweeter version of the same, suan but female, Tamina, subtly different and less heated, Ciriel, musky and delicate but cut with the acridity of fear.

In addition to Comus and the seven suan guards, she had slaked her lust on a further five males, ranging from the fat young suanthrope in the roof garden to Khian-Shu himself. The councillor had made a fitting culmination to her heat, leaving her vagina blissfully inflamed and providing the satisfaction only possible from a male of her own genotype. Now that her frenzy had died, she felt concern for those males on whose backs she had left the bloody marks of her passion, and also for Jasiel, the small acyonthrope she had chased from Khian-Shu's bedchamber. Comus in particular she regretted, although it gave her a wry amusement to think that he would probably be more concerned with his shirt than with his back.

Such considerations were, however, minor. During the brief conversation they had held after copulating Khian-Shu had revealed that the ancient Lord Pallus was now dying and that the council had chosen the giant suanthrope Otomos as his successor. Her brain, now clearer, swam with thoughts and emotions, not the least of which was to wonder how Pomina must feel squealing out her lust on her lover's monstrous penis.

2

First Seductions

Warm sunlight flooded the chamber, illuminating the glossy red and black of Tian-Sha's fur as she lay sprawled, face down on her pallet. Her only movement was the slow twitching of her tail. The previous night had been the first hot flush of her season, a clear, urgent need to use her vagina again and again. Twice in the night she had filled her vagina with the tip of her tail and brought herself to a fast, urgent climax, and her sleep had been uneasy and fraught with erotic dreams. Day had brought a dizzy feeling, as if her head was filled with cobwebs, while her need had become a steady, insistent ache.

With a sudden, angry motion she pushed herself up from the pallet. Splashes of water on her face and vulva went some way to clearing her head, and a deep draught refreshed her. She selected a pomegranate from a bowl of fruit and went to stand at her window. Outside the sun was already well over the horizon, bathing Suza in its radiance. The air was still and hot, with the heads of storm clouds visible beyond the horizon. Unsheathing a single claw, she slit the skin of her pomegranate, revealing juicy pink seeds beneath.

She began to eat, using her tongue to extract seeds from pith; the muscular tip working with all the precision of a finger. As sweet juice filled her mouth she recalled the night, moving across rooftops and walkways, sensing males, picking out individual scents, stalking, catching, bringing cocks to erection, filling herself and filling herself again, and again . . .

Shaking her head, she forced the thoughts of her need away. Promising herself that on the coming night she could indulge her passion to the full, she turned from the window and stalked out of her chamber.

Despite her nakedness and the obvious state of arousal of her vulva, few gave her more than a cursory glance as she walked. Many knew her and knew that she was on heat, but her manner showed no inclination to dalliance. To the occasional proposition she gave curt responses, hurrying on before the male scent could break her resolve. Only when she reached the chambers of the councillor Urzon did she break her stride, pausing to sound the brass gong that hung outside the door to his chambers. The suanthrope appeared, greeted her with a familiar grunt and led her inside. A single glance at her swollen sex was followed by an understanding nod.

'Arabica? Wine? Laudanum to ease your heat?' he offered.

'Arabica. In milk if I may.'

'Certainly for a suan, just possibly for a true-girl. We shall see.'

Urzon crossed to a bell-pull, gave it a precise series of sharp tugs and then continued.

'So, the charts for the buttresses are complete?'

'Not entirely. I intended to complete them last night but was unable to focus. My visit is on another matter, not architectural.'

'Indeed?'

'Yes, in short, I coupled with Master Khian-Shu last night and learnt of the selection of Otomos as Lord Presumptive.'

'No surprise there.'

'Indeed not, yet in the female citadel it is not welcome news, or at least not altogether.'

34

'Indeed so. Yet you must accommodate yourselves to the situation.'

'You mistake me. I am a pragmatist as you know. Otomos will be Lord, the populace will not have it otherwise.'

'Absolutely. When both soldiery and agrarians hail him as a hero how else could it be?'

'Quite so, but some would risk civil strife to further their own ends.'

'The Mistress Rufina for one, and her followers. Many more female felians and true-girls resent the idea but accept its necessity. Alla-Sha, I think, has more intelligence. We know all this.'

'Yet your knowledge lacks detail.'

'You offer to supply it?'

'Yes.'

'And in return?'

'When Pomina is Lady – which we both know you intend – I wish her support for the female council.'

'You are young . . .'

'So is Pomina herself.'

'Yes . . .'

Urzon's reply was broken by the chime of the gong, swiftly followed by the entry of a plump true-girl whose belly showed the swell of pregnancy.

'Eomaea, my pleasure,' Urzon addressed her. 'Do you have milk yet?'

'Yes, Master Urzon, from yesterday.'

'Perhaps then you could prepare Arabica in milk.'

Tian-Sha and Urzon turned their conversation to architecture as Eomaea busied herself at a side table. Removing her kirtle, the courtesan began to massage her breasts, squeezing one and then the other until the white spots of milk began to form on the areolae. Scenting the sweet-sharp tang of true-girl milk, Tian-Sha found herself running her tongue tip over her lips. Eomaea bent forward, presenting the full seat of her bottom to the room as she began to milk herself into a shallow earthenware dish. The thin silk of the girl's culottes hid little, if anything stressing the size and firmness of her buttocks. Her labia also showed, twin lips of flesh heavily grown with black hair that formed a plump ball beneath its silk wrapping.

Although largely indifferent to the magnificence of Eomaea's rear, Tian-Sha realised that this was not the case for Urzon. His male scent pervaded the room, yet its familiarity and her determination to retain control had allowed her to keep her responses hidden. Now she knew his cock was swelling beneath his robes as his scent was becoming ever more rich and hard to resist. The waft of coffee filled her nostrils, bring momentary relief. Eomaea stood, performing the last motions of the ritual and then taking up two silver vessels.

'Master, Tian-Sha,' she spoke, offering the drink.

Naked but for her culottes, Eomaea's beauty was on full display. Her nipples stood proud from her heavy breasts, with runnels of milk coming from each and down on to the swell of her distended belly.

'Have you long?' Tian-Sha asked, trying to fight down her urge to mount Urzon and bring him to erection against her sex.

'Days only,' Eomaea answered. 'I see you are in season yourself.'

Tian-Sha swallowed, her resolve crumbling at the mention of her condition. Opposite her Urzon was grinning and displaying a notable bulge in the front of his robe.

'Be welcome,' he spoke, 'but mounted, and Eomaea is to hold your wrists.'

'I . . . I doubt I am able,' Eomaea responded quickly.

'Tie me then,' Tian-Sha said, abandoning herself to what she so badly needed.

Urzon's smile broadened in response. Tian-Sha rose and parted her legs to stand braced with her wrists crossed in the small of her back. Eomaea quickly put down the vessels and cast round for ties, her motions flustered and clumsy.

'By my pallet,' Urzon instructed. 'Jasiel paid me a visit last night.'

Eomaea scampered away, quickly returning with two lengths of plaited silk cord. Tian-Sha stood still and allowed her wrists to be strapped together, keeping her claws from Urzon's body. He waited, admiring her breasts and belly but doing nothing to risk bringing her into a frenzy before he was safe. Only when Eomaea stood back did he pull up his robe, exposing the extended spiral of his penis.

Tian-Sha lifted one long leg and spun, her balance perfect despite her tied hands. With her back towards Urzon, she straddled him and lowered the neat, hard globes of her bottom into his lap. Her buttocks settled to either side of his penis, with her vulva pressed against his balls. Growling at the feel of the thick shaft against her sex, she began to rub, moving her bottom back and forth. Urzon quickly attained erection, his cock hardening to a rigid bar in-between Tian-Sha's buttocks. Her tail lay on the swell of his stomach, its tip curled back, flicking gently.

Reaching forward, he cupped her buttocks, each firm ball of flesh filling a hand. She felt herself lifted, rising until she was seated on his hands with his erection standing beneath her vagina. The tip touched her, making her hiss with desire at the feel of bloated cock on tender vulva.

'Down then, my pleasure,' he grunted and began to lower.

With her hands strapped helplessly into the small of her back, Tian-Sha could only give in to the feeling of being filled with penis. She hissed as her vaginal walls twisted to accommodate his shape, arching her back and wriggling her tail at the ecstasy of mating. He released her bottom and it plumped on to his thighs, the last quarter or so of his penis jamming into her with a vigour that made her hiss. The full mass of his cock was now inside her, a sensation that made her feel full to the point where his erection seemed to invade even her head. The leathery skin of his legs was hot against her bottom fur, while the coarse tangle of his pubic hair rubbed against her anus.

The feeling was as familiar as it was wonderful, an exquisite blend of tactile pleasure and relief at being entered. Yet it was also different, for usually when she mated her power and size gave her control over all but the largest and strongest of partners. Urzon was big and might have handled her until his greater age had begun to tell, but now she was tied and so under his control.

Normally, once mounted on a penis, she took off at a frantic pace, eager to drain the sperm from it and go on to the next. Now she had no such choice and knew it was Urzon who would control the pace of their mating. As a suan of experience and notorious virility, he was unlikely to be hurried. His big hands clasped her by the thighs and she knew for sure she was to be taken slowly. She gave a shiver of frustration as he began to move her on his erection but said nothing, knowing that her protests would only amuse him. As Urzon began to bounce her slowly on his penis, Tian-Sha surrendered herself to a long, slow pleasuring.

Eomaea stood to the front, her fingers fluttering nervously on the swell of her pregnant belly. Tian-Sha could see that the courtesan was eager to join herself and Urzon but waiting for a command.

'Touch my breasts, Eomaea,' she spoke, keen to make the choice before Urzon decided on some more exotic practice.

The girl smiled and stepped forward, obediently taking the lowest pair of Tian-Sha's breasts in her hands, then moving upwards, rubbing each pair of

38

nipples in turn. The motion mimicked that used by felian females to start masturbation, and Tian-Sha was at once glad for Eomaea's experience. Having her breasts touched also removed some of the frustration of being tied, and as Urzon's teeth gently took the tip of her tail she settled down to make the most of her circumstances.

Her pleasure built, with the need for her clitoris to be touched becoming ever greater. Only the knowledge that Urzon was waiting for precisely that moment stopped her. Once her clitoris was under Eomaea's fingers she would come, and if they chose to continue touching then she would continue to come, losing any shred of dignity in a display that she knew had been jokingly compared to a suan girl's rutting frenzy. Then would come the final self-betrayal. When in control of sex it was a point she could not reach, a point from which she always retired, if only because her clitoris became unbearably sensitive. Yet the knowledge of what was going to happen to her could only delay the moment, and as her brain began to reel with pleasure she heard herself crying out for Eomaea's finger.

It came immediately, a soft touch to her vulva, the finger questing between her lips, finding her clitoris and beginning to rub. Tian-Sha screamed and screamed again. Her hips were bucking frantically, her bottom bouncing on Urzon's cock, her wrists straining against the silk bonds. Blackness filled her head as the peak hit her, every muscle in her body locked hard, then once more she peaked and she was slipping down only for Urzon's hand to catch her firmly by the waist. Eomaea's finger left her clitoris . . .

'No, my pleasure,' Urzon ordered. 'Keep it there, make her come again. Make her act like a suan girl stuck on a Baluchi!'

Tian-Sha gave a single half-hearted growl which came out more like a sob. Once more her body began to be

39

bounced on Urzon's erection and once more Eomaea's finger touched the agonisingly sensitive bud of her clitoris. Immediately she was writhing and squirming on his cock, wriggling her bottom with abandoned desire, rubbing herself desperately against him, behaving, in fact, exactly like a suanthrope girl in rut. Urzon laughed at her and put his hands to her wriggling bottom, spreading the cheeks in a way that she knew showed off her anus and the junction between his cock and her vagina. As the air touched her anus she came again, screaming out. Neither of her tormentors stopped, both pacing her, bump for bump and rub for rub in an expert rhythm. Her own scent was strong in her head and she could feel the drips oozing from the glands that flanked her anus and those of her vulva. For an instant a new scent joined them, the sharp, feminine tang of her own urine and then she came once more and it happened.

Urine erupted from her bladder, spraying out around Eomaea's finger to splash the girl and Urzon's legs. The suanthrope laughed as Tian-Sha screamed out her orgasm even as the urine pooled around her vulva and his balls. His hand gripped her buttocks, opening them wide. She felt a thumb touch her anus, rubbing the oil from her glands into the tight hole. Through the dizziness of her orgasm came the thought that she was about to be buggered while sat in a pool of her own pee and then the cock inside her jerked hard and she felt sperm flood into her.

This time when her climax faded the torment was over. Tian-Sha slumped down on Urzon with a rich, sleepy feeling of satisfaction. For a long moment she stayed still and Urzon made no move to disturb her. Then she felt his hand on the silk at her wrists. She pulled herself forward and looked up at the girl who had brought her past the normal limits of ecstasy.

Eomaea was standing back, her face set in a knowing smile, her huge breasts, swollen belly and plump thighs spattered with urine. Her culottes were also soaked, the thin silk clinging to the wet mass of her pubic hair. On her breasts the pee was mixed with milk and, on her thighs, with the juices of her vulva. Tian-Sha returned her smile, mixing it with a slight baring of her fangs to indicate to the girl that the act would not be forgotten. Eomaea returned a nervous giggle.

Otomos sat splay-legged on a heavy chest, his face set in a frown. Pomina lay across his lap, face up and naked in contrast to his full dress of deep-red cloth. One of his hands was laid on her chest, absently fondling her breasts and teasing one nipple after another to erection in a distracted manner. Opposite him sat Lomas and Urzon, both in full council regalia.

'Too overt a display will sour your popularity,' Urzon was urging. 'You must be seen to mourn. Some still doubt your ability, and without popular support a challenge might yet succeed.'

'By who?' Otomos snorted.

'Be cautious, my son,' Lomas advised. 'You are a hero and have no need to do more than wait to secure the Lordship. In particular avoid all duels – challenge nobody and ignore all provocation.'

'What?' Otomos demanded. 'And appear a coward! Never! Besides, who would dare challenge me?'

'Probably none,' Lomas replied. 'Yet only if you were to die in an honour duel would a challenger avoid the wrath of the populace. The greatest danger is that a skilled man might goad you into a challenge and so secure choice of weapons. In particular avoid arbalestiers.'

'A coward's weapon,' Otomos sneered.

'But effective,' Urzon remarked.

Otomos gave a loud snort and pointedly gave his attention to Pomina's breasts. She moaned softly in response and arched her back, pushing her chest up into greater prominence.

'Furthermore,' Lomas continued, 'take heed of Rufina. She has no more scruples than a wasp and is equally malignant. Nor does she care for the law.'

'Rather she should take heed of me,' Otomos answered.

'Just so,' Urzon put in, 'but be vigilant none the less. We do, as it happens, have a source of information. I am honour bound not to reveal her name, but suffice to say that she is niece to Alla-Sha and no friend of Rufina's.'

'You work your wiles,' Otomos grunted. 'I am a warrior and prefer to be blunt. Let Rufina know that if she so much as scuffs the law I'll take her into the fields and stake her out for agrarian use, personally.'

'Doubtless a popular move,' Urzon joked, 'but not a wise one, at least not until you are the Lord.'

'Popular indeed,' the giant suanthrope rejoined. 'Indeed, were a Baluchi to piss on her they'd make it the Lord in my stead.'

Otomos chuckled at his own wit.

At a long bench in the hall of essences Comus sat, to outward appearances absorbed in the study of a vial of liquid that gleamed a deep orange in the sunlight. His mind ran on a very different course, considering the conversation he had earlier held with the councillor Xerinus.

Rather than issue a summons to his fine chambers beneath the citadel wall, Xerinus had visited in person. This was not entirely unprecedented as there was at least a possibility that the two were father and son, yet it was sufficiently abnormal to arouse Comus' immediate interest. Xerinus had begun with the information that the council had appointed Otomos as Lord Presumptive; news irksome but hardly unexpected. The councillor had then implied, without ever issuing a direct statement, that should Comus choose to challenge for the Lordship he might expect a minimum of two votes in council. The conversation had then become trivial, allowing Comus no hint as to how he might challenge Otomos, or gain a majority of the council's support.

Since then Comus' mind had been fixed on the possibilities brought up by Xerinus' visit. To him, attaining the Lordship had long been a dream, and he had expended great effort in gaining popularity in the city. Along with many of the more perceptive among both true-man and felian cliques, he doubted Otomos' suitability to rule. None could match Otomos and his Uhlans in battle, which fact the populace of Suza took as evidence of the giant suanthrope's heroic status and suitability for the Lordship. Yet the tactics and subtleties of each victory had been dictated by the Lord Pallus and Khian-Shu.

The prospect of Otomos as Lord gave Comus both distaste and unease; the first from the inevitable vulgarity of a suan supremacy, the second from the fear of a running war which Suza could not ultimately sustain. Of one thing he was certain. His own qualities – among which modesty did not come high – were better suited to the Lordship than those of Otomos. This had seemed immaterial, with the great bulk of the populace and the council in support of the giant suanthrope. His sole chance of achieving his ambitions had seemed to be for Otomos to fall in battle and for a demand to rise for a wiser, more cautious Lord. It had not happened, and once Otomos was Lord it would become impossible. Yet now, with his dreams seemingly dashed, he had been offered a half-chance of success.

By mid-morning he had considered every apparent option. Shortly before noon he had sent his apprentice, Ciriel, to make an appointment with the courtesan Zara. The apprentice returned quickly, bringing Zara, and was promptly sent to gather poppy seed in the fields beyond the wall of Suza.

'So, Zara, my pleasure,' Comus addressed the courtesan as Ciriel turned them a last curious glance. 'I am fortunate that you could be so prompt.'

'It is my pleasure,' she replied. 'I was to be mud-girl in the higher suan bathhouse but preferred to attend you. I have pleaded exhaustion.'

'I am flattered,' Comus responded.

'I am a trifle sore today, also.'

'Just so, such is the nature of your art. Today I wish a brief satisfaction, following which I have a task for you for which I shall exchange this vial.'

'And its effect?'

'To ameliorate the mood. A single drop, placed in a drink or applied to the inner skin, will soften even the most dedicated of spoilers and debauchers. Rather than beat you or grease you with oil of pimento – as I understand was done recently – they will sit and stroke your breasts and hair, taking their love-play in more easy fashion. As the sheer magnificence of your bottom causes you to be so often summoned to take the whip I imagine it will be of use to you.'

'Certainly, and in return?'

'I wish a sample to be collected, a rather unusual sample.'

'Is that not Ciriel's task?'

'Ciriel lacks the necessary skills, and, frankly, the courage. I wish a quantity of sperm, suan sperm.'

'Simplicity.'

'From Otomos.'

'Otomos!'

'Two vials?'

'Three.'

'So be it. I will be here for the remainder of the day. Do not rush the deed or allow him to think you desire more than the experience of his lust. Also, tell nobody.'

'Just so. You wish satisfaction first?'

'Indeed, now what shall I do?' he mused. 'Come between those glorious breasts, or maybe along the crease of your equally exquisite bottom – well oiled. Perhaps, but that might tempt me to bugger you. Would you dispute my entrance?'

'No, yet I would prefer a more gentle treatment. Last night the Mistress Rufina put me to the torment of whip and cock. For the cock she made use of a bronze homuncule. Its head bore a conical tip that she obliged me to take in my anus.'

'Painful, but delicious. Not your anus then, nor your buttocks if they are whipped sore. Rufina is cruel to spoil you so.'

'Not cruel, except in her lust. Simply indifferent to the wants of others.'

'As you say. Pull up your kirtle then, I shall enjoy your breasts.'

Zara knelt and lifted her kirtle, displaying the heavy globes that decorated her chest. As Comus stood she cupped them in her hands and pushed them together, offering a soft groove of flesh for his pleasure. He smiled at the sight as he began to undress, removing his clothing piece by piece and folding each garment with meticulous care. Even when he was naked he postponed his pleasure, instead reaching to a high shelf and taking down an earthenware flask.

'Oil of urtica,' he remarked, removing the stopper and pouring a measure of thick green liquid into the valley between her breasts. 'Fresh this morning.'

Zara gave a low purr as the viscous liquid pooled against her skin, then a moan as the warmth penetrated.

'Effective, as you see,' Comus said and laid his penis into the soft caress of Zara's flesh.

He began to rub, rapidly gaining an erection as the feel of her body and the heat of the unguent had their effect. Zara also was showing excitement, the day to day event of giving a man the pleasure of her breasts enhanced by the warm and unfamiliar feelings. Her nipples had quickly popped out and her sighs matched his as his cock continued to rub and his thighs squashed into her breasts with ever greater urgency.

He performed slowly, taking his time in the warm, sticky embrace, holding back until her eyes were shut and she had began to moan deep in her throat. Only then did he push his shaft down deeper until only the head protruded from between her plump pillows of flesh. With two hard thrusts he came, splashing sperm over her neck and chin, then across her face as he pulled back and finished off in his hand. Zara made no effort to rise, but lifted a fat breast in one hand and began to lap at the mixture of sperm and unguent. With her face set in bliss her fingers went to her vulva and began to rub, bringing her quickly to a peak as Comus watched with an indulgent smile.

Following a fastidious toilet performed with a small sponge, Comus dressed and made himself comfortable on the couch. Zara washed and dressed, her every movement betraying nervousness.

Zara made her way to the hall of courtesans, intent on food and a period of meditation before tackling Otomos. Once there she seated herself at a table and ordered fruit, honey-cake and wine from the servitor. With most of the girls on appointments for the afternoon, she was alone and remained so until Eomaea arrived and joined her.

'Not yet down to the sanatorium?' Zara greeted her friend.

'No, but soon,' Eomaea responded, seating herself with care. 'How goes your day?'

'Well enough, although Rufina whipped me last night and my bottom is still ablaze. And you?'

'Frustrating. I aided Urzon to couple with Tian-Sha

46

but had no time to take my own pleasure. Since then I have been attending the Lord with medicines, towels and whatever, and never once able to pleasure myself. Yet I have some fine hearsay!'

'Which is?'

'Urzon and Tian-Sha would not speak in front of me and they had no charts or books. Some scheme is afoot.'

'Suza seethes with schemes, why, myself . . .'

Zara broke off, her desire to better Eomaea's story suddenly overcome by the memory of Comus' request for secrecy.

'Yes?' Eomaea urged.

'I . . .' Zara began and glanced around as if checking the room while struggling for what to say.

'Come, tell me!'

'I can't,' Zara stammered. 'I am sworn to secrecy.'

'Oh Zara!'

'I can't. I am sorry.'

'But . . . oh, never mind. Are you needed later?'

'Not until a glass before sundown. I was supposed to be a mud-girl but cried off because of my bottom.'

'Good, you can massage me in the hall caldarium. In return I'll soothe your poor behind.'

'A good offer.'

The meal over, they made their way to the caldarium. At the entrance both girls stripped, casually shedding their clothes and placing the garments on pegs. Zara followed Eomaea within, admiring her friend's soft back and full bottom as they went. Always full-figured, Eomaea had put on weight while she was pregnant and was now much heavier than Zara at both breast and bottom. The effect, mixed with Eomaea's swollen belly and milk-ready teats, gave Zara a strong urge to be mothered. The idea of having her bottom soothed fitted well with this, offering both the comfort of being made better and the arousal of her friend's touch.

Eomaea took towels and spread them on a dais, then

lay with her hands folded behind her head so that her swollen belly was the highest part of her body. Zara stood looking down at her friend, admiring the plump swell of thighs, breasts, sex and most especially midriff. Eomaea's skin was exquisite, a pale tan and the texture of satin, as if freshly oiled.

'You are beautiful,' Zara remarked, touching a fingertip to Eomaea's belly.

'As you are.'

'Your skin has an exceptional glow. What unguent do you use?'

'I don't, at present. I simply rub my breast milk in. To good effect, as you can see.'

'Might I?'

'Surely. Come, climb up on me.'

Zara crawled on to the dais and straddled Eomaea's legs with her bottom resting on the pregnant girl's thighs. The action spread her vulva to the warm air of the caldarium, making her realise how wet her sex was. Eomaea had put her hands to her breasts and was pulling at them, making the fat pillows of flesh wobble and shiver against her chest. Zara watched in delight as the droplets of milk began to form, swelling to join and pool, then breaking to run down the creamy skin in pale rivulets. The smell of milk was thick in the air, blending with the tang of caldarium spices and the hot smell of the girl's sex.

Leaning forward, Zara put her hands to Eomaea's breast, wetting them with milk. With her belly pushed against her friend's her arousal became keener still. Also her bottom was up and open, a position she enjoyed for entry. She kissed Eomaea's nipple, tasting the milk as her friend giggled in response. As she sat back a drop of warm sweat trickled down between her bottom cheeks, touching her anus and sending a new thrill through her body.

The milk had began to flow freely, rising in little

48

spurts from Eomaea's nipples with each squeeze. Zara's hands were wet with it and she began to smooth it on to Eomaea's belly. Zara began her massage, rubbing gently until the skin was wet and then using her fingertips to soothe away the knots of tension in her friend's abdomen. Eomaea continued to massage her breasts, supplying Zara with fresh milk and leaving her skin and the surface of the dais awash with the pale fluid.

The glossy smoothness of Eomaea's skin increased as the milk was rubbed in, as did the girl's sighs of pleasure and the urgency with which she was squeezing her breasts. Zara continued the massage, trying to ignore the ache in her own sex in order to bring her friend the full ecstasy of the experience. Soon she had fluid dripping from her vagina to pool between Eomaea's thighs and a prickling, urgent sensation throughout her sex and also on her anus. Still she continued the massage, enjoying the feel of her friend's flesh, the huge, heavy breasts, the plump hips and thighs, the distended belly and the soft swell of the pubic mound. Only when she felt Eomaea's thighs start to try to open did she choose to take the massage to its inevitable conclusion. The motion was an instinctive desire to spread the vulva, a feeling with which Zara was entirely familiar.

She dismounted, allowing Eomaea to bring her legs up and open. As the damp pink centre of the girl's vulva came on display the scent of sex strengthened, filling Zara with the urge to taste her friend. Yet she knew that the more slowly she took it the greater would be the strength of the climax when it came. Putting her fingertips to the insides of Eomaea's thighs, she began to stroke, each movement coming ever closer to the swollen mound of the girl's sex. Eomaea arched her back in pleasure, squeezing her breasts to send twin fountains of milk high into the air. Some splashed her own face, more falling on her belly to make a pool in the navel. Zara giggled at the sight and planted a gentle smack on the bulging tuck of her friend's bottom.

'Now, Zara, pleasure. Make me come,' Eomaea sighed.

Zara knelt forward and began to kiss the roundness of Eomaea's belly, tasting the salt of sweat and the richness of the milk. Sliding her hands beneath her friend's bottom, she hugged the swollen belly to her face, revelling in the feel of taut flesh. Putting her mouth to Eomaea's navel, she sucked up the milk from it and swallowed. Her hands squeezed Eomaea's plump bottom cheeks, then delved between to touch the warm crease and dig a small finger into the anus.

'Dirty little wretch,' Eomaea sighed. 'No, don't take it out. Lick me now.'

Zara slid her finger deeper up her friend's bottom and transferred the attention of her mouth from belly to sex. Burying her face in Eomaea's rich curls, she began to lick, lapping at the wet flesh to get the distinctive taste of the pregnant girl. With each lick the labia parted under her tongue, squirming beneath the pressure. Then Eomaea would sigh as her clitoris was bumped and push herself yet harder against Zara's face.

As Eomaea's sighs rose in urgency Zara began to wriggle her finger in the wet embrace of her friend's anus, teasing the little hole open and stroking the hot, puffy flesh of the interior. She felt the ring tighten, then start to pulse and she knew that Eomaea was coming. Sliding a thumb into the girl's vagina, she found that too undergoing the contractions of climax. Her tongue tip found the clitoris and began to lap faster, then faster still as Eomaea groaned and called out Zara's name. Then the plump thighs had locked tight around her head and both holes had clamped tight on the intruding digits. Eomaea came with a long groan, her whole body shuddering again and again until it was over and both girls sank down into the pool of warm milk that covered the dais.

Quickly recovering herself from the passion of

50

Eomaea's orgasm, Zara found the need to come herself unbearably strong. So was her urge to be mothered by her friend while she climaxed.

'Now me!' she squeaked. 'I want . . . I want to rub myself with your lovely breasts in my face!'

'Squat down. I'll kneel.'

Zara responded, rocking back on her haunches until her bottom touched the warm tiles of the dais. Eomaea rose and gently took Zara's head to cradle it between her breasts. Zara sighed as her face was smothered into the plump, moist breast flesh. Spreading the lips of her vulva with two fingers, she began to rub at her clitoris. Eomaea's breasts felt huge in her face, two fat pillows of flesh, each heavy with the delicious fluid they had been sharing. She nuzzled, letting the two fat globes slap on her cheeks as she rubbed herself. Eomaea giggled and hugged Zara close, smothering her in breast flesh. In response Zara licked, tasting milk and filling her with the need for a nipple in her mouth. She pulled back, gaping.

Eomaea immediately offered her a breast, holding it out and pulling Zara's face gently down on it. Zara began to suckle. Her mouth was full of the milky taste, her body sticky with it, yet still she needed more and as she felt the muscles of her lower body start to contract she knew what would give the finest pleasure.

'Squeeze, do it in my face!' Zara begged.

'No!' Eomaea laughed.

'Why not? Please!'

'No. Not until you tell me your secret.'

'Eomaea!'

'Now tell me, or I won't do it!'

'That isn't fair!'

'Tell me!'

'I . . . Oh you wretch! The Master Xerinus plans to stand down from the council on the death of Lord Pallus and seek election for Comus the essencier, that is all.'

'Only that?'

'That is all. Now wet me!'

'Sweet slut! Here's some milk for you then, little Zara.'

Zara pulled back, opening her mouth as her friend cupped the flesh around one bloated nipple. Her eyes were locked on the hard, red-brown bump, her fingers rubbing hard at her clitoris. Eomaea held back one more taunting moment and then squeezed. Milk spurted full into Zara's waiting mouth, then again, across her face. As she felt the wet and tasted the sweet-sharp fluid Zara began to come. Eomaea squeezed again, and again her milk sprayed Zara's face, catching her cheeks and nose.

As her climax hit, Zara leant forward, taking Eomaea's nipple into her mouth and sucking, sucking until her mouth was full of the delicious fluid, sucking until it ran from the corners of her mouth. For one, long, glorious moment everything dissolved in bliss. With her mouth stuffed with soft breast flesh and firm nipple, with milk soaking her body and filling her mouth, with her bottom thrust out behind as if seeking entry, with her clitoris burning under her finger, her whole existence was complete.

Then it had passed and she was coming down. She sat back, panting and grinning at her friend with milk running down her chin and on to her breasts and belly. The dais was awash with milk, sweat and girl-juice, as were both their bodies. Eomaea returned the smile and then hugged Zara's head back on to her chest, not in passion but in warmth and friendship.

In the chambers of Rufina, the councillor was seated in a pillared alcove that looked out high above the rooftops of Suza. An elaborate dress of deep blue leather clung to her body, covering her from neck to ankle but leaving her breasts bare. Golden caps topped her nipples, while rings and clasps decorated her hair and arms. In one hand she held her long whip, while her face was set in an expression of intense concentration.

On the blue-tiled floor lay Igalia, a suan courtesan and sister to Otomos. She was rolled on her back and her plump thighs had been pulled up to her chest and bound in place, with her arms strapped into the crook of her knees and her ankles lashed together and fastened back hard. The position left the bulging lips of her sex thrust out, entirely unprotected, as were the undersides of her broad buttocks and the prominent hoop of her distended anus. Parts of her fat breasts were also vulnerable, squashed out between her chest and thighs, in some instances with the nipples revealed.

As Rufina mused she would occasionally flick the suanthrope's breasts or vulva with her whip, making Igalia wriggle and squeal but never come close to a climax. For all the courtesan's desperation, her tormentor's mind was clearly elsewhere, the anguish of her victim no more than an idle amusement to aid her thoughts. Since Igalia had arrived and been bound for Rufina's amusement the sun had crossed the zenith, and the plump suanthrope was now squirming with discomfort and the need to climax.

She knew the game, knew that not until she was writhing in a puddle of her own juice would Rufina apply the whip to her clitoris and relieve her anguish. Only then would the councillor expose her own sex, squat over the suanthrope's face and take her pleasure of the thick, muscular tongue. The tiles beneath Igalia's bottom were already damp and she knew that it would be soon, or so she imagined.

Reaching her conclusion, Rufina stopped tormenting Igalia's vulva, dropped the whip, rose and strode towards the arch that led from the chamber. Igalia's eyes followed her, curious at first and then in alarm as Rufina took up a cloak.

'Mistress!' the bound suanthrope squealed.

Rufina gave no answer.

'Untie me, Mistress! I beg!' Igalia went on, her alarm now rising to panic.

'Silence, sow!'

'But, Mistress, I have further appointments!'

'I said silence! Now stop squealing. I have an important matter to attend to and no time to concern myself with your petty demands. Besides, I may wish to continue to amuse myself with you when I return.'

'Mistress!' Igalia squealed.

Rufina left, only to throw back a final comment.

'And if you soil the floor I'll have you chained under a public sump for a week.'

Igalia was left wriggling in her bonds.

Rufina walked briskly, making her way around the base of the citadel along broad corridors decorated with rugs of colourful weave and areas of polished mosaic, each depicting some long dead Lord or councillor of Suza. None drew her attention, nor did she acknowledge the people she passed, but kept purposefully on until she came to a tall door that gave entrance to the citadel stable block. Here she paused, feigning interest in a tapestry until she was alone, and then she pushed quickly through the door.

As she entered the atrium she winced at the smell of beasts and dung, but pressed on, pausing only to take her cloak up to avoid soiling the hem. Coming into the long, open channel that ran between the citadel wall and the stalls, she gave a brief upward glance to the row of enormous heads that stuck out over the split-level doors of the stalls. The Baluchitheria ignored her absolutely, continuing to chew mouthfuls of hay or watch the sky in the peculiar manner of their kind.

The clang of a pail alerted Rufina to her target and she pushed through one of the inset gates. Within, the ursanthrope Hoat stood by the side of a Baluchitherium, his great shaggy head rising close to the top of the beast's foreleg. On seeing her he gave a grunt of surprise but inclined his head in an approximation of the traditional gesture of respect.

'Do you wish to take a beast out?' he rumbled.

'No,' she replied, her tone softer by far than that she had used with Igalia. 'I wish to converse with you.'

'Me?' Hoat queried.

'Just so,' she answered. 'You are a great man, Hoat, the most powerful in Suza, and yet you work as a stable hand. All too evidently you are capable of greater things. Does this not irk you?'

'I have shelter, food, occasional female company. My position is fair. Who else could harness and saddle the beasts?'

'Just so, none. Your strength is unequalled. You should not be a stable hand. You should be Lord.'

'Lord?'

'Indeed. The Lord Pallus is dying. The cliques squabble among themselves. Now is the time for a strong male to come forward, a male with no allegiance other than to Suza. You are that male.'

'How? Who would support me?'

'Myself, as Lady.'

'You are not Lady.'

'I will be shortly. Alla-Sha is to step down on the death of her mate.'

'And the male council?'

'They will see reason.'

He grunted, his face setting into a grimace of concentration and doubt.

'Think,' she wheedled, 'first choice of courtesans, beauties such as Zara, Eomaea and even Jasiel at your feet, not shunning your cock but begging to have it put to them. As Lord you could have other ursanthropes brought down from the north – females.'

Hoat gave a low grunt, still doubtful but less so.

'What of you? You have always shunned me?'

'Not so,' she purred, 'but it takes courage for a woman to approach so great a male as you. Now I can resist no longer, and as my chosen mate the male council will have little choice but to accept you.'

'Many true-girls become uneasy at the sight of me – you have always been entirely without passion.'

In answer Rufina reached out and tugged aside the leather apron that hid his genitals. He looked down, his mouth drawing up into a grin. Barely flinching, she cupped his scrotum, drawing her nails slowly over the rough skin, once, twice, and then curling her hand around the thickness of his penis.

'I will be yours,' she assured him. 'Without reserve once we are Lord and Lady, accommodating you in any way my body is able. For now, to prove my word, allow me the privilege of bringing you to climax.'

Hoat's only answer was a deep growl of passion. His cock had already began to stiffen in her hand, and as she tossed at it the shaft thickened and filled, becoming first turgid and then rigid, a bar of glossy red-brown flesh some four hand spans in length and too thick for her hand to circle. It projected close to the horizontal, aimed at a level with her chest as she altered her grip and began to tug on it.

She smiled and looked up to him as his growls grew deeper and more urgent, then closed her eyes and put a hand to one gold-topped nipple. With the bud firm in its cup she began to twist gently, all the while jerking at Hoat's penis with ever more speed and longer strokes.

A huge hand took her head, touching lightly but with evidence of a strength far beyond her power to resist. Thinking that she was to have her mouth drawn down on to Hoat's cock, she opened wide in resignation. Yet he made no move to force her, only stroking her hair. Still sure that he would make her suck unless she

56

hurried, she increased the pace of her masturbation to a frantic bobbing.

Hoat growled, a new note, deeper still. Rufina felt his cock spasm and quickly tried to angle it away only to discover it rigid beyond her strength. Even as she tried to step back a jet of sperm burst from the tip, catching her between her breasts and splashing over the immaculate leather of her dress. A second gout erupted, sending a long line of thick, yellowish droplets in an arc across her cleavage to soil her cloak and midriff. Gritting her teeth but shamefully aware of the stiffness of her nipples and the dampness of her vulva, she finished him off over her front, amazed at her own action even as the copious discharge of viscous fluid oozed and bubbled down her front.

Feeling deeply disturbed, she thanked Hoat, confirmed their agreement and left with as much grace as she could manage, all the while holding her expression to one of serene goodwill. Only when she was clear of the stable atrium did her air change to one of deep disgust. In the corridor beyond she stopped, chose a suitable alcove and, taking a square of silk from her sleeve, she began to wipe the thick clots of yellow come from her breasts and bodice.

Zara perched herself on the edge of a low wall. The afternoon heat was at its greatest and all of Suza seemed roasted beneath the sun. The stone beneath her buttocks was at first uncomfortably hot, briefly irritating her whip marks. Enquiry had revealed that Otomos had gone to inspect a mosaic newly completed in his honour, and the walkway above which she perched seemed his most likely route back to the Uhlan barracks. Now she awaited him, her belly fluttering with nervousness.

Her judgement quickly proved accurate. Accompanied by three Uhlan Wardens, he appeared, his great form resplendent in half-armour, harness and the deep red garments of his rank. He was clearly in good humour and joked with the Wardens as the group approached, then stopped to appraise her.

'Lord Otomos,' she purred.

'Zara, is it not?' he answered, then turned to his companions. 'A favoured courtesan among the councillors. Fine breasts if only two of them, and a backside to match my sister's. Show it, girl.'

Zara smiled and moved her hips to display the roundness of her bottom, thinly veiled by her culottes.

'Fine,' Otomos grunted. 'Fat but firm, as a female's buttocks should be.'

All three Wardens made noises of agreement.

'May we speak, my Lord?' Zara asked.

'By all means,' Otomos answered. 'What is it?'

'A matter of my art, my Lord.'

'Indeed? Walk on, you three. I'll be on shortly.'

Zara watched as the Wardens passed, answering their lustful glances with a smile and another flash of her bottom. One spoke, words she did not catch, and the other laughed in response.

'So?' Otomos demanded.

'Do you know that with your rank you might have me?' she asked sweetly. 'Even before your formal elevation to the Lordship.'

'As a captain I may demand any courtesan I please,' he answered. 'Yet you little true-girls fall faint at the very thought of my cock. I need a suan girl to satisfy me. You are well grown, but doubtless tight-cunted like all your sort. Why should I trouble when I have Pomina and every other ripe suan slut in the city begging for me?'

'Might I not try, my Lord?' she wheedled.

'In the cunt?' he responded in disbelief. 'You'd best have a good oil. Aren't you scared of being split? It takes a suan girl to accommodate me, as I thought the whole of Suza knew.'

'I thought, perhaps, in my mouth, Lord,' Zara said softly.

He shrugged, ran his eyes over the plump swell of her haunches and then gave a thoughtful nod. Zara jumped down from the wall and swayed towards him, then turned and offered her arm. Without warning his hand caught the seat of her culottes and pulled them tight up into the crease of her bottom and between her labia. She gave a cry of surprise and shock, only to lose her breath as she was lifted and thrown casually across his shoulder. With her bottom to the fore and her culottes pinched tight into her sex, she was carried to the Uhlan barracks and within.

The sight of her near-naked, upthrust bottom caused a roar of mirth from the Uhlans, accompanied by suggestions as to what Otomos should do with his burden. He replied with coarse humour, assuring them that Zara would not go unfilled. Upside down with her hair covering her face and her kirtle fallen to display her breasts and hamper her arms, she could do nothing. When one Uhlan commented on the recently whipped state of her bottom, Otomos planted a fresh smack on her quivering cheeks. Another called out, asking for a view of her sex. Immediately Otomos obliged, hooking a thick nail under the gusset of her culottes and ripping them away. Zara gasped as she was stripped and then once more as a leathery finger opened her vagina. She began to kick her legs in helpless frustration, resulting only in fresh gusts of rude laughter.

She was carried into his tower, Otomos taking the steep stairs in great bounds that had her clinging in fear to the back of his harness. Two doors were kicked open and slammed and she found herself in his private chambers. Setting her down on the floor, he tore off her kirtle with a single jerk, leaving her stark naked and dizzy with her hair disarrayed and the blood singing in her head.

He began to strip, peeling off harness and clothing

until he stood naked but for boots and greaves. Zara put a hand instinctively to her pubic mound at the sight of his genitals protruding from beneath his belly flap, to which action he returned a sour grin.

'Don't fret girl,' he said, sitting down on a padded stool. 'I'll not force that little slot. Fruit? Wine? Or straight down to pleasure?'

'Now, please, my Lord.'

'Then kneel for it, and keep that big backside stuck out while you suck, it reminds me of my Pomina's.'

'Yes, my Lord.'

Zara knelt before Otomos, then swallowed as he spread his knees to reveal the full expanse of his genitals. The great thick cock hung below its protective pad, resting coiled on the bulging scrotum within which his balls squirmed slowly.

'Here then, my pleasure,' he grunted. 'This is what you need. Have you ever seen such a fine one?'

She shook her head numbly, her eyes transfixed on the enormous cock before her. Otomos took it in his hand, pulling it out of its recumbent coil to stretch, thick and twisting, towards her mouth. Zara swallowed hard and parted her lips. Otomos laughed and reached out, taking her by the hair in an unbreakable grip. Zara gaped wide, then wider still as the huge penis was fed into her mouth. Her jaw ached and she could feel the strain in her lips, yet she began to rub her tongue on the leathery foreskin and make sucking motions on the tip.

It stiffened quickly, spreading her jaws until they could go no wider. The head emerged from the prepuce, jamming into the back of her throat until she began to gag and was forced to pull back. Otomos gave an indulgent chuckle and allowed her to adjust her head, then once more locked his grip.

'Come, my pleasure,' he instructed. 'Come with the Lord Otomos' cock in your unworthy mouth.'

Zara obeyed, putting one hand to the plump mound of

her damp vulva and the other to the bulge of his scrotum. Manipulating his balls and sucking on his penis, she began to masturbate, rubbing her clitoris towards climax. Overwhelmed by the sheer erotic force of her act, she became aroused fast, high on the feel of his monstrous genitals and the thick musk of his scent. As her climax began to rise she briefly slid a finger inside her vagina, comparing the tight hole with the girth of the erection in her mouth. The thought of attempting to accommodate him was the final touch and she climaxed with her head ringing with the impossible horror of being taken by her scruff and put on his cock with neither warning nor the chance to build up her natural lubrication.

Peak after peak tore through her body and all the while she sucked hard on his penis and moulded his balls in her hand. Coaxing her clitoris to response with an expert hand, she held the climax until the blood began to sing in her ears. At that she stopped, denying herself the pleasure of fainting on his cock. Placing her juice-dampened hand on the base of his shaft, she gave her full attention to his pleasure. He grunted deep in his throat and altered his grip on her head, twisting up a handful of brown curls.

'Now me,' he grunted and pulled her head sharply forward, jamming his cock down her throat.

She took it, feeling her mouth twist around the hard spiral. For a moment it was bearable and she began to suck, keeping her bottom well pushed out and enjoying the sensation of absolute fullness of mouth as she prepared for his orgasm. Abruptly he pulled her yet further on to himself, jamming his meaty glans into her gullet and starting a pumping motion. Unable to breathe, she began to mouth desperately at his erection. She could feel every movement of the glans in her throat, stifling her as the pressure built in her head. He gave a furious grunt and jammed it yet further down. The muscles of her neck spasmed in protest, once, twice, squeezing the intruding cock head in a desperate reflex to reject it.

Otomos squealed and his cock jerked in Zara's mouth. Suddenly her throat was full of not just meat but sperm. Zara began to choke, clogged by her mouthful of cock and gagging on the thick fluid. Otomos held her head, forcing his glans deeper still into her throat. His grip relaxed, just for an instant and with a frantic effort she jerked her head back. The sperm burst from around her lips and splashed in heavy gouts on to her chest and thighs. Once more he jammed his erection deep into her, holding her hair as eruption after eruption of come burst out of him. Even when it had stopped he held her, draining the last drops of fluid down her gullet. Unable to breathe, she could only shake her head and make desperate pawing motions with her hands. Only when her face began to redden and her writhing became truly desperate did he release her, only to ejaculate once more, full in her face. She fell back on to her haunches, spluttering the thick, creamy pig-come from her nostrils and lips.

With her cheeks bulging and her face a rich puce in colour she ran from the room in blind panic, followed by the coarse bellow of the suanthrope's laughter. Unheeding of her naked, sperm splattered body, she fled the barracks, the laughter of the Uhlans and comments on Otomos' sexual prowess following her bouncing bottom as she retreated.

In the hall of essences Comus was inspecting Ciriel's crop of poppy seed when Zara burst in. Ciriel's mouth opened in an O of shock as the courtesan bent across the bench and disgorged a mouthful of a thick, white substance into a beaker. Comus' own mouth twitched slightly into an amused smile. Zara sat down, panting and shaking her head, her huge eyes round and bright.

'You met with success, I assume?' Comus questioned, eyeing the beaker.

Zara swallowed hard and took a deep breath.

'I did,' she finally answered. 'He . . .'

'A moment, my pleasure,' Comus interrupted. 'Ciriel, perhaps you could place this seed in the jar, the quality is excellent.'

Ciriel rose to obey, again casting a questioning glance back over her shoulder.

'This is for an experiment, but recall my request for secrecy,' Comus explained to Zara. 'As you may imagine, Otomos would be less than amused should word come to him. He would consider the act impudent at the least, which would be awkward. I trust you appreciate the need for discretion?'

'Absolutely,' Zara responded. 'Indeed, Eomaea sought to trick it out of me but I told her a lie.'

'Good girl. What then of the experience?' Comus enquired. 'You seem no more than slightly discomfited.'

'It . . . it was terrible but wondrous,' Zara replied. 'His organ is vast, larger in proportion even than those of the Baluchiteria. To take it in my cunt I would need more lubrication than I can myself supply and perhaps as long as a quarter glass of being opened by fist.'

'Remarkable.'

'He made no move to force it on me, but took pleasure in making me choke while I sucked. My confusion and discomfort was a rich joke to him, and also the other Uhlans, yet I am not hurt. He also allowed me to take a climax myself, though doubtless more for his vanity than my pleasure.'

'He was not surprised by your request?'

'No more than might be expected.'

'Perfect. Thank you, my pleasure. Here, your vials of ameliorant. There is water in the trough if you wish to wash and perhaps I can offer you a cup of muscat?'

Zara accepted both.

* * *

From the roof of the female citadel tower the Lady Alla-Sha looked out across Suza and the plains and hills beyond. Her choices were stark: accept Otomos, step down from the Ladyship or try to prevent the ascension of the suanthrope. Even when on heat her erotic tastes had always been refined, and she had accepted few true-men, and never the coarse, rutting passion of the suan genotype. Nor was Otomos any ordinary suan. He had been fathered by Lomas, while his mother had been from the far south, a woman of imposing bulk and strange, uncouth habits. Yet even she had not had the thick, plated skin of her son, while the size of his tusks and genitals was out of normal proportion even on his massive body. It was also said that when he came enough sperm was produced to fill the largest of wine goblets. Indeed he was said to regularly perform the trick at Uhlan feasts.

Alla-Sha gave a shudder of distaste at the thought. To step down would be so easy, either to the rank of councillor or altogether. Yet to do so would leave the Ladyship vacant and open to the machinations of Rufina. Already Rufina's faction enjoyed a majority in the female council. The twin true-girls, Zirina and Ilana, were younger sisters to Rufina and supported her every move. That alone allowed Rufina a great deal of control. Indeed, it had only been the strength of Lord Pallus that had so far curbed her excesses. Jasiel, the Mistress of Courtesans, although a felian, had long been a rival to Alla-Sha and was known to enjoy Rufina's more refined erotic torments. The sole suanthrope, Soumea, was Pomina's mother and an ardent supporter of both Otomos and her daughter. While no supporter of Rufina, she could not be counted on to back Alla-Sha.

The thought of subservience to Rufina was as galling as the thought of mating with Otomos was repulsive. For years Rufina had regarded Alla-Sha with malice and envy that showed with every glance. As the eldest child of Lord Pallus' first mate, Rufina also regarded the Ladyship as hers by right. If it became hers in reality, then Alla-Sha could expect to find herself spread on a public whipping frame as soon as the vindictive true-girl could engineer an excuse. The sole comfort was that it was impossible to see Rufina accepting Otomos as mate, yet that in turn raised disturbing possibilities.

The soft, ineffectual Pomina as Lady would be little better than Rufina, destroying the balance of power between male and female citadels. Nor was any other female suan a practical candidate. Indeed, a period of suan supremacy was to be avoided at any cost, and objectively the choice was worse than that of Otomos and Rufina as Lord and Lady. For over three thousand years Suza had stood on its isolated hill, first as a citadel built by true-men, then as a town as genomorphs of various types fled from persecution in the western lands. The fugitives had brought a horror of bigotry and a pride in their own type. The females of each genotype also bred true, so that a male might father any of the types but females always bore in their own image. These factors had allowed an otherwise heterogeneous population to live together, as indeed had been intended by the genotypes' original creators.

Now there were true-men, suans with their piglike characteristics and three types of felian, tigranthropes like herself, with a blending of tiger traits, oncanthropes and acyonthropes, their plasms taken from panthers and cheetahs respectively. The blend had proved strong, with each genotype providing its own skills and the faults of each balanced by the virtues of the others. The town had flourished to become a city, resisting or overcoming its neighbours until it now stood as the strongest state among the dozen or so that vied for local supremacy. The entire cone-shaped hill was now cloaked with buildings, a great warren with the citadel at its peak and the five-hundred-year-old great wall surrounding it.

Most other states had a strong predominance of one genotype or another, and that often proved a weakness. Twice only across its history had Suza come close to falling, and both times had been during a period of suan supremacy. The very aggression and lack of tact that made suans such good soldiers too often led to miscalculation and a tendency to act too soon. With Otomos in unchallenged leadership the same was likely to happen again, and whatever the male councillors might think, Suza was not strong enough to resist an alliance of all her enemies. Few seemed able to see this, just as few had her knowledge of the city's history and the mistakes of the past.

With a deep sigh Alla-Sha turned back towards the stairs, then turned for a final look out across the shimmering brown and green tones of the city.

3

Manipulation by Sodomy

Comus the essencier sat at his workbench with a small vial in one hand. It contained twenty-seven drops of a clear, thick oil and gave off a rich, musky smell so thick as to be almost rank. Its distillation had required painstaking work, using a system of retorts and jacket-clad cooling spirals. Now it was done, and he had what he had set out to produce – triple distilled suan musk from Otomos himself.

Taking up a flask of bright, pale-green oil, he poured half the contents of the vial into it. A brief shake mixed the two oils, and the scent of apples filled the air. Comus inspected the mixture and then shook his head. Taking up another flask, this time of a rich brown fluid, he added five drops, then shook the flask once more and again inspected the results. The colour was now a yellowish green, while the smell combined those of apples, coffee and musk. Now smiling, he transferred a measure of the mixture to a silver vial and sealed the vessels. Turning to the main body of the hall, he called for his apprentice. Ciriel appeared, emerging from a side room.

'Ah, Ciriel,' he addressed her. 'Tonight I intend to seduce your friend Pomina. I require your advice as to her preferences.'

'Pomina?' Ciriel answered. 'But Mentor . . .'

'Yes, yes,' Comus responded, 'I know what you mean

to say, that Otomos will tear me limb from limb and so forth. Your concern is appreciated but I intend to have her anyway. Come, you may explain while I bathe and dress.'

'Mentor . . .'

'No more, Ciriel, or I shall feel obliged to slap your pretty bottom. Now, what of Pomina?'

'Otomos takes her with great vigour, and always to the same plan. First he lifts her by the scruff and spanks her until her juice is running freely, then he puts her on his cock, sometimes face up, sometimes down. His strength is terrifying. When on his cock she cannot even touch the ground, yet he seems barely to notice her weight.'

'I fear that I am unlikely to be able to reproduce this erotic feat. Does she not enjoy more refined play?'

'Yes, when she and I play she likes to be coaxed slowly to her climax with attention paid to her whole body, especially her breasts. She enjoys being oiled and lightly spanked, also tickled.'

'Tied?'

'Now and again.'

'Has she learnt to enjoy her anal responses?'

'She thinks it depraved but giggles if she is touched there.'

'A shame. So few appreciate the exquisite pleasures of anal play.'

'It is degenerate, Mentor.'

'Yet delightful, as you yourself can vouch.'

Ciriel's cheeks coloured but her mouth turned up at the corners, drawing a knowing laugh from Comus. While they had been speaking he had undressed, handing each piece of clothing to her until he stood naked. She took his clothes away while he walked to the small washroom that opened from the hall. Climbing into the low stone trough, he began to splash water on to his body. Ciriel quickly returned, and shrugged her gown from her shoulders at the arch of the washroom. Beneath it she was naked. Small and compact, her body was neat rather than opulent, with slim hips, pert breasts and a tight, bulging bottom that was undoubtedly feminine despite lacking weight and size.

Comus watched as she took soap and worked up a lather. Joining him in the trough, she began to soap his body, forcing him to close his eyes and think over the formulae of complicated essences to prevent his cock from growing erect. Even when she massaged the soap into his cock and balls he managed to remain detached, although it was evident that she was making an effort to arouse him.

Despite all his cock had began to swell when she finished washing him and as she stepped from the trough she turned him a smile that left no doubt as to her enjoyment of his response. He returned what was intended to be a look of reprimand, at which she dropped the towel on the floor.

Bending to pick up the towel, Ciriel gave a display of her bottom that was all too clearly no accident. Not only did the trim, hairless lips of her sex show, but the puckered hole of her anus. Both were favourite receptacles for his cock, but instead of taking advantage of her display he allowed her to towel his body dry.

'May I speak freely, Mentor?' she asked as she stroked the towel across the muscles of his chest.

'As always.'

'Then please take my advice and leave Pomina to Otomos. She is pretty and playful, but if you wish a suan girl, then there are many others who would be happy to accommodate you. Some even enjoy sodomy. Not that they would admit to it, but I know. Aphelia, for instance, is as pretty. Close to the last full moon I caught her pleasuring her bottom with her fingers. We three could play together. Shall I send for her?'

'Another time, Ciriel, my little one,' Comus replied.

'Tonight I must have Pomina. No other will do. For now I wish to be rubbed down. Use my normal oil but with a dash of apple and apply your hands only as necessary.'

Ciriel obeyed, fetching the oil and rubbing it into his skin in a practised manner but deliberately avoiding his genitals. Only at the end did she touch his cock, but with an unmistakable firmness of purpose. Her hand curled around the shaft, rubbing the oil in and then starting a slow and purposeful movement. It began to harden and her stroking became more urgent.

'That is pleasant,' Comus sighed, 'but perhaps unwise.'

'Not so, Mentor,' Ciriel answered. 'I intend to masturbate you and then perhaps you will forget about Pomina.'

'Ciriel,' he said warningly and gently removed her hand from his penis.

'Or I could suck,' she urged, cupping his balls in her other hand. 'I'd kneel for you and take you in my mouth. I'd roll your balls over my tongue and kiss your anus. I'd suck until you came and play with the sperm in my mouth or lick it from your hand . . .'

'Ciriel,' he repeated more sternly and again took her hand away.

'Think of my lips, soft and warm on your beautiful cock,' she continued. 'Think of my mouth running with your sperm. Or you could do it inside me, deep in my vagina . . .'

'Ciriel, I have warned you,' Comus cut in. 'Stop tormenting me or I'll not only slap your bottom to a ruddy pink but leave you tied for the night with a measure of oil of pimento in your rectum. Do you recall how it burns?'

'Yes, Mentor,' Ciriel answered, 'but not so much as it does when your penis is coated with it and in my bottom.'

'Ciriel!'

'Sodomise me,' she urged. 'I'll hold my back in to keep my bottom round as you like it. I've been practising the control of my ring as you said I should. You can put your beautiful cock-head in and I'll squeeze with my hole until you come in me. I'll . . .'

'Ciriel, Ciriel,' Comus interrupted, 'you tempt me almost beyond endurance. I'll gladly sodomise you tomorrow, and do all the things you say, but for now I need a full quantity of sperm for Pomina. You wouldn't want your friend to be disappointed in me, would you?'

In answer she pulled back from him and went on to all fours. The position left her entirely open to him, with her buttocks apart and her anus pushed up. The little hole winked as she tightened her ring, taunting him to put his penis to it. Comus closed his eyes and stepped from the washroom. Behind him she gave a muted cry of frustration.

He went to sit on the couch in his chamber, trying to ignore the warm feeling in his cock and push the memory of the lewd, winking invitation of Ciriel's anus from his mind. Yet he knew how tight she was, and how she had learnt to control her anal ring to pleasure him, employing a skill equal to that the best courtesans had with their vaginas. When he buggered Ciriel she would squirm and mewl as his cock moved inside her rectum. Also she would talk to him, telling him how it felt to have his cock up her bottom, describing each moment from when her ring first opened to accept him to the very climax and beyond while she masturbated as her bottom-hole oozed sperm on to her eager fingers . . .

With a desperate effort he tore his thoughts away from her even as she walked in, still naked and swaying her slim hips as she walked.

'I'll dress myself,' he announced.

She ignored him, but came over, turned and abruptly sat her trim little rump in his lap, then wiggled her bottom to ease his penis into the cleft between her cheeks. He could feel the dampness and warmth of her vulva pressed against his balls while her small, round buttocks wiggled in his lap, a sensation too good to resist. Worse still, the bottom-hole he had been trying so hard not to think about was now rubbing on his cock shaft. She had greased it with his bath oil and it felt slick and spongy.

'Bugger me, or I'll pee on you,' she announced.

'Ciriel, no,' he ordered. 'Get up. I'm going to have to beat you.'

'I'll do it,' she threatened. 'I'll do it all down your balls, then you'll have to take me. Think how easily it would go in, all soft and easy in my bottom. Please, Mentor, do you not like my bottom?'

'I adore your bottom, as you know,' Comus answered, trying desperately to control himself. 'Now . . .'

Something warm and wet was trickling down his balls and down over his thighs.

'There, I've done it,' Ciriel sighed.

Comus could do nothing, but lay back as the warm pee trickled over him. Ciriel began to rub her bottom on his penis, back and forth to move her oily crease on his rapidly hardening shaft as her urine splashed out over him. Giving in, Comus lay back on the couch and took hold of Ciriel's bottom. She lifted it obligingly and giggled, knowing she had won. She bent forward so that her vulva showed, still with pee trickling from the hole. His cock was now fully hard and glossy with oil and urine. Taking it in his hand, he nudged it forward, pressing the tip between the lips of her sex. The head disappeared into her vagina, then the shaft as she sank down on to him with a long, pleased sigh.

The flow of her urine died away, leaving him warm and damp from belly to anus as he began to bounce her on his penis. She giggled and cried out in pleasure as

72

they coupled, occasionally wriggling her bottom on his erection in pure joy. Only when he once more lifted her to withdraw his cock from her vagina did her passion become more serious. Her breathing deepened as his erection popped from her hole and she reached back to pull open her buttocks. Comus once again took hold of his cock and began to rub it on her, only this time not between her sex lips but against the well-oiled ring of her anus.

He allowed Ciriel to control her own penetration, watching as she gradually lowered her bottom on to his cock. Her anus was quickly straining against the tip of it, struggling to keep him out as she held herself tight shut. Then abruptly she allowed herself to relax and her sphincter opened like a pink, fleshy flower, accepting first the head of his cock and then the shaft, bit by bit until she was once more sat pertly on his lap only now with the full length of his erection embedded in her anal passage.

Comus took hold of her buttocks and pulled them wide, treating himself to a view of her sphincter stretched taut around his penis. She was moaning and moving up and down, controlling the rhythm of her own buggery. He made no move to stop her but simply watched, feeling his excitement rise at the sight of her beautiful young body riding on his penis. Her rear view was a model of innocent beauty, long black hair hanging to the small of her back, smooth olive-toned skin, a neat waist flaring gently to her hips, the neat globes of her bottom, all showing the sweet beauty of young womanhood. Then – in a contrast which Comus found particularly alluring – there was the actual crease of her bottom, spread wide and with the shaft of his penis embedded in her anus.

He concentrated on the view of her bottom as she rode, feeling his pleasure build slowly towards climax and occasionally reaching out to caress the soft pear of her bottom. Her own responses built as well, her bouncing changing in pace from rapid, shallow thrusts to long, slow pulls that took his cock almost free of her rectum only for her to fill herself slowly once more. She also played with her breasts, belly and thighs, stroking her skin in long, sensuous motions. These began slowly to focus between her legs, her hand going to squeeze his balls or touch the junction between penis and anus as if to confirm just how debauched an act she was enjoying.

Comus had begun to feel that he could hold back no longer when Ciriel suddenly put her hand purposefully to her vulva. He tensed, listening to her rising moans and waiting for the delicious moment when her anus would go into the climactic spasm around his cock. She was bouncing fast, jamming the sensitive flesh of his penis head into the soft tube of her rectum again and again. At last he could take no more and grabbed her by the hips, taking control even as she gave the first cry of her climax. Her anus tightened on his cock, then began to spasm, squeezing and squeezing as his erection seemed to swell to impossible proportions and then burst, jetting sperm deep into her bowels. She screamed as it happened, her own climax lasting far beyond his, so that she was still bucking her bottom frantically on his cock even when it had began to soften and retract from her.

Spent, she leant forward, allowing his cock to pull slowly free of her bottom-hole as it lost its rigidity. When it came free she made no move to rise, but stayed in place as Comus watched his sperm run from her slowly closing anus and down on to the sweet pink lips of her sex.

'That was beautiful, I thank you,' she sighed. 'Are you glad you didn't go off chasing after Pomina?'

'You are incomparable as always,' Comus sighed. 'Tomorrow must suffice for Pomina.'

Ciriel made no reply but pulled herself up from his

body. Turning to him she gave a look of sulky resignation and then sat down on the couch.

'As usual I have been unable to resist either your body or your impudence,' Comus continued. 'Still, at least I will have the satisfaction of beating you.'

'Beating me!' Ciriel squealed. 'Why?'

'Why?' Comus echoed. 'Because you have seduced me from my purpose, that is why. What is more, I shall beat you in public, and when you become aroused again I will allow the crowd to take turns with you. Is that reasonable justice for subverting my will?'

'Yes, Mentor,' Ciriel sighed, 'but perhaps I would be better whipped in private, or at most with a select few invited to enjoy my arousal?'

'No,' Comus responded. 'It will be public, and short of Otomos or Hoat chancing by you may expect to have your vagina used by any who care to.'

He rose, ignoring her attempts to have her punishment changed as he washed and dressed. Then, with Ciriel held firmly by the ear, Comus left the hall of essences. Moving at a brisk march, he took her to one of the major passages. Here torches provided adequate illumination while citizens were coming and going. A colonnaded window provided an ideal whipping post and Comus made short work of strapping Ciriel's wrists to a pillar. Naked and with her small, round bottom stuck out to the passage Ciriel provided an appealing spectacle and a crowd soon began to gather.

By telling each newcomer that he intended to beat his apprentice for impudence, Comus quickly had a sufficiently large audience for his purpose. Then, borrowing a leather belt from a passing suanthrope, he set to work on Ciriel's squirming bottom. She writhed and thrashed under the beating, making no effort to hide the most intimate details of her body as she danced in the pain of her punishment. The crowd watched in delight, one or two criticising the technique of her beating and more commenting on the oiled state of her bottom crease and the amount of thick, sticky fluid that was running down the inside of her thighs.

As the state of her arousal became increasingly apparent, cocks began to be pulled out among the audience. Seeing this, Ciriel began to make her bottom dance with yet more energy, but Comus took no notice, planting smack after smack across her nates until both were an angry red and her initial gasps had turned to deep, loud, sobs.

Only then did he stop beating her and offer her to the crowd. For a while Ciriel continued to jump from foot to foot, unable to control herself in her pain. A crack of the belt across her thighs put a stop to this and she moved to position herself for entry. She stood with her ankles set apart and her back dipped to an elegant curve that left her well-thrashed bottom thrust out to the audience and her open vagina freely available. Unable to move her hands, all she could do was look back with an expression of nervous anticipation on her pretty face and wait to be taken.

The men of the audience used her one by one, politely offering each other the next use of her vagina. Several took the opportunity to fondle her breasts and bottom, or to masturbate her to make her come while they had their cocks inside her. Sperm had soon began to run down her thighs, then to fall in thick clots on the floor, until she was standing in a pool of male come and her own juice.

Intent on fair play, Comus allowed each male to take her and also several of the females to explore her helpless body. Only when the last of a group of burly suanthrope guards had ejaculated over her well-beaten bottom did he call a halt. Untying Ciriel's wrists, he put her across his shoulder and set off once more for the hall of essences. There he washed her and applied soothing oil to her bottom, vagina and anus. He then took her to her couch, only to become aroused once more and bugger her. When they finally slept it was on her couch with her head cradled into the crook of his shoulder, showing the deep intimacy of the beaten girl to the one who has punished her. Her mouth was set in a sleepy smile of the deepest satisfaction.

The courtesan Zara lay back on a cushion, naked and masturbating in an idle fashion but with her thoughts only half on the sensations of her vulva and nipples. Of more importance to her were the intrigues of Suza, in which she thought to discern a pattern. After serving the council the previous night she had been dismissed, leaving Xerinus alone with Ilarion. This was unusual. The two brothers often spoke together after council meetings, but usually only to discuss epicurean refinements. Wine, spice, coffee and erotic diversion were favourite topics, but in all cases she was welcomed to provide a third viewpoint and the benefits of her body. That she had been dismissed despite offering to stay could only mean that the conversation had involved secrets. Given that they had been discussing the succession to the Lordship, the nature of the private discussion seemed obvious. Neither true-man approved of Otomos as Zara knew. Thus it seemed likely that they planned to scheme against the giant suanthrope's succession. How this was to be accomplished she had no idea.

The following day she had been summoned by Comus the essencier to perform a most unusual task. The nature of this had puzzled her, as had the risk it involved. Comus was known for his caution and would not risk confronting Otomos without good reason. Undoubtedly he was involved in some intrigue.

At her evening appointment with Xerinus she had discovered a link between the two events. The councillor had used oil of urtica to grease her breasts for his cock.

It had been strong, and poured not from a sealed vial but from a minim-cup. From its freshness she knew that no more than a day could have elapsed since it was made, and it could only have come from the same batch she and Comus had used. Xerinus had visited Comus.

Thus the councillor's intrigue seemed certain to involve Comus, who was a favourite of Xerinus and possibly the councillor's son. Comus was handsome, vain and intelligent. He was also well known and popular owing to the nature of his trade. In due course he might well have been a candidate for the council. Yet to challenge for the Lordship, and against Otomos, was the act of a fool.

Comus was no fool.

Nor did he act without reason; yet his reason for wanting a quantity of Otomos' sperm was beyond her.

The thought of how she had collected the sperm brought her mind back to the pleasant sensation of her body. With one hand between her thighs and the other on a breast, she had been slowly working herself up, a half-conscious masturbation that aided her thoughts. Now it became more direct as she thought of the blend of arousal and fright she had experienced with Otomos' cock jammed into her mouth and throat. Concentrating on the sense of absolute helplessness it had brought, she put a finger to her clitoris and pulled her legs up and open.

The curtain of her outer chamber rustled, signalling the arrival of a visitor. Zara spat a curse and half-rose, only to fall back to the cushion. With her eyes closed and her finger working hard on her clitoris, she shut out the world, focusing her mind on the suanthrope's gigantic cock and how she had been stripped, told to kneel, made to suck, held down on his cock, being unable to breath, swallowing come, choking . . .

Zara came. Her thighs were clamped tight on her hand and her teeth were gritted as the climax built and exploded in her head, only for her to lose concentration before it was really over and open her eyes to see who had arrived.

'Slattern,' Rufina's voice sounded from the arch that led from her inner chamber.

'Mistress, I . . .' Zara began, only to stop short at the sight of Rufina's expression, a hard smile that conveyed both derision and amusement.

'I have work for you,' Rufina stated. 'First – as doubtless you have been prying on your appointments and gossiping with your fellow sluts – what hearsay have you collected?'

'Little, Mistress, save only that the calligrapher Tian-Sha visited Master Urzon this morning.'

'What of it? He is Master Architect. She illuminates his charts.'

'She had no charts, and would not speak while Eomaea served arabica in milk.'

'Perhaps useful, although I am told she is in season and so likely came merely to slake her lust on his fat pig's cock. What else?'

'Nothing new, Mistress.'

'Then get up and put this on.'

Rufina took a leather leash from beneath her cloak and threw it to the ground. Zara reached for it, only to find her hand trapped beneath Rufina's boot.

'What you are about to do,' Rufina spoke, 'is not for idle gossip, nor for you to ponder on. You will do as I say, no more, no less, and afterwards you will put the incident from your mind. Am I clear?'

'Yes, Mistress,' Zara squeaked.

'Then come.'

'Might I not wash? What of my clothes?'

'Where you are going it will make no difference what you have been doing with your fingers, nor that you are nude. Now come, or do I have to whip you again?'

Zara fixed the leash and collar to her neck and

79

hastened to follow as Rufina strode from the chamber. As Zara had anticipated, Rufina chose the smaller corridors and walkways, and her curiosity and unease rose as they ascended the city. Twice they emerged into the moonlight, only to plunge once more beneath black-mouthed arches. Rufina gave no hint of their destination, and only when they came out into the main corridor that ran beneath the citadel did Zara realise their location. Here Rufina took the leash in her hand and hurried forward, only to stop before a high door.

'This is the stable block, Mistress,' Zara said in puzzlement.

'I realise that, stupid girl,' Rufina snapped. 'Now follow me.'

Within, Zara found her nose assailed by the reek of the Baluchitheria and their dung. Puzzled as to Rufina's intentions, she allowed herself to be led to an empty stall, where her leash was attached to a peg as if she had no more volition than a draft beast. Rufina left, closing the inset door to leave Zara in blackness relieved only by the faint moonlight from the door grill high above her.

She waited, wondering if the councillor intended to test some new erotic torture on her, and if so, why it needed to be done in a Baluchitherium stall. Anticipation of the climax that such treatment would eventually bring mixed with trepidation for the pain it might involve and relief that whatever Rufina intended did not involve one of the great beasts. Then came the rumble of a deep voice and Zara realised that her fate was not to be so very different.

' . . . that I can do, be it Otomos or any other.'

Even as Zara recognised the bass tone of Hoat's voice the inset door opened once more and the ursanthrope himself pushed through. He bore a torch, which cast red-orange light into the stall, illuminating the high walls, the carpet of filthy straw that littered the floor and the vaulted ceiling high above. On seeing her his face broke into a broad grin, to which Zara responded with a shy smile. Rufina followed him and closed the door firmly as Hoat set the torch in a sconce.

'Mistress, am I to pleasure Hoat?' Zara asked tentatively.

'Yes.'

'By hand, I trust? Or perhaps between my breasts or bottom cheeks?'

'No, in your cunt, and from the rear.'

'Mistress!'

'Do you dare dispute me?'

'But . . .'

'He wants your cunt and he wants you kneeling. Now get down!'

'Mistress! I lack the capacity! For this task you should have chosen Igalia!'

'Stop whining!' Rufina spat. 'Now get down in the straw and stick your fat backside in the air!'

'It is not such a trial,' Hoat rumbled. 'Tian-Sha takes close to half . . .'

'Tian-Sha!' both true-girls cut in.

'Indeed,' he went on. 'She comes to me whenever she is in season.'

'Another slut, for all her fine airs,' Rufina remarked. 'Now get down, Zara, or I'll have Hoat take a beast quirt to you.'

Zara gave a nervous glance at the thick, double-ended lash that hung on a nearby wall. It was designed for the thick hides of the Baluchitheria and definitely not for a girl's tender skin, yet she had no doubt that Rufina was as good as her word. Once she had been whipped Hoat was certain to mount her anyway, and the thought of attempting to accommodate his penis was certainly tantalising if also terrifying.

Then there was the position she would be in: collared and leashed, upended on the filthy stable floor. She

81

looked at the straw with distaste. It steamed faintly and smelt of Baluchitherium, also of mould. Evidently the stall had been recently occupied and not cleaned for some time. It was filthy, but she was going to be mated in it, with her face in it. Entry from the rear pleased her, providing deep penetration and the bliss of offering her bottom to her mate. Normally, though, she was mounted while kneeling on silken cushions or at least a rug, and by lovers whose genitals were in proportion to her own. Now she would have to kneel in a pile of filthy straw and offer herself to the massive, shambling Hoat, the very size of whose cock was a topic of tremulous speculation in the hall of courtesans. Once done, she would at least be able to boast of her exploit to her peers, having taken a cock that made even Igalia nervous. With that thought in her mind Zara stepped forward and sank to her knees among the straw. The rank stench became stronger as she put her face down and lifted her haunches, offering her naked bottom.

'Stupid girl!' Rufina spat. 'How is he to mount you with a limp penis? Suck it first, you little fool!'

Zara rocked back, smarting with the injustice of Rufina's remark. She had been told to stick her bottom up and she had done it. For a moment she opened her mouth to protest, but caught sight of the heavy quirt on the wall. Then her indignation was swept from her head as Hoat dropped his leather apron to the floor.

Faced with the huge cock and balls that hung from his groin she could only stare and part her lips in submission to what she was expected to do. Hoat held his penis out and rolled down the foreskin to expose the meaty glans, its flesh moist and red-pink in colour. A strongly male scent assailed Zara's nose, putting a hard lump into her throat even as she felt one nipple pop out and then the other. Hoat stepped forward and reached down, taking her leash in his hand. She found herself trembling hard as he pulled her forward by the neck, slowly, bringing her face ever nearer his monstrous penis.

Zara gaped wide, remembering how she had strained to take Otomos' cock into her mouth just hours before. Despite the length of Hoat's organ, it was mercifully less thick, if only by a narrow margin. The glans touched her lips and she tasted the salt and the flavour of bear, then it had plugged her mouth, a thick wedge of flesh that had her jaws straining and pressed her tongue back and down. Moving her cheeks and tongue as best she could she began to suck.

He hardened quickly, filling her mouth to nearly the same, straining state that Otomos had done earlier. Only where Otomos had done his best to jam the full three hand spans of his penis down her throat, Hoat remained content for her to suck on his fist-sized glans while he masturbated the long tube of dark red-brown flesh that stood between his groin and her mouth.

With his cock a straining erection in her mouth, Zara began to suck more eagerly, aware that a mouthful of sperm would save her a sore vagina and also having to put her face down in the revolting old straw. Hoat gave a low growl in response and tightened his grip on her leash, pulling another section of penis into her mouth. Zara fought back the urge to gag as the tip nudged the back of her throat, instead reaching up to take the great hairy mass of his scrotum into her hands. Again Hoat growled.

'Pull back, Hoat,' Rufina's voice sounded. 'She aims to make you spend in her mouth and so rob you of your treat.'

Hoat hesitated and then Zara felt the pressure on her neck relax and the fat penis head that filled her mouth was slowly withdrawn.

'Now, on your knees,' Rufina ordered. 'Face well down and backside well up. Let's be sure your cunt is properly offered.'

Zara obeyed, dropping to all fours and crawling

round to present them her rear view. Trembling hard and with her eyes tight shut, she put her face down to the filthy floor. With her fists clenched on two handfuls of dank straw and her senses swimming with the taste of bear's cock and the scent of mould and dung, she spread her knees and thrust her bottom up to full prominence. The dampness between her legs immediately produced a cool sensation, not just on her open vulva but between the ample cheeks of her bottom and on her anal ring. All of it was showing, a display which she loved to make for its very vulnerability, yet which had never before been offered to so huge a penis.

'She is wet and open, as you see,' Rufina remarked casually, 'yet her cunt is tight for one used so often. This may serve to ease her passage.'

Zara looked back, finding Hoat looming over her with his great shaggy legs set apart and his penis sticking out from his groin like a small log. Rufina was holding out a jar to him. He took it and ran a finger around the interior, bringing out a thick lump of some rich cream. Zara watched as he leant down to her, then felt the cool of the cream as it was applied to her, touching not the open hole of her vagina but the tightly puckered ring of her anus.

'No!' she squeaked, half-rising in fright at the prospect of attempting to accommodate Hoat in her rectum.

Rufina began to laugh as Hoat's hand settled on to the small of her back and pushed her back down gently but with a strength far beyond her means of resistance. Helpless, Zara could only clutch tighter at her fistfuls of dirty straw. Then she felt his glans touch between the raised cheeks of her bottom, squashing the cream out over her anus and up between them. Her legs began to kick in an agony of frustration as he used the tip of his cock to smear the cream in, down, on to her sex and into the hole of her vagina. She gave a gasp of relief as

84

she realised that she was not going to be buggered, then another as Hoat's glans poked at the entrance to her vagina. Zara found her mouth open and eyes wide as her hole strained to accommodate the massive head.

It felt enormous, a great ball of flesh prodding at an impossibly small hole. She felt the cream that had been put up her vagina squash out at the sides, then her hole was stretching, opening until her hips seemed to be coming apart. Rufina was still laughing, a cruel, mocking sound directed at Zara's impotent struggles and desperate panic when she had thought the huge cock was going to be forced into her rectum.

'One day, Zara, I will have you buggered,' she taunted, 'but not today. Just know yourself fortunate that Hoat is not so debauched as to prefer the feel of rectum to that of vagina. Come now, Hoat, she is a courtesan, there is no need to be so gentle.'

Hoat's hands took Zara's haunches. The mouth of her vagina was full of penis, stretched to what seemed an impossible extent. He gave a sudden push, shoving her open mouth into the straw. His fingers held her substantial buttocks like a normal man might have held two eggs, gripping her whole lower body as he pushed himself inside her. The sensation was too powerful for her even to think of spitting out her unexpected mouthful of straw and dirt. Instead she simply held her position as her vagina filled with what seemed an impossibly large quantity of cock flesh. Then it bumped on her cervix and stopped, leaving her with the impression that her whole body was full of bloated erection, not just her vagina but every part of her. Her head especially seemed to be bursting with penis, a sensation that had her moaning and clutching at the ground.

Rufina laughed to see the state Zara was in and then Hoat began to move his cock. Zara gasped as she felt it stir inside her, pulling slowly back then sharply in to

85

push hard on her insides and knock the breath from her lungs. As he began to fuck her she felt her control slipping quickly away, until there was nothing she could do but pant out her emotions into the straw. He was holding her, totally in control of her sex, using her vagina as he pleased. Dimly she was aware that no more than half of his huge cock was inside her, yet it had become the very focus of her existence as she was ridden at his pleasure. With each push his balls would swing against her thighs, the coarse hairs tickling her vulva to produce ever more ecstatic responses from her clitoris. Her breasts were swinging too, the fat, dangling globes rocking back and forth to the motion of her fucking with the nipples rubbing against the rough stalks of the straw.

With a loud, broken sob she reached back to find her vulva. She kept her face down, her mouth wide and full of straw and dirt, the taste and smell of which had become an element of what was happening to her. Her fingers found her clitoris, touching the little bud to bring a new ecstasy. Hoat's balls slapped against her hand as she began to masturbate.

Rufina's cruel laughter sounded again in response to Zara's surrender to the feel of the cock inside her. With the mocking sound ringing in her ears and her body bucking on Hoat's cock, Zara began to come. For a moment it was building, the muscles tensing around the penis at the centre of her body. Then it came in one great rush. With her feet drumming on the floor and mouth working on its filthy contents she came, her control quite gone save for the finger on her clitoris. At the very peak of her climax she screamed Rufina's name, then again as the orgasm subsided, more quietly thanking her tormentress for what was happening to her.

The response was a short, derisive snort, but it was lost on Zara. As her vagina had tightened on Hoat's cock in orgasm he had began to increase the pace of his pushes. She had no time to recover herself, but was lifted bodily, still in climax but helpless to prevent him doing as he pleased. With a squeak of alarm she threw out her hands to balance herself, only to meet loose straw and something soft and damp. He began to move her faster on his cock, leaving her toes scrabbling in the straw. Her last vestige of control went and she found herself being tossed like a doll on his invading penis, fucked with a frantic jerking motion that robbed her of the ability to do more than gasp and grunt in helpless passion.

Then it happened. Her vagina had seemed impossibly full, but suddenly it was as if his cock had blown up to twice its already huge size. She screamed as her insides strained, bucking in desperation and kicking out with her legs. Something wet exploded from around the mouth of her vagina, soaking her thighs and drenching her pubic mound. Hoat grunted and jammed himself into her, forcing his penis hard against her cervix to make her scream again. Without the slightest warning she climaxed herself, her body overcome by the sheer intensity of his orgasm. For what seemed an age she was writhing and wriggling on the end of his cock, coming to peak after peak as he drained his sperm inside her. When finally it was over he released her hips and she slid off his penis to collapse on the floor.

Zara sank face down in the straw, sore and exhausted, no longer caring about the dirt and smell. Vaguely she was aware of the opening of the inset door and of the faint sound of Rufina and Hoat in conversation, but she was too far gone to find interest in whatever scheme they were hatching.

On the ledge high above the stables Tian-Sha perched motionless. It had been her intention to spend the best part of a glass easing her need on Hoat's cock. She had done well in the evening, taking male after male until her belly was swollen and her vagina ran with sperm. Mating Hoat would have allowed her to rest yet to keep herself filled, but on reaching the ledge she had detected the scents of Zara and Rufina.

That Rufina should have chosen to have Zara mated by Hoat was no great surprise. Tian-Sha knew full well that Rufina took pleasure in the erotic anguish of others. It was as if the councillor fed on the feelings of girls under the whip, with their vaginas filled to capacity or undergoing any of the more subtle torments she might devise. The helpless shuddering climaxes that she induced in her victims seemed to give Rufina an especial satisfaction, as if it milked them of their most powerful and intimate emotions.

Putting a true-girl to the ursanthrope's cock was merely a new refinement, unusual only in that Rufina normally hated anything that might involve soiling her own precious hands or offending her senses. Tian-Sha had waited, enjoying the scent of Hoat's arousal and also Zara's. During the mating she had kept herself aroused by stroking her sex with her tail tip, but when Rufina and Hoat emerged from the stable she had frozen to absolute stillness. Her orange and black markings blended well with the shadows and the flickering light of Hoat's torch, while her cloak of camel hair broke her outline and hid the pale fur of her front. Thick culottes of black silk also covered the pale fur of her sex.

Not that the concealment had been necessary. Neither true-girl nor ursanthrope had thought to search the wall above them. Each word was clear to her, Rufina's reminder of some important task, Hoat's grunted assurance, Rufina's reiteration of the importance of following her instructions.

Rufina then made her way from the stables, leaving Tian-Sha aware only that some intrigue had been hatched that necessitated Rufina's involvement with

Hoat. Zara had clearly been a treat, brought to ensure that Hoat complied with whatever Rufina asked of him. Despite her ignorance of details, Tian-Sha felt certain that Rufina's scheme would be of benefit only to Rufina, and undoubtedly not to Hoat.

She considered dropping down, only to reject the idea. For all her sexual intimacy with Hoat she could not be certain where his loyalties lay, and Rufina had clearly gone to great lengths to gain his support. Nor was it possible to trust Zara, who could only be relied upon to hold a secret until her next session under Rufina's whip.

With a hiss of anger and frustration she began to make her way along the ledge. With most of Suza below her and the moon bright in the sky she could make out details not just of the city but of the plain beyond, with the river showing as a broad band of silver and the hills in the distance. It was these to which she set her eyes as she left the stable area and began to make her way down across the roofs.

At the wall she paused, waiting until a lone suan guard appeared from a watch house. His scent was strong in her nostrils: male, suan and slightly aroused, perhaps from the indulgence of a serving girl in the watch house. To emerge from the shadows, pull his cock hard and mount him would have been the work of a moment, yet she held back. Only when he had disappeared in the dark tunnel of a corner turret did she come forward, and then not to accost the guard but to swing herself over the parapet and start down the wall.

She had chosen the place carefully, a high bastion the outer wall of which was invisible from within the city. The stones were large and worn, allowing her claws purchase between their joints. With great care she let herself down until she was no more than twice her own height above the ground, then dropped. Sinking to a crouch she looked up, seeking for sight, sound or scent that might indicate that her departure had been noticed. Only the faint scent of the guard was detectable and that was as before, showing neither the acrid tang of fear nor the strong musk of aggression.

Turning her face to the fields, she cast about for a different scent, quickly isolating it among the varied mammalian smells of livestock. A dozen of them were evident, the high, adapted racing camels that alone of riding beasts showed no fear of felian scent. A quick run brought her among them, where she selected an unbranded female and mounted. Urging the beast into a steady trot, she set off to the east.

The first flush of dawn found her in an area of low, barren hills well to the east of Suza. The air was silent but full of scents – thyme, sage, vine and animals. Only one of these stirred her, a bitter musk that both set her claws out and made her uncomfortably aware of the heat in her sex. There was more of the ape than the human in the scent, and it was exclusively male.

Its origin, she knew, could only be a group of beta-male cynocephalids. The half-human creatures were common in the hills, and occasionally seen near the city, where the brilliant turquoise and scarlet of their faces, buttocks and genitals caused great amusement. They were moderately intelligent, yet a characteristic streak of destructive malice in their characters made them impossible to tame. The alpha-males were also a problem. Massive, vicious creatures, they defended their harems with both violence and paranoia.

Tian-Sha brought the camel to a stop. All night the mental vagueness that came with being on heat had been rising and the strong male scent on the dawn breeze was now threatening to overwhelm her. Mating would ease the strain, yet to offer herself to the baboon-like half-humans was an act so debased that the mere thought sent a shiver the length of her spine. Suan soldiers did it, it was true; indeed, luring one of the females away from a group in defiance of the guarding alpha-male was considered a fine act of bravado. They were said to couple with great eagerness, offering their neatly formed, sky-blue bottoms willingly to any male with the courage to approach. Yet they were suan and gross by nature, she was felian, and while she might be expected to mate any man in Suza during her season, male cynocephalids were a different thing altogether.

Imagining the jokes at her expense that would pass among the soldiery and agrarians if she gave in to her lust, she angrily set the camel back into motion. It responded well, moving with a power and speed far beyond its unadapted relatives and also with moderately good temper. With her tail and head-hair streaming out behind her, she urged it to its fastest gait, her temptation pushed aside by the pleasure of speed.

Taking its own head, the camel made for a low gully, reaching yet greater speeds on the flat sand at its bottom. As the gully became deeper the scent of cynocephalids became stronger, yet she continued to urge the camel on, determined not to surrender her dignity. Brackish pools began to appear, sheltered from the full sun by the cliffs now passing on either side of her. Another gully joined the first, coming in at right angles to form a broad, flat area in which a small lake had formed. There, clustered on the shore between cliff and lake, were the cynocephalids.

Their scent hit Tian-Sha like a blow. She caught her breath, holding it in desperation as she tried to steer her mount away. The camel ignored her, unfazed by the half-men but avoiding the lake with all its race's dislike of open water. One of them noticed, rising to call a warning in their harsh, screeching speech. They had been drinking from the lake or working to put out their fire. There were around ten in all. Now they hastily snatched up clubs or rocks and turned to face the oncoming camel.

Realising that they thought they were being charged,

Tian-Sha made a desperate attempt to slow down, abandoning her efforts to hold her breath as she did so. For a moment the camel paid no heed and she suffered a dreadful vision of going down under a hail of missiles when they reached the cynocephalids. Then it stopped, so suddenly that she came close to losing her balance.

Kneeling by the edge of the lake, the camel put its head down to drink, paying no attention to the half-men other than to ensure that they remained within the range of its vision. Tian-Sha dismounted and turned to face them, her head swimming with the need to mate and a telltale trickle of moisture running down the inside of one thigh. The scent was too strong, her need too powerful, and with a last, regretful shake of her head she accepted what she was about to do.

They faced her, each wary, each far from confident, their turquoise and scarlet faces set in expressions of fear and doubt. None reached the level of her chin, and their eyes kept flicking to her hands and feet, as if expecting her to unsheath her claws at any moment. Moving slowly, Tian-Sha undid the clasp of her cloak and let it slip down, then pushed her culottes down over her hips. Stepping away from her garments, she stood naked before them, the hardness of her nipples and the damp of her labial fur revealing her excitement.

The foremost of them, both taller and broader than the others, moved forward a step, then put his hand to the scrap of uncured leather that hid his groin and squeezed the bulge beneath. Tian-Sha smiled and, putting a hand to her sex, she pulled her labia open to show the damp pink centre of her vulva.

The display removed their last doubts and the clubs and stones fell to the ground. They formed a broad ring around her, moving quickly from human stance to the quadrupedal squat of a baboon, seemingly comfortable in neither position. She turned, as uncertain as they were, knowing only that when suan guards boasted of mating females it was always the pale-blue buttocks that were offered to their cocks. Reasoning that if she was to accept their cocks then it was no worse to do it in the position they favoured, she sank to her knees.

The largest immediately came forward, circling her to approach from behind. With a final sob Tian-Sha raised her haunches and lifted her tail, offering her vulva in a gesture that represented the final surrender of dignity to the needs of her body. With her face pressed to the ground she waited, desperate to have her vagina filled. His hands closed on her hips and his cock touched her sex lips, nudging once, twice and then finding the wet entrance to her vagina and sliding within.

It was done, the cock was inside her and she could no longer back out even if she had been able. With her face pushed down into the dirt Tian-Sha abandoned herself to the ecstasy of having a penis inside her and was quickly sighing and growling to herself with as much pleasure as if it had been a lover whose cock she was accepting. After a while the shamefaced gesture of putting her face down came to seem pointless and she lifted her head, only to find herself looking at the legs of a cynocephalid.

He took her hair, pulling her head round towards his groin. The penis was in front of her, the same startling blue as their faces and bottoms, only with the protruding head a furious scarlet colour. She hesitated as he pushed it against her lips. The tip was soft and moist, tasting of their musk. Unable to stop herself, Tian-Sha opened her mouth and promptly had it filled with stiff, eager penis. She began to suck as the others closed in.

A leg was thrown over her back as one mounted her, then began to rut his cock in the soft fur at the nape of her neck. Then they were all around her, their cocks rubbing on her fur, in her armpits and against her neck. One slid beneath her and started to rut between her dangling breasts, rubbing his balls between the lowest pair and his cock between the two higher ones.

The one inside her took hold of her tail, holding it up to get at her vagina but in doing so managing to jerk at it as he rode her. For Tian-Sha the action of having her tail pulled was the perfect detail to her ravishment. Her world dissolved into a place of cocks, balls and musk. Willingly she allowed them to use her, handling their erections as best she could, sucking and fondling while other used her fur to rub themselves on. When the large male came in her another immediately replaced him, only to ejaculate before he was inside and spray her bottom crease with come. The one in her mouth also came and was replaced as quickly. Soon she was wet with sperm, not only her bottom and in her mouth but on her face and in both armpits. More come soiled the fur of her back and neck. The one who had chosen to ride her had ejaculated in her hair, and two had soiled her dangling breasts.

Lost to everything except her pleasure, she would lift her bottom when each of them had come in her, offering the haven of her dripping vagina to yet another cock. Again and again this happened, and again and again she climaxed, until at last her urgency began to give way to satisfaction. Then her tail was taken in a mouth gently but firmly and once more hands took her by the hips. Horny thumbs spread her buttocks open, stretching her vagina wide and she gave a long hiss of pleasure. A cock prodded between her buttocks, just above the vagina. She raised her bottom, trying to take the erection inside herself only to have it pulled back and then put once more between her cheeks.

Too late she realised that the cock was at her anus. She tried to turn but with her head held by the one in her mouth and her movements hampered by the others, it was impossible. She knew that the crease of her bottom was slick with sperm, that her arousal would already have made her anus loosen and pout, yet she was powerless to prevent the cynocephalid from attempting to bugger her. He pushed, straining her bottom-hole as she realised to her utter horror that her instinct was not to keep the penis out but to allow it in. Yet for a moment she held, using her last reserves of decency to try and stop it, only to give in and relax her ring.

It happened immediately. Her eyes opened wide at the shock of her anus popping and then the cock was up her, in her rectum, which no male had ever before invaded. A great wave of shame went through her as the cock was forced to its full length in her bottom. She was being buggered, and not even by a man but with the slim blue cock of a cynocephalid. Then it began to move inside her, pushing with short, sudden motions each of which seemed to knock yet more air from her lungs. With a groan she sank down, lying herself on top of the one who was rutting her breasts, only to have the one in her mouth pull her head sharply up to restore the comfort of his erection.

Only when the sudden flood of sperm into her rectum failed to arrive did she realise than the one up her bottom must be among those who had already come once, indeed, probably the large one who had first entered her vagina. Instead it was the cock in her mouth that jerked and flooded her with come. Another replaced it, one who had been using the warm hollow of one of her armpits and she tasted her own sweat as she began to suck him.

One by one the others finished, leaving Tian-Sha to concentrate on the sensation of being buggered. To have a penis in her rectum created a terrible sense of disgrace, as she was breaking one of the strongest taboos of Suza. Yet, worse, far worse, was the fact that instead of the sensations of pain – both sharp and bruising – that she had expected, the cynocephalid's

95

cock produced a warm, stretched feeling in her bottom-hole, combining a delicious fullness with a curious sense of relief.

Yet it was impossible to ignore, and before long she had slipped a hand back between her thighs and begun to masturbate. Rubbing at her clitoris with her mind firmly fixed on the cock that was moving in and out up her bottom, it was not long before she started to come once more. The climax was different from those achieved with cocks in her vagina, less intense but more drawn out, rising like a wave until her feet were drumming frantically on the ground and then breaking as her anus contracted in frenzied spasms on the intruding cock.

The effect was too much for the cynocephalid and he came in her rectum, producing a demented chittering as his sperm drained into her. Then his cock was being pulled out, leaving her kneeling with her anus gaping open to the cool morning air. Despite herself she stayed down, hoping that another male would refill her bottom-hole even though it felt sore and loose.

None took advantage of her and eventually she came to realise precisely how she must be looking on all fours with her fur sodden with sperm and not just her vagina but her anus wide and ready to accept any cock whose owner was willing to put it in her. Sitting down quickly, she made a hasty check to ensure that she had not been caught enjoying such depravity. Only the camel returned her glance, its large eye expressing absolute indifference to either of the supposedly disgusting acts she had just committed. The cynocephalids had lost interest and had began to move off along the shore of the lake, their indifference to their recent conquest as marked as that of the camel.

Filled with a deep sense of shame and an even deeper sense of satisfaction, Tian-Sha stood and turned to face the lake. Torn between her instinctive dislike of immersion in cold water and the need to wash her body, she stayed irresolute for a moment. Her tongue normally sufficed, but now not only was her fur slick with sweat but she had sperm in every crevice of her body and coating her face, bottom and breasts. With a rueful shake of her head she plunged into the lake. Washed and feeling sexually satiated yet hungry for food, she paused just long enough to take a drink of milk from the camel's teats before once more setting off to the east.

4

The Choice of Tools

Tian-Sha stopped at the crest of a hill. For most of the day the camel had moved swiftly to the east, covering a distance that even the swiftest of runners would have taken three days to cover. Now it stood tethered to an acacia in a hollow while she crouched to inspect the valley ahead.

Below her was the city of Alaban, a great arc of houses facing the river. These were of the same sienna stone as Suza but squatter in form and divided by open gaps instead of corridors and stairs. Nor did it possess the malachite and lapis lazuli that decorated Suza's finer buildings, although many low domes were faced with scarlet and gold. There was also the deep purple-brown of the wine houses, a colour resulting from the ritual pouring of libations on their walls each year.

Across the river from the city a bulge of land within the meander showed the brilliant green of rice paddies. Numerous ditches cut through this and to the south, where further cultivated land showed as a strip of green at the foot of a rocky hillside. Behind the city was the vineyard itself, an amphitheatre of vivid blue-green running around the bow of the river from immediately below her to a point where the heat haze made the vines seem a single, shimmering wall of green. This was the source of Shiraz of Alaban, a wine greatly prized in Suza and elsewhere. Indeed, on the river road below the bluff she was on, a massive wain, drawn by Baluchitheria, was leaving the city gates; the stacked amphorae in the back showed its nature.

A new and uneasy alliance existed between Suza and Alaban. Historically they had been set against one another, with Suza generally the more powerful. Then, when the city of Grurahn had sought to conquer Alaban, Suza had offered support. It had been the first of Khian-Shu's gambits, and the defeat of the Grurahnians the first of Otomos' triumphs. Since then Suza and Alaban had existed in friendship undercut with the memory of their old enmity. Tian-Sha had been there only once before, coming with Ilana, the Mistress of Tomes, to copy scrolls. For five days she had sat under the dome of their central library, writing out information that was being exchanged on a strictly even and heavily supervised basis. Having little shared feeling with Ilana, Tian-Sha had spent her evenings with the heavy-set suan guide who was in fact her guard. He had proved voluble and provided her with a great deal of information – information that she now intended to exploit.

The gates were open, with a single guard visible. This was a suan, a bored individual leaning on his pike while agrarians streamed into the city from the fields and vines. With the sun sinking slowly towards the hills behind her, Tian-Sha started down the slope. The felians of Alaban would recognise her as an outsider immediately, yet with luck and a degree of boldness she would be able to pass.

In the vineyards the grapes were beginning to show the purple flush of ripeness. Agrarians were scattered here and there, thinning excess growth or weeding between the rows. Tian-Sha made for one of the smaller groups, two true-men and a suan who were packing away their tools. They paid her only cursory attention, not even troubling to acknowledge her until it became obvious that she was approaching them.

'What prospects do you see for the vintage?' she asked.

'Until yesterday there had been too little rain,' one of the true-men replied. 'Last night there was a storm to the south, and more threaten, so there may now be too much.'

Tian-Sha made a light joke of the man's pessimism, which brought grins to the others' faces. Their conversation quickly became casual and when they set off for the city she walked with them. Her explanation of being an apprentice to a Suzan wine merchant was accepted without question, to the point of their providing recommendations as to where her mentor should buy. They also offered her wine from what remained in their flasks. She accepted and deliberately spilt a quantity down her chest.

At the gate the suan guard no more than glanced at her, and it was a glance not of aggression or even suspicion, but simply of lust. Tian-Sha passed under the high arch of the gate and into Alaban, praying that the scents of wine and her heat would mask that of her nervousness. In Suza each gate guard included a felian, but she had not seen any on her previous visit to Alaban and so it now proved.

Within the city the interest that was shown in her remained purely sexual. Those few felians she did pass gave her no more than curious glances. It was as she had hoped, those that recognised her as not of the city assuming that she had a right to be there merely because she was there. Even when she had left the three agrarians nobody interfered with her.

Not troubling to hide her curiosity at the strange, open walkways of Alaban, she made her way around the curve of the city until at length she came to a long, low structure of weathered stone. This, she knew, was the building in which those men and women who had been assigned the lowest and dirtiest tasks of the city lived.

They were technically criminals, those who had repeatedly offended against the city's complex code of laws. Tian-Sha had learnt something of this before, and to her it seemed as abstract as it was complex.

Before the building grew a great cypress, from the lower boughs of which hung cages made of bronze rods. In four of these miserable captives squatted – the latest uptake of malefactors, being displayed to the public before joining the work gangs. Tian-Sha walked on, showing no more interest in the spectacle than might have been expected of her.

The sun was now poised above the western bluffs and gave a deep orange light that reflected from the scarlet and gold of the Alaban domes to create a splendid pattern of rich colours in the city. Now hungry and with her heat rising with the dusk, Tian-Sha began to look for a means of assuaging both urges. Being so thoroughly ravished by the cynocephalids had proved more satisfying than she cared to admit to herself, and she also wanted a fresh mating to put the experience behind her.

A fellow tigranthrope provided for all three of her wants. He was a splendid young male, tall and sleek furred with a fine penis and balls covered in soft black down. Within moments of making her offer Tian-Sha found herself being mated in a narrow gap between two houses. Food followed, river fish in strong herbs washed down with wine of the city. Having eaten to repletion they shared a flask of bittersweet essence and made love for a second time, then a third. Only when the moon had risen to its zenith did she go, leaving her lover sprawled in a contented sleep.

Moving across rooftops and along darkened alleys, she made her way to the cypress from which the four criminals were suspended in their cages. Not once was she challenged, her evident state of arousal providing all the reason she needed for prowling the city in the dead of night. Yet the streets of Alaban proved a hard place in which to select her own mates, and twice she was propositioned by eager males – a true-man and a suanthrope. Both times she allowed them to take her from behind in swift, active couplings that left the men far more exhausted than her. It also enabled her to keep a reasonably clear head until she reached her destination.

Crouching in the angle of a wall, Tian-Sha contemplated the occupied cages. Two were clearly impractical, hanging side by side and containing large male suanthropes. The remaining two hung from separate limbs, one holding a jet black oncanthrope, the other an acyonthrope whose yellow and black fur was evident despite the dim light. Scent told Tian-Sha that the black felian was male, the other female. Both lay curled on the wooden floors of the cages, asleep.

Pulling herself quickly into the boughs of the cypress, she ran out on to a heavy limb and swung herself down to catch the bars of the acyonthrope's cage. Reaching a hand inside she touched the occupant gently on her shoulder. The response was immediate, the acyon-thrope's eyes snapping wide and her mouth opening to show ready fangs. Tian-Sha moved her hand to stroke the girl's yellow fur.

'I am Tian-Sha,' she stated. 'Of Suza. I am here to take you out of Alaban.'

'Why?' the girl answered.

'For my own ends, but I assure you of freedom.'

In response the yellow and black girl wrinkled her nose. Tian-Sha did the same, testing the quality of the girl's scent for veracity just as her own was being tested. The acyonthrope's scent showed fear, both immediate and lasting, also anger and sorrow, but gave no evidence of duplicity. Doubt showed in her eyes, then faded as she completed her assessment of Tian-Sha's scent.

'Do it then,' the girl stated, suddenly eager, 'if you are

able. I am chained by the neck and the bars and lock are stout enough to hold a grown male suan.'

'I have the means – king's-water,' Tian-Sha said and motioned the acyonthrope to move back in the cage.

Reaching within her cloak, she produced a glass vial bound with bronze. With great care she removed the stopper and placed the narrow spout into the keyhole, pouring half the contents into the lock. Fumes quickly began to rise, causing both females to wrinkle their noses in distaste, while the hiss from within had them glancing nervously around.

A sudden change in the tension of the bars signalled the demise of the lock mechanism and the careful application of Tian-Sha's claw slid back the catch. The process was repeated with the lock that had held the girl's neck chain to the bars and then she was free.

Together they dropped from the cage and ran. Without exchanging a word they smelt out the movements of the guards and crossed the wall, then hid in the shelter of the reeds that covered the narrow strip of ground between the river road and the river itself. Neither sound nor scent suggested that their departure had been noticed, and Tian-Sha found the nervous energy that had sustained her through the escape changing to exhilaration.

'And now?' The acyonthrope asked.

'First, what is your name?' Tian-Sha responded.

'Xerafina.'

'Then, Xerafina, know that we are bound for Suza. I have a racing dromedary in a hollow on the bluffs. We do not go directly to her, though, but first to the river, then across and to the south as if headed for one of the cities with which Alaban is in enmity. Using the drainage ditches to conceal our scent we may re-cross the river some way to the west and so back up into the hills and to the hollow where my camel is tethered.'

Xerafina responded with a nod of understanding and

followed Tian-Sha without protest. Even during her immersion in the cold waters of the river she gave no more than quiet mews of distaste and they found Tian-Sha's camel without incident. Once mounted and making steady progress to the west with no evidence of pursuit, Tian-Sha at last allowed herself to relax.

'Tell me then,' she asked. 'What did you do to earn your place in the cage?'

'I made copies of coins,' Xerafina answered.

'The metal discs you use in barter?'

'Yes.'

'Why is that a crime? It must take skill and time to make them, surely the council would welcome the provision of more?'

'No, they think of it as theft. Worse than theft indeed, as the coins may be exchanged for any item.'

'Thus everybody benefits. Who is the loser?'

'The city.'

'Not so, they simply have more coin while you have more goods.'

'That is what I reasoned, but I was caught and thrown into the cage. In three days I was to be given justice, whipped naked at the tail of a cart and put to work preserving the workings of the city's sewers.'

'Crime is a subtle concept in Alaban,' Tian-Sha answered. 'In Suza you would be considered impudent at worst. I doubt we would even trouble to whip you, except that our Mistress of Castigation might wish to take pleasure in your pain and misery.'

'The suanthrope Othon, who runs the work gangs, is of a similar bent. He understands every nuance of pain, female pain in particular.'

'As does Rufina, and that brings me to the nature of your task.'

In Suza, the activity of early evening was drawing to a close. A few windows still showed the yellow-orange

105

light of torches, while only the occasional squeal or scream broke the silence. Among the most lively places was the great bathhouse reserved for the more elevated ranks. This was a long, windowless building from which numerous chimneys rose among gables and domes of blue lapis. Within, numerous small chambers opened from a central hall. Each chamber was devoted to a specialist technique, while the hall contained a great bath of warm mud richly scented with apple oil. In this the patrons lolled, half-immersed, taking their ease over cups of wine and dishes of delicacies. Almost exclusively suanthropes, with only an occasional true-man among them, their manner was one of pleasant indolence.

Very different was the manner of Zara, who was making up for her skipped duty as mud-girl. She was naked and her body had been oiled, yet she was running sweat both from the warmth of the air and from her exertions. All day the mud tanks on the roof had been warming in the sun, and she now had to control their valves to regulate the temperature of the bath as well as serve the patrons. The service involved not only distributing wine and food, but attending to the patron's sexual needs. When summoned she would kneel on the tiles that surrounded the bath and bend forward, seeking under the mud for penis or vulva. As she masturbated the patrons their hands would usually explore her body, fondling her bottom or breasts to leave her filthy with mud in addition to the sweat and oil. Occasionally a finger would be inserted into her vagina and she would be obliged to visit the douche chamber to clean herself.

Yet despite the effort needed for her work, her mind was on other things. Being used for Hoat's pleasure had left her sore and faint, but not so spent as to prevent her from realising that the event was abnormal. For Rufina to subject her to erotic torture was normal, if unusual in that it had been done in the stable. What was unusual was that Rufina had not expressed her own pleasure at Zara's expense. Rufina's habit was to bring her victims to ecstasy and then stand above them and masturbate. Rather than do this, she had remained detached, not even troubling to take Zara to her couch for the night. Clearly some more important matter had been weighing on her. After spending the day considering and rejecting explanations for the councillor's behaviour, Zara had concluded that only one fitted with all she knew. If Rufina wished to please Hoat then it was for a reason. It was not for sexual satisfaction. Rufina's choice in males was for weak, pliable individuals. Hoat was pliable but hardly weak. Indeed, his virtues lay solely in his strength and size. He was neither cunning, nor well connected, nor skilled in any craft more refined than those needed to tend Baluchitheria. Thus Rufina needed a feat of strength.

Had her requirement been within the law, she would merely have demanded it of Hoat, or summoned a work gang for that matter. The task had to be clandestine. It was also sure to involve Rufina's desire for power and status. The Lady Alla-Sha was widely expected to step down rather than accept Otomos as mate. Rufina was the inevitable successor, except in that she was no more suited to Otomos' embrace than Alla-Sha, less if anything. Of all the males in Suza, Hoat alone might hope to challenge Otomos and win. This then, was Rufina's strategy.

To be the sole person to be aware of Rufina's strategy was useful to say the least. Not that it was wise to attempt to apply leverage to Rufina. That route led only to pain and humiliation beyond her ability to absorb. Yet to warn Otomos would bring favour if he won and make no difference if he lost. Then, with the favour of the future Lord she might hope for preferment, a Mentorship, perhaps a place on the council . . .

'Zara! Wine!'

The call cut through Zara's daydream, rousing her to attention as she saw that it was Lomas himself who was demanding her service.

'My apologies, Master,' she stammered as she scampered to obey.

Lomas did not reply to her, but turned to make a comment to his companions. Zara failed to catch the words but found herself blushing at the quality of the laughter that answered the remark. Having filled their vessels and presented her bottom for a gentle smack of encouragement, she took the empty wine flagon to the storeroom. Here, as she struggled with the seal of a new amphora of muscat, she returned to her daydream.

The knack, she was sure, was to appear to support all possible factions but to do as little as possible. That way whoever won was likely to be grateful but she was unlikely to suffer for supporting a losing clique. To Rufina, she knew, she was no more than a puppet, expected to show loyalty and do as she was told without question. Rufina invariably assumed stupidity in those who succumbed to her erotic tortures, and also confused fear with respect. Both faults Zara was determined to take advantage of, while always retaining an outward manner of doglike obedience.

Leaking Rufina's plans to the suan clique was clearly a good idea, but risky unless timed so that the information came too late to be of any practical value. Should Rufina succeed and then learn that Zara had betrayed her, Zara's future would be grim to say the least. Providing sexual satisfaction single-handedly to a group of one hundred agrarians would be the best she could expect, and that would be after the public whipping and being marked. Yet with Rufina as Lady she might expect a similar fate from simple malice. Undoubtedly Otomos had to be warned.

Providing information of Comus' intentions would be safer, but less satisfying. Besides, should Comus succeed he could be relied upon to reward his supporters. Comus at the least should be treated well, perhaps offered the chance to bugger her, or better still, brought a new girl who could be persuaded to accept his cock in her anal passage. Only the most hedonistic males of Suza indulged in buggery, and those were largely among the élite. The populace as a whole considered the act degraded, and those who enjoyed it kept their preferences a careful secret. The same was true of the girls, with only a select handful of true-girls indulging themselves. Rufina, inevitably, took a special pleasure in the penetration of her victim's anuses, but always in private.

As her thoughts turned back to Rufina, she remembered the way having to spread her anus on to the pointed head of the homuncule had added a new torment to what had already been a powerful experience. The same was always true of anal play, her shame blending with her pleasure in a way that always produced exquisite climaxes. That had been true from the first, when Ilarion had taken her by surprise as she bent to lift a tray from the ground. She had been sucking his cock, and her own juice had run down between her cheeks. When she had felt the head of his cock at her anus she had thought it was a mistake, only to find it in her bottom-hole and then fully up her rectum. He had buggered her and masturbated her with his hand as he did it, bringing her to a squealing, breathless orgasm before coming himself. Afterwards she had run from the room in confusion, unable to believe that she had come over so dirty an act. Within a month she had been asking for his cock in her bottom-hole as a favour.

Zara's hand was on her bottom. Her longest finger lay in the oily crease, moving slowly down and in, towards the inevitable target. The open amphora stood neglected, while the laughter and calls from those in the mud bath were no more than background noise. Slowly she burrowed her finger down into the meaty embrace of her bottom, intent on finding her anus, stroking it, teasing it open . . .

'Zara!'

She jumped and spun at the call, her cheeks flaming to scarlet as she saw the bulky form of a suan male in the archway.

'You are supposed to be serving,' he said. 'We wish more wine. What are you doing, masturbating?'

'I . . . er . . .' Zara tried as her cheeks coloured to a deeper red.

The suan grinned in response, then turned back to the hall.

'Little Zara is masturbating in the storeroom!' he announced.

'One too many cocks in her hand tonight, I expect!' another voice called back.

'Bring her out, she can do it in the pool,' a third suggested.

The call was taken up with enthusiasm and Zara found herself dragged out on to the tiled ledge that surrounded the mud bath. Several suans were nearby, grinning as they advanced.

'No!' she laughed. 'Not in the mud! Have me here if you must!'

'We prefer it in mud,' one answered. 'It cools the balls during coupling.'

She backed away, trying to look serious but unable to stop herself giggling. Then her bottom bumped against a man's legs. Zara screamed as strong hands gripped her legs and pulled. Her balance went, only for her to be caught around the waist. More hands gripped her wrists and she found herself stretched between four burly suanthropes, each clutching a limb.

'No boys, not in the mud! Please!' She laughed as she realised their intention.

Her protest had no more effect than she had expected. To the jeering calls of the other patrons, the four suanthropes began to swing her, counting each time her body lifted out over the glutinous surface of the mud pool. Each time she expected them to let go and her heart jumped in anticipation of being dropped into the filth. Only on the tenth swing did one of them call out as the arc of the swing began.

'No!' her despairing squeal rang out even as they released her limbs.

Then she was flying through the air, out over the mud pool. She hit the surface with a stinging impact and a sticky plop, then vanished beneath it. Having failed to stifle her scream in time, she was rewarded with an instant mouthful of filthy ooze. For a moment her orientation went and she was struggling in what seemed an infinity of mud with neither up nor down. Even as the first twinge of panic hit her she found the bottom and pushed herself quickly up.

Zara struggled to her knees, lifting her head, then her back and finally her bottom above the surface of the mud. Before she could react or even scrape the mud from her eyes they had seized her by the hair. Once more her face was pushed beneath the surface of the mud, even as other hands gripped her hips.

Even as she struggled to pull her head back out of the mud, something hard was probing between the mud-slimed cheeks of her bottom. It nudged her anus, then between the lips of her vulva, finding her vagina on the third push and sliding inside her. She felt her flesh twist and knew the man who had mounted her was a suan and then the hand in her hair had mercifully pulled her head out of the muck and she was gasping down mouthfuls of air along with a good quantity of mud. Quickly wiping the slime from her eyes, she found herself faced by the man whose hand was locked in her hair, or rather by his mud-smeared genitals.

111

'Suck me,' he demanded, pushing his erection towards her face.

His huge cock reared in front of her, so thick with slime that only the angry red of the glans was uncovered. The grip on her hair tightened and she found herself being pulled towards the filthy erection. It nudged her lips, seeking entry to her mouth. Zara moved her head to the side, intending to spit out her mouthful of mud before sucking his cock.

'Suck it, I said,' the man demanded.

Before she could find the breath to explain her face was once more plunged into the muck, her mouth filling with it to the back. She came up spluttering and gagging, only for the cock to be pushed unceremoniously into her, mud and all. He tugged her hard on to his groin by her hair, forcing her to suck even as his cock pressed mud into the back of her throat.

She began to choke, the memories of sucking on Otomos' giant cock flooding into her mind. It was the same now, except that it was a wad of dirt that was clogging her windpipe and not more than the end of the penis she was sucking. She also had a cock in her vagina, the movement of which was helping to lift her towards total loss of control. With no choice, she swallowed. As the thick clot of mud slid down her throat she gagged, an action that proved too much for the man whose cock she was sucking. He came, spurting come into the back of her throat to make her gag again and again until he had drained his load into her mouth.

As he pulled back, Zara was left gasping for air. Coughing and spitting mud in time to the thrusts of the suan in her vagina, she struggled for control, only to have her head taken once more and the thick spiral of a suan's cock thrust into her mouth. Hands grabbed her dangling breasts as others closed in on her, kneading them in the mud. Someone started to pull at one of her nipples, tugging down as if milking a cow. The cock inside her rammed deep and then jerked, splashing come out around the mouth of her vagina.

Expecting to be filled again, she lifted her bottom, only for a palm to land hard on her meaty cheeks, spraying droplets across the hall and making her choke on her mouthful of cock and mud. Again it happened, and as an arm closed firmly around her waist, she realised that she was to be spanked. It was typical of suans, a good spanking being used to open a girl's vagina before she was fucked. Only now her vagina was already open and it was being done simply for the pleasure of seeing her put through it.

They laughed as they beat her, not just one but several of them slapping at her buttocks until the two meaty balls were throbbing with pain and showed red where the slaps had cleared mud from her skin. She kicked and writhed, sending sprays of mud across the hall and all the while sucking on the thick spiral of penis in her mouth. Twice the suan in her mouth complained when an especially hard swat made her close her teeth on his shaft. It happened a third time and he pulled out, contenting himself with masturbating over her face. Zara closed her eyes as she realised his intention and then his sperm was added to the filth that already coated her face and hair.

Her bottom had begun to throb, with the initial pain of spanking fading to be replaced by the warm glow of satisfaction and need that always followed a well-applied beating. She began to groan and squirm her bottom upwards for more, harder punishment. Her knees slid slowly apart, opening her sex and lowering the plump swells of her belly and pubic mound until they met the surface of the mud. Her breasts were already in it, and both were being handled, while her mouth was agape, eager to have another penis pushed into it.

Abruptly the spanking stopped and her mouth was

immediately rewarded with its third erect cock. She began to suck, now revelling in the taste of soil and male as she stuck her bottom up again in the hope of entry. No cock touched her hole, but a hand did, two fingers slipping inside her, then a third – thick, soft fingers that caressed the inside of her vagina with skill and familiarity.

Realising that it was a woman who was exploring her, Zara tried to look back, briefly glimpsing the full, heavy chest and wide shoulders of Soumea. The big female suan had her eyes locked on Zara's rear view and one hand on her own vulva, masturbating while she explored with the other. Then the man whose cock was in her mouth had jerked her head back round and she returned to concentrating on his pleasure.

Barely had she began to suck when he came in her mouth, ejaculating just as she started a long stroke of her pursed lips. He pulled back and the second spurt caught her in the face, only for him to once more plunge his penis deep into her throat. She was left with a long thread of sperm hanging from her lower lip and yet more on her nose and across her cheeks.

Soumea's fingers had left Zara's vagina, but only for an instant. The big, motherly suanthrope's hand cupped Zara between the thighs, pressing mud to the vulva, then squeezing to fill the cavity of the vagina with the warm, thick mess. Zara gasped, opening her mouth only to have a fresh cock inserted in it. As she began to suck, Soumea began to masturbate her, rubbing her clitoris while pushing the handful of mud further and further up her vagina. The motion on her clitoris was expert, the result of long years of practice, and Zara quickly began to come. As it happened the cock in her mouth erupted sperm down her throat, adding to the ecstasy of the climax.

From the point of her climax events became a blur for Zara. She was still dizzy with pleasure when the next

114

cock was put in her mouth and was vaguely aware of Soumea's climax. From then on it became a welter of cocks and fingers, groping her body and probing her vagina and mouth. Several times she was rolled over, and more than once her head went under the mud, both accidentally and on purpose in order to fill her mouth with it.

More than once handfuls of mud were pushed into her vagina to improve the sensation for the cock that was about to follow. At one point a finger invaded her anus beneath the surface of the mud, revealing the presence of a sodomite in the crowd. Having been so comprehensively used, Zara half-expected to be buggered, but whoever it was contented themselves with a brief manual exploration of her rectum, lacking the courage to commit so debauched an act in public.

She quickly lost count of her own orgasms, remaining only vaguely aware that it was generally female fingers that brought her off. The cocks in her mouth and vagina also blended together, one following another until it seemed that she was forever full of penis at both ends. Again and again penises erupted inside her, filling her womb and mouth. More came over her, splashing her breasts, face and bottom with come which mixed with the mud to form a glutinous paste that filled every hollow and crevice of her body. She was repeatedly obliged to swallow mud, even to eat it from some of the female's vaginas, until her belly was swollen and she felt as if she had taken a full meal. A great deal of it also went up her vagina, making her feel ever more bloated. She had lost all sense of anything beyond the responses of her body by the time they started to tire of her. She was sore from entry and from rubbing herself; her nipples felt stretched and her tongue ached, while her mud-filled stomach felt distended and fat.

Zara crawled from the mud, exhausted. With what she was sure was the last of her energy she squeezed the muscles of her vagina, expelling a thick worm of mud and come that landed on the tiles beneath her with a sticky plop. Then she collapsed to the tiles, utterly soiled, smarting both from cocks and her beating but filled with a deep sense of sexual consummation.

Dimly she was aware of the patrons laughing and congratulating one another. One voice speculated on how many times she had climaxed, another remarked on the state they had left her in and wondered if it was possible to send for another mud-girl. A third suggested taking her to the water chamber for a dunking and then a fourth, louder and deeper joined in, first complaining that he had been deprived of his share of cunt and then volunteering to dunk her.

With mud caking her face she was unable to open her eyes, but guessed that the newcomer was Otomos himself. A hand gripped her, closing around one plump thigh and lifting her clear of the ground with no more effort than that required had she been a doll. She squeaked at the treatment but he took no notice, simply carrying her by one leg into a side room. Knowing her fate, Zara braced herself as she was flung out into the air. Then the cold water hit her and she was beneath it, then out again as her ankle was grabbed and she was lifted once more. Again and again she was dunked, until finally she was clean and could open her eyes. As she had suspected it was Otomos who had caught her. He was naked, and as he dumped her dripping body on to the tiles she found herself looking up at his monstrous cock, which was already beginning to swell and uncoil.

'Get up girl,' Otomos ordered. 'Don't you want a decent cock after all those weed-thin members?'

Zara struggled to obey. Her belly and stomach both felt heavy, swollen with the mud and come she had taken in. As she pulled herself into a crawling position she could feel both hanging beneath her just as her fat breasts hung from her chest. Otomos reached down and

116

took her by the hair, then pulled her head hard on to his cock. She gaped as it was thrust down her windpipe, making her gag. This drew an approving grunt from him. He hardened quickly, fucking her head with short, sharp thrusts each of which jammed his cock well down her throat. By the time his erection had swollen to its full, magnificent size she was gasping for breath and scrabbling at his legs and balls.

Once ready, he dropped her on to the tiles and stood, preening his erection and looking down at her as if wondering what to do. Feeling faint, Zara scooped her big breasts into her hands and held them out, offering her cleavage as a slide for his cock. He peered down, contemplating the fat globes of flesh with relish only to shake his head.

'No,' he announced. 'I'm going to fuck you. With a fat little slattern like you it's got to go in at least a little way.'

Zara could do nothing, but found herself lifted once more and placed on the tip of the giant suanthrope's erection. It felt huge against her vagina and then the thing that she had fantasised about again and again since sucking his cock actually happened. He jerked downwards and the enormous knob of his penis was forced roughly into the entrance of her vagina. She cried out in pain, only for the sound to turn to a whimper as he slid her slowly down on to his cock. Her vagina felt stretched to impossible dimensions, bursting with penis to fill her whole body with the sensation of being fucked.

She was far beyond responding with more than gasps and grunts of shock and excitement. Otomos seemed not to notice, but bounced her on his cock, rubbing the knob in her vagina as he held her body easily in his grip. Zara's breasts were flying up and down with the motion, also her hands and legs, while her flesh quivered in waves with each push. Then he came, deep inside her, filling her already stretched belly to make her cry out.

Once more he pushed himself in, sending a spray of mud and sperm out from the mouth of her vagina. She felt another eruption deep in her vagina and then he was pulling his cock slowly out of her.

Otomos grunted with satisfaction, then dropped her. Zara squeaked as her sore bottom smacked hard on the tiled floor. Utterly spent, she collapsed back on to the floor, then watched with glazed eyes as he casually drained the remaining sperm from his cock all over her belly and breasts. He stamped from the room.

Zara put one hand to her vulva and began to masturbate while she rubbed his sperm into her breasts with the other. Soon she was rubbing at herself in a shameless frenzy, all her plans for warning Otomos of Hoat's intentions lost in a whirl of sex and exhaustion.

Comus rose from the couch. Strong moonlight from a window illuminated the chamber and the face of the sleeping Ciriel. Her expression was serene, suggesting nothing of their earlier passion or her beating. She stirred as his weight shifted from the couch, then threw out an arm. One eye flickered open, then the other.

'Comus? Mentor?' she asked sleepily.

'I'm sorry to wake you,' he answered.

'You are going picking?'

'No, I am going to Pomina.'

'But . . .'

Comus made no reply but bent to retrieve the cords that he had earlier used to lash her to the pillar. Before she could rise he had taken a wrist and twisted her arm up behind her back. She squeaked in protest as her other arm joined the first and his hand fastened on to her wrists.

'Mentor! This is foolish! Tie me if you wish, but then have me. I'm still soft and open . . .'

'Not this time, my little one,' Comus chuckled as he lashed her wrists tightly.

Ciriel continued to struggle and make entreaties as Comus tied her up. He ignored her, pausing only to pat her bottom in response to an exceptionally debauched suggestion. At last she was secure, face down on the bed with her wrists lashed tight into the small of her back and her ankles drawn up to her bottom and tied off on her wrists. He had also gagged her, making a ball of a pair of silken culottes and forcing them into her mouth. A twist of cord secured them and her bondage was complete.

Comus then began to dress, selecting garments carefully and talking to himself as he did so. Ciriel pleaded with her eyes and squirmed in her bonds but to no avail. He selected scarlet breeches, a loose white shirt and highly polished black boots, completing the ensemble with a sash of heavy black silk. When attired to his satisfaction he applied carefully selected essences and fetched the vial of musk from the workroom. Ciriel watched him, occasionally tugging at her bonds or attempting to spit the gag from her mouth.

'My apologies for your discomfort,' he stated as he moved to the chamber door. 'You will, however, come to realise the necessity of this in due course. I will be back before dawn, I imagine, so stay on the couch for the best comfort. If you feel the need to wet yourself then squirm to the floor, as otherwise both our couches will be soiled. Farewell.'

Comus left Ciriel wriggling futilely on the couch and set off across the city. He whistled as he went, the sound resounding oddly in the empty stone corridors and narrow stairwells. On nearing Pomina's chambers he slowed and proceeded with greater caution. Intending to slip on to her couch and open the vial beneath her nose, he was concerned not to find himself applying his wiles to the terrible Otomos instead of the succulent Pomina.

To his surprise a light showed in her outer room. Approaching cautiously, he peered within, finding her seated in front of a mirror as she brushed out her long, silky hair. She was dressed only in undergarments, but as was usual for female suanthropes these were of some complexity. A loose chemise covered her top half, laced over her breasts to show intriguing slices of soft, pink flesh reflected in the mirror. Culottes covered her bottom, not the simple silk garments worn by most girls, but a confection of lace and gauze. A gap allowed her tail to protrude, leaving the small spiral of pink flesh showing in a deliberately tempting fashion. Her seated position meant that these were stretched taut across her plump buttocks, a sight that caused Comus to wet his lips in anticipation.

Moving stealthily back, he gave her gong the softest of touches. Presently Pomina appeared, looking at him with mild surprise as he gave a polite inclination of his head.

'I was picking moon asphodel in a roof garden and saw your light,' he explained. 'I have had the luck to obtain something rare which I had hoped to show you. So many dance attendance on you during the day, and I thought that now might prove a suitable hour?'

'I was cleaning my hair,' Pomina answered. 'My Lord Otomos visited me in the mud bath this evening and well, you know how things are.'

'Indeed,' Comus answered, 'the most exquisite pleasures invariably require a great deal of ablution afterwards. May I enter?'

'Certainly,' Pomina offered, 'but you said you had something for me?'

'Indeed,' Comus replied and brought out the silver vial. 'It is the essence of a fruit called a musk apple. I was fortunate in obtaining some from a Transnegran merchant. As apple oil is your favourite body unguent I thought you might be the one to whom I might offer its first use.'

'Was it not expensive?' Pomina asked.

'Expense?' Comus replied with a dismissive motion of his fingers. 'What is expense next to knowledge? Yet it is true that it is not something I intend to waste, and you may be sure I will not be offering it to any but the most refined of the populace. I bartered this vial for three measures of tincture of scarlet.'

'I am flattered,' Pomina answered, 'but why me? Why not my mother, or another Mistress?'

'Were it merely a rare and exotic essence,' Comus said, 'that would be my choice. However, it is more than that. It is not a perfume for experienced matrons or practised courtesans. It is for the young, the innocent, those whose beauty is fresh and simple, with nothing of the contrived.'

'Then I shall try it,' Pomina answered, her voice ringing with pleasure at his flattery.

Comus handed her the vial and watched as she delicately removed the cork and sniffed the contents. At first her expression was one of doubt, then surprise and finally delight as her pretty mouth opened into a smile.

'It's . . . it's wonderful,' she declared. 'Strange, and I can see it's foreign, but I've never known a scent so heady, so, so stirring.'

Putting the vial to her nose, she inhaled deeply. Comus smiled.

'Truly exquisite,' she sighed. 'It makes me want to take everything off, every last stitch.'

'Do so then. I shall enjoy the view.'

'Really? I thought your taste ran more to lighter bodied girls, like Ciriel.'

'Ciriel is exquisite, as are you. My tastes are not so narrow. Indeed if she might be compared to a fine perfume, essence of Jasmine perhaps, then by comparison you might be thought of as . . . why, as apple essence, rich, full and sweet.'

Pomina giggled and took another sniff at the vial.

'Strip then,' he urged, 'slowly, until you are naked. Then, if you wish, bring yourself to climax for me.'

121

'I couldn't, I'd need to be mounted,' she answered, 'or at the least taken there with your tongue.'

'Nothing would give me greater pleasure than to oblige,' Comus responded.

'I need to be filled, I do,' she sighed, 'but do you dare?'

'Why not?' he answered. 'You are beautiful. It is hardly an act of bravery to mount a pretty girl!'

'What of Otomos?' Pomina asked uncertainly. 'He is jealous and likely to take our coupling as an insult, should he discover.'

'Let him be jealous,' Comus answered. 'I need you. I need you urgently.'

'But Comus, he may challenge you! You could never hope to win!'

'No, not while he awaits the Lordship. He would do nothing that might turn the council and people against him.'

'You are wrong. You don't know Otomos,' Pomina sighed. 'I want you though, and all the more because of what you're risking to have me.'

Pomina sat back on a couch, her fingers going to the front of her blouse. Comus watched in genuine delight as she began to unlace the front, tugging each pair of breasts free as the laces came loose. With the lace free of the last two eyelets, her whole chest was exposed, all twelve breasts sitting snugly together. They quivered as she giggled in response to the quality of his attention and Comus felt his cock begin to harden in his breeches.

Abandoning reserve, he leant forward and pressed his face in among the soft breasts. Pomina giggled again as he began to kiss and lick at them, then sighed as his lips found a nipple. Comus slid his hands beneath her, finding the gap between chemise and flesh. She sighed again as his fingers began to caress the velvet soft skin of her back, and arched her back to press her breasts more firmly into his face.

Knowing he had his victory, Comus began a slow, methodical exploration of Pomina's breasts. Using not only his mouth and tongue but the fringe of his hair and the lightly stubbled sides of his face, he teased each breast. Her nipples came erect easily, a brush of stubble or a brief lick being all that was needed to make each little rose-pink bud pop up. All the while he stroked her back and the nape of her neck.

Pomina's initial giggling response slowly gave way to a deeper, rawer passion, until her hands had locked into his hair and her sighs had began to turn to squeals. Her thighs had already been spread by his body, but had now begun to clench and open, while he could feel the plump swell of her pubic mound pressing damply against his chest.

Only then did he stop and pull back to strip. Pomina stayed in place, her breathing deep and slow, all twelve of her breasts flushed pink and with the crowning nipples projecting hard from their tops. Her huge eyes were fixed on him as he removed his clothes, watching the exposure of his torso, then the unfastening of his trousers and lastly locking on his crotch.

Comus was close to erection, his cock swollen with blood and projecting firmly out towards Pomina. Her thighs were spread, the bulge of her belly and pubic mound showing, ripe and feminine beneath the gauze of her culottes. A froth of lace hid the details between her legs. Her willingness to be entered showed in her eyes, and if she was disappointed by the failure of his penis to match up to Otomos' monstrous organ then she showed no sign of it. Comus, however, intended the full enjoyment of her plump young body before putting his cock inside her.

'Kneel,' he instructed, 'I will explore your sex from the rear with a subtle intimacy I believe you will enjoy.'

Pomina giggled and began to squirm round on the couch to present her bottom to Comus. He watched, enjoying her wriggling motions and her eagerness to please him. In position, she raised her bottom for his inspection and looked back with an expression of mischievous delight. Comus paused to admire the two long rows of dangling breasts and the fat, well-displayed bottom in the tight culottes.

'For the full enjoyment of this,' he continued, 'I must tie your wrists. Perhaps if you would care to cross them behind your back?'

Once more Pomina giggled. Her smile broadened at the suggestion as she obeyed. Comus came forward, pressing his cock in among the lace ruff to draw a grunt of pleasure from her. Retrieving the chemise lace from beneath her, he set to work to strap her wrists firmly into the small of her back. As he tied her he rubbed his cock in the lace of her culottes, bringing himself to full erection and drawing giggles and grunts from her.

Pomina's giggling took on a nervous quality as Comus tightened the lace to render her helpless. He was aware of his reputation, and knew that any girl finding herself tied in a kneeling position with her bottom available to him must be intensely aware of her anus and his predilection for sodomy. The idea amused him and he gave her bottom a prod with his erection to enhance her uncertainty. Pomina squealed, at which Comus chuckled. Her wrists were fixed, but as an added refinement he tied the lace off around her tail, drawing another squeal from her.

Kneeling and tied, Pomina presented a fine rear view. Her culottes were stretched taut over her ample bottom, the transparent gauze doing nothing to hide her charms but serving to exaggerate the size and roundness of her hindquarters. At the top her tail stuck out of its lace trimmed slit, jerking slightly with every movement of her tied hands. Below, an expanse of embroidered gauze covered the main spread of her bottom and the deep cleft at the centre. The gauze ended in the lace puff where the culottes ran between her thighs. This, Comus knew, would have an opening at the centre, allowing access to her vagina and bottom as necessary.

Burrowing his fingers in among the lace, he found the slit and pulled, exposing the plump, bare lips of Pomina's sex and part of the equally plump tuck of her bottom. Extending his tongue he began to lick, touching the groove that separated her bottom-cheeks with little flicks, each of which brought a new sigh of contentment from her. He placed his hands on her cheeks and pulled them open, exposing the deep cleft of her bottom and the tight, pink hole of her anus. Again she sighed, but on a new note, nervousness now showing along with her pleasure.

Comus smiled to himself, delighting in her response to having her bottom-hole inspected. It was inches in front of his face, a puckered ring of pale flesh, with the little creases meeting at a central hole that was clearly virgin. It was also moving slightly, clenching and unclenching in her nervousness.

'Do not be concerned,' he said softly. 'I do not intend to sodomise you. Yet still . . .'

He leant forward and planted a firm kiss on her ring, matching the pucker of his lips to that of her hole.

'Comus!' she squealed as his lips pressed to her anus.

He flicked out his tongue, briefly probing the tiny hole but finding it too tight for insertion. Pomina squealed again, rapture mixed with shock at the pleasure of the debauched act of having her anus kissed. Comus moved lower, running his tongue down over the smooth, taut skin that separated vagina from anus. Pomina's sex was neat: trim inner lips within a deep furrow formed by fat outer lips. In contrast her clitoris was large, and now protruded from the centre of her vulva, firm and hard in her excitement.

Comus began to explore her with his tongue. Without hurry he investigated every fold and crevice of her sex, licking and kissing while Pomina's sighs and squeals became increasingly urgent. Yet with her wrists tied she could do nothing, only remain passive as he indulged himself in the pleasures of her body.

Her vagina quickly began to run, then drip, the juice oozing from the hole in a richly scented trickle that covered his face as he licked and kissed at her. Its taste was intensely feminine, musky and stronger than the taste of a true-girl's cunt. She had also begun to writhe her bottom, clearly desperate for entry. Comus planted a final kiss on the taut bud of her clitoris and sat back, taking his cock in his hand.

Pomina adjusted her position, spreading her knees and thrusting her bottom up to make herself as available as possible. Her culottes stayed partly open, leaving the well juiced shape of her vulva peeping out from a field of lace ruffles. It was a target Comus found impossible to resist. Stepping forward, he put his cock in among the lace.

He probed, sliding his cock between the frills of her culottes to find the fat, yielding flesh of her bottom. The lace tickled his cock and balls, adding to his urgency to be inside her. Pushing deeper, he felt his cock touch the damp flesh of her sex. He pushed again and she opened, her vagina accepting the full length of his penis with one easy, fluid motion. Within her he could feel the spiral of her vaginal walls, which guided his cock in a twisting pattern as he began to fuck her.

Pomina began to squeal, not the delighted squeaks of foreplay but loud, urgent noises that Comus knew would be ringing out into the night air over Suza. With his cock inside her, her fat bottom pressed to his front and his mouth full of the taste of her juice, Comus found himself glad that he had made such thorough use of Ciriel's bottom earlier. Had he not done so he would already have come in Pomina. As it was, he was ready for a long, protracted session of love-play.

Sliding his hand beneath her belly, he began to masturbate her. He kept his pushes short and brisk while touching her breasts, rubbing the nipples and running his hand along them to make them swing and slap against each other. Pomina began to buck and her grunting and squealing became more urgent. Then he tweaked her clitoris.

She climaxed, an explosive orgasm to the sound of desperate squealing and bucking motions so violent that Comus had troubling keeping his erection sheathed in her vagina. Curling his other arm beneath her belly, he took a firm grip on her, holding her while she writhed on his cock and stimulating both her breasts and her vulva. At length her orgasm began to subside, but he continued to manipulate her body.

'No,' Pomina gasped, 'that is too much. I can't . . . Comus, no!'

Once more she came, screaming out with a volume that he was sure would be audible beyond the walls. Again he continued to twiddle her clitoris and stroke her nipples.

'No, Comus, not again!' Pomina gasped. 'Comus, no! Comus!'

Again she came, this time with a frantic piping noise that was interspersed with gasps and grunts and ended with her collapsing in his arms. Comus relaxed his grip and took hold of her by the thighs. She was sighing and panting as he pushed his cock deep inside her and began the ride to his own orgasm. Each push brought him nearer, and she was squealing again when his cock exploded inside her.

Comus withdrew, pulling slowly back to free his cock and then squeezing the last of his come into the ruffles of her culottes. Pomina rolled to the side, and as her huge brown eyes met his, Comus saw a look of wonder and satisfaction deeper even than those he received from Ciriel after her favourite combination of beating and buggery. Seating himself on the couch, he pulled her head into his lap, cuddling her to him only to find her mouth opening around the now limp form of his cock and starting to suck.

He relaxed, making no effort either to encourage or deny her. She continued to suck, working her lips and tongue on the soft flesh of his penis. As his cock began to respond Comus focused on the picture of her as she lay, nude but for her soiled culottes, which did nothing to hide the beauty of her bottom. Then there was the criss-cross of ties that bound her wrists and the loop that fixed them to her little pig's tail. Best of all, even though he could not fully see it, was the thought of her pretty, piggy face with the mouth open around his slowly swelling cock.

Tempted by her helplessness and the fat swell of her pouted buttocks, he reached out and patted one bottom cheek. Pomina thrust her bottom out even before the flesh had ceased to wobble. Encouraged, Comus planted another, firmer smack on her bottom, resulting in an increase of the eagerness with which his cock was being sucked.

With his cock now stiffening quickly in her mouth he began to spank her. As her buttocks reddened and warmed she became ever more excited, bucking and pushing her bottom out while growing ever more attentive to his cock. He was quickly hard, while the red flush of her beating was showing through the gauze of her culottes.

Fired by the desire to beat her and the obvious relish with which she received it, he pulled her head from his cock and took her across his knee. Pomina squealed in delight, then in pain as his hand smacked hard down on the seat of her culottes.

He beat her firmly, aiming the blows to both the weighty cheeks of her big bottom and to her chubby thighs. She quickly began to kick and squeak, then to thrash and squeal as her pain grew and her ability to control her body slipped away. Comus' cock was now fully hard and wedged among her breasts with the soft flesh rubbing on it as she struggled. After a space he tore away her culottes, leaving her red, quivering buttocks sticking nude from the mess of torn fabric. Pomina yelped at the treatment but kept her bottom well up.

Then, suddenly, she threw her leg across his and began to rub herself on him with a frantic, unreserved urgency. Comus laughed at the sight and increased the force of the beating. Pomina screamed, then once more began to make the curious piping noise that had accompanied her third orgasm. He continued to slap, bouncing her fat bottom beneath his hand as her climax tore through her and, at the very peak, kicking her midriff high to spread her bottom. As her soft cheeks flew apart he planted a last, powerful slap full across her vaginal lips and anus. Pomina screamed.

Comus allowed her to come down in her own time, contenting himself with stroking her inflamed bottom as she lay gasping and panting over his knee. His cock was still hard, yet he was content to wait and soothe her from her spanking until she was ready. At last Pomina slid from his lap, landing on the floor with a fleshy slapping noise. Slowly, and struggling because of her bound wrists, she managed to right herself and crawl to him. With her reddened bottom thrust out among the ruins of her culottes and her eyes swimming with pleasure, she took him in her mouth. Comus sighed as she began to suck, and with the well-beaten girl kneeling between his knees, he took his second climax in her mouth.

Their love-making continued for some time, more gentle and slow, but leading to many more climaxes for Pomina and finishing with a third for Comus. This was taken in the groove of her naked, well-beaten bottom with his cock rubbing between her fleshy cheeks.

Although her anus was well lubricated with apple oil, he held back from buggering her. Yet when he did press the head of his penis a little way into her well greased sphincter, her response was not a grunt of indignation but a little squeal that conveyed apprehension but also excitement.

He left her face down on the floor with sperm between her buttocks to add to the apple oil and her own juices. She sighed with regret as he announced his departure, but made no move to stop him.

'That was exquisite,' he declared as he started to dress. 'An experience of true erotic beauty. May I dare to hope that we will now become regular lovers?'

'You are a wonderful lover, Comus,' Pomina sighed. 'Return soon, but be careful of Otomos.'

'To the pit with Otomos,' Comus answered.

'Please?' Pomina urged.

Comus made no response but continued dressing. Once clad, he bent to kiss her as she lay exhausted on the floor. Then, with a last courteous nod, he left.

Later, having released Ciriel and calmed her sulks by applying his tongue between her thighs, Comus at last found time to rest. As he sank into a satisfied sleep his last thought was to wonder whether the risky and difficult process of obtaining and distilling Otomos' sperm had in fact been necessary.

5

To Cheat a Mistress

Otomos sat splay legged on a couch, his face set in an expression of obstinate boredom. Urzon stood by the window with his heavy buttocks settled on the ledge. For some while the councillor had been attempting to explain the virtues of diplomacy to Otomos, yet he had met with little success.

'This talk wastes time and debases a man; also the city,' Otomos objected in response to Urzon's repeated insistence that a diplomatic excuse was necessary before war could be declared. 'Our enemies know we covet their land as we know they covet ours. Why trouble to pick a quarrel? Why warn them of our intentions? The man's way is to gather an army and attack.'

'Thus gaining us a reputation for unprovoked aggression,' Urzon went on.

'Just so,' Otomos snorted, 'to keep them in fear of us.'

'And better prepared and defended,' Urzon pointed out. 'Not that outright attack is without its virtues. We might – for the sake of argument – create a dispute with, say, Tyoch, and then move unexpectedly on, say, Alaban. Yet . . .'

'A fine plan,' Otomos interrupted once more, 'let us call Khian-Shu and put it into effect forthwith.'

'No, no . . .' Urzon responded hastily, only to be cut off by the sound of the door gong.

A bellowed demand from Otomos led to the appearance of Tamina.

'A girl!' Otomos called in pleasure. 'Enough of this babble then, Urzon. Let us take her fore and aft. I have dice somewhere, I'll roll you for who has her cunt first!'

'I will gladly pleasure you, my Lord,' Tamina said hastily, 'but I have news.'

'What?' Otomos demanded.

'I fear it may make you angry, my Lord,' Tamina went on, 'but I know that it is my duty to tell you. Pomina has coupled with Comus the essencier! I came to her chambers this morning. She was revelling in having committed the act!'

'Pomina? That popinjay Comus? Why?' Otomos exclaimed, rising to his feet as his complexion took on a dark tinge.

'I do not know,' Tamina went on, 'but she admitted to everything! She had a new perfume, very rare and exotic. He gave it to her and then mated her, in several positions and with many refinements. She says it lasted the space of five glasses!'

'He knows Pomina will be Lady and seeks her favour,' Urzon broke in. 'He aspires to the council.'

'He would do better to seek my favour,' Otomos grunted, 'and coupling my Pomina is no way to do that.'

'It is a small thing,' Urzon stated, 'you have many lovers and every suan girl in Suza vies for your attention; also many of the bolder true-girls and even some felians.'

'Pomina is mine,' Otomos answered. 'I mean to make her Lady. If she is seen coupling with every posturing popinjay in Suza I will become a laughing stock. I must challenge him!'

'Not so,' Urzon replied. 'If you issue a challenge it will merely show spite and envy. These are not suitable traits for a Lord.'

'How can I not challenge him and keep my pride?' Otomos demanded.

'Your pride should be undented,' Urzon went on.

132

'His mating of Pomina does not mean that she has a preference for him. Indeed, it was probably done merely in appreciation for the gift of this exotic essence; a deed of gratitude – simple propriety.'

Otomos grunted doubtfully.

'Therefore,' Urzon continued, warming to his task, 'should you challenge him over such a small matter you will seem ungracious. Worse still, you are the foremost warrior of Suza, he is an essencier. If you slay him the populace will not talk of your prowess but of cowardice!'

'Cowardice!'

'Exactly that. Where is the glory in defeating a man who makes no more physical exertion than to pull herbs? He does not even own a sword! No, Otomos, if you challenge him every last citizen of Suza will think of you as a coward, nothing more.'

'Never!' Otomos spat. 'So be it. I will pay no heed to him.'

Grumbling faintly, Otomos sat back down.

In a chamber set high against the wall of the female citadel Rufina and her sisters sat at breakfast. Both Zirina and Ilana shared Rufina's stamp of height and elegance, but neither carried her air of stern power. In appearance they were identical, as they were in dress, with loose robes of deep blue covering all but their heads, hands and feet.

Two male courtesans knelt at their feet, both true-men and both naked but for leather collars set with brass studs. Both bore the fine red tracery of the Mistress's whips on their backs and buttocks, and both had straining erections which they were careful to maintain in case of need. Neither woman paid much attention to the men, save to occasionally flick one or the other with her whip.

Rufina took a lazy bite from a honey cake, then

signalled Zirina with an almost imperceptible nod. In response Zirina immediately reached forward and pushed her man brusquely to the floor, leaving him lying flat with his erection projecting upwards like a flagpole. She laughed at the ease with which she had pushed him down, then rose to stand over his supine body. Rucking her leather dress up around her waist, she presented her naked quim and bottom to the room.

'What do you see, worm?' she demanded.

'Your cunt, Mistress,' the man answered.

'Idiot! Brainless lump of meat!' Zirina snapped. 'You see nirvana, heaven, that to which you ultimately aspire yet can never hope to achieve!'

'Yes, Mistress.'

'And what is your deepest desire? No, what is the most you dare hope for?'

'To watch you masturbate, Mistress, and perhaps to be permitted to do the same myself.'

'Do you think we want to watch you jerking your disgusting little cock?'

'No, Mistress.'

'Then keep it stiff but no more than stiff, while you watch.'

She began to masturbate, stroking her sex with long, elegant fingers while beneath her the man became increasingly desperate. His hand was on his cock, tugging gently and occasionally going faster as if in the hope of stimulating an orgasm. Each time this happened Ilana would flick her whip out, catching the man's testicles or thighs with the lash. Once more he would go back to the slow, nursing motions that kept his cock erect but never allowed orgasm. Rufina laughed as she watched her sister torment the man, then slid her own hand up under her dress to gently stimulate her sex.

Zirina began to moan softly, then, with a sudden, abandoned motion, she sat herself neatly on to the man's lap. Rufina sighed as she watched the penis disappear inside her sister's body and then turned a despairing look to Ilana as Zirina began to ride the man. The position was anything but refined, with the true-girl's dress hitched high and her legs cocked well apart to display both the junction of cock and vagina and the tight dimple of her anus. Zirina was heedless of her undignified exposure, bouncing on his cock and moaning with increasing urgency. Suddenly white sperm erupted from the mouth of her vagina, plastering his balls, which in turned smeared Zirina's anus and the tuck of her bottom. Again Rufina shook her head as her sister began to masturbate frantically, rubbing at her clitoris as she sat astride the man's cock. Zirina came with a long cry of pleasure, then slumped forward. The man's cock pulled slowly free of her vagina, then flopped against his thigh, its skin liberally coated with both her juices and his come.

'You lack control, sister, as always,' Rufina remarked. 'You must learn to restrain your passion and never to take a cock inside you when you have said you intend to deny it to your victim.'

'I apologise, sister,' Zirina gasped. 'It was more than I could resist.'

'And what did we agree if you failed again?' Rufina demanded.

'To lick you while I myself am teased with the whip,' Zirina answered.

'Exactly,' Rufina replied. 'Now crawl to me, and keep your dress high.'

Rufina watched as her sister dismounted and crawled obediently across the floor. The front of Zirina's dress had fallen loose, allowing her breasts to swing free within. Taken by a strong urge to have her sister's chest naked, Rufina moved forward and tugged the soft leather sharply down, leaving both soft, pink orbs hanging free in the air, their nipples stiff and red beneath them. Zirina gave a muted sob but came on,

135

placing her head meekly between her sister's knees. Rufina opened her thighs and slid forward, pressing the moist flesh of her vulva into Zirina's face. Then, with her dress rucked about her middle to leave bottom, quim and breasts naked, Zirina began to lick her elder sister.

'Come, Ilana, beat her,' Rufina ordered as the moist tongue began to explore her vulva. 'Not hard, but enough to bring to her an understanding of her condition.'

Zirina shivered at the words, but increased the pressure of her tongue on her sister's vulva. Rufina watched as Ilana rose, smiling, and gave the out-thrust ball of Zirina's bottom a playful tap with the sting of her whip. Again Zirina shivered and pulled her back tight in, offering the open spread of her bottom to her twin. Ilana flicked the whip down, drawing a sharp cry from Zirina. Rufina smiled to herself and closed her eyes, allowing the sensation of being licked to build up. Ilana continued to whip her sister, delivering short, precise blows of the whip, each of which brought a little gasp from Zirina and increased the urgency of her tongue work. Rufina was in no hurry, intent on leaving her little sister's bottom thoroughly welted before she climaxed. Indeed, her mind was focused on the thought of the small, round white bottom becoming gradually redder and sorer as the whipping continued, and of her sister's feelings as she was beaten by her twin with two men looking on.

Only when Zirina had begun to play with her breasts and produce little, doglike panting noises, did Rufina reach down and take hold of her sister's hair. Recognising the signal, Zirina began a frantic lapping motion with her tongue. Rufina sighed, spread her thighs wide across her sister's face and began to come. The orgasm built slowly to a peak, then broke in Rufina's head, making her cry out despite her best efforts at control. At the very peak of her climax the feel of tongue on clitoris suddenly became too much, and she pushed her sister firmly back even as she heard the firm smack of the whip on the girl's bottom.

Rufina opened her eyes to find Zirina with her face to the floor and her bottom high. She was masturbating, with her legs open as the whipping continued, indifferent to the intimacy of her display. Both men were watching surreptitiously, Ilana's still nursing his erection. Zirina came, crying out her pleasure and pushing her bottom out to the whip, then collapsing to the floor. Ilana laughed, bent briefly to kiss her twin sister and then turned to the man she had been tormenting.

'Show little Zirina how it should be done,' Rufina ordered.

Extending one booted toe, Ilana pushed the man down on to his back. He went over and she gave him a contemptuous prod with her toe, then pulled up the front of her dress. He swallowed at the sight of her naked sex and took hold of his erection, holding it up as if expecting her to lower herself on to it. Ilana sneered and spat in his face, then spread the lips of her vulva and pushed out her hips, positioning herself as if about to urinate on him. Zirina had risen and was watching, while Rufina felt a thrill of pleasure at the prospect of watching Ilana soil the man's face.

The door gong sounded. Ilana quickly covered her sex and her sisters both responded with noises of irritation. An angry demand by Rufina was answered by the sound of her door being pushed open, then by the entrance of three women. Rufina looked up, her momentary annoyance changing to an expression of amused malice. Alla-Sha stood at the head of the group, her slender, white furred body clad in loose black silk that served to emphasise her natural elegance and poise. Behind her was Soumea, the Mistress of Refectory, her solid body covered in an elaborate confection of dark-blue cloth. The third woman was Jasiel, dressed in loose culottes of deep-blue silk worn low on her hips, otherwise naked.

'Lady,' Rufina addressed Alla-Sha with no more than the faintest hint of mockery. 'May we assume that this visit is formal?'

'It is,' Alla-Sha answered. 'Perhaps if you could dismiss your playthings?'

The two men rose and left. Alla-Sha waited until the door had closed and continued.

'I wish to put my resignation before the council. Soumea and Jasiel are ready to accept. Can I assume you will also do so?'

'You may,' Rufina said, making no effort to hide her pleasure at the news. 'Indeed I had been expecting this visit, although perhaps not until the demise of my father.'

'Should I have waited until the election of Otomos, he would have had the right to enjoy me as part of the celebration,' Alla-Sha replied. 'Thus, as my final act as Lady, I chose to set the election for Ladyship immediately before that for the Lordship, and for the celebrations to run concurrently. I trust you will enjoy your success and the subsequent pleasure of Otomos' phallus, Mistress Rufina.'

'I shall accept it as a Lady should,' Rufina answered coolly.

'That I would like to watch,' Alla-Sha retorted. 'Ilana, if you have a stylus and parchment you may make out my declaration.'

'A pleasure,' Ilana answered and turned to a chest of inlaid rosewood.

They waited as she extracted her tools and created the declaration of resignation with a few deft strokes of her stylus. Alla-Sha then took the parchment and laid it in clear view, then accepted the re-inked stylus from Ilana.

'I now resign,' Alla-Sha declared and marked the parchment with a complex flourish.

One by one the others added their marks, each in order of seniority and finishing with Jasiel. Alla-Sha then acknowledged the three true-girls with the most perfunctory of nods and left, followed by Soumea and Jasiel. As the beautiful acyonthrope left, Rufina called after her.

'Return in two glasses, Jasiel, I wish to celebrate.'

The yellow-furred girl accepted the appointment with a nod and closed the door, leaving the sisters alone. They waited, listening until it was certain that their conversation could not be overheard. Rufina took a peach and bit into it, tasting the sweet juice as it ran over her tongue, then swallowing.

'It is time,' she stated. 'Ilana, sister, go to Zara and tell her to proceed.'

'It is perfect,' Ilana remarked, 'the vile creature will be thinking of his morning wallow, they may catch him on the way.'

'Ideal,' Rufina agreed, 'his blood will be thick and his temper high. Return with Zara afterwards, sister, to be sure we have what we want.'

Ilana rose, and left.

Still smarting from the insolent behaviour of Comus, Otomos stamped towards the bathhouse, intent on his midday wallow, food and a ripe courtesan or two. Urzon walked beside him, doing his best to turn the conversation to more neutral topics than the etiquette of duelling.

'It is simple,' Otomos declared. 'A man must respond to an insult with a challenge. Only thus can honour be maintained. If the challenged one accepts his fault, then he may apologise and honour is satisfied. Otherwise he must fight or be branded a coward and worse.'

'True, true,' Urzon replied, 'for a captain or mentor, but as you know well, duelling is considered beneath councillors and forbidden to the Lord.'

'I am not yet Lord,' Otomos answered. 'I am Captain of Uhlans.'

'Yet the situation is far from the ordinary,' Urzon insisted.

'True, yet . . .' Otomos began and then stopped as they rounded a corner.

To the side of the passage ahead was Hoat, naked and with his massive buttocks moving rhythmically as he fucked a true-girl who was kneeling on a window sill of appropriate height. As they approached, Otomos saw that the girl was Zara, and that her face was set in an expression that combined ecstasy with disbelief. Some two spans of thick, dark bear's cock were hidden inside her vagina, and with each push a further span would briefly disappear.

'There's one who likes her cock,' Otomos remarked. 'A fuck would calm my nerves. Let us take her when the bear has finished.'

Even as he spoke Hoat grunted and sperm erupted from the mouth of Zara's vagina to splash liberally on to the floor. For a long moment he held his cock deep inside Zara, then gave a final flurry of quick, hard pushes that had her gasping with pleasure. Once more he stopped, then began to ease his cock out, vacating her hole but leaving a long strand of sperm joining the lower lip of her vagina with his erection. Then the strand of sperm broke as he stepped back to leave Zara with her vagina a gaping pink hole from which their mixed juices ran.

'Our timing is fortunate,' Otomos grunted cheerfully and put a hand to the front of his tunic. 'Ho, Zara my pleasure, hold that pose. We've more cock for that fine cunt of yours.'

Zara turned, her expression still breathless and dizzy. Seeing the suanthropes, she managed a smile and adjusted the set of her knees to lower her vagina to a more convenient level for entry.

'That's my girl,' Otomos grunted, 'an ever willing fuck.'

Hoat turned, his great cock swinging out into the passage to scatter droplets of Zara's juice and his own sperm. He grinned at the suanthropes as they drew level, then, reaching down, he took up the hem of Otomos' fine red cloak and, quite casually, wiped his come-slick cock clean.

For a moment the scene froze. Otomos stared at his cloak, his mouth wide and his eyes set in an uncomprehending stare. Urzon also stared, looking at Hoat with incredulity. Hoat held his insolent grin, while Zara remained in place with her bottom stuck out in the hope of entry.

It was Otomos who broke the tension. With a roar of outrage he leapt forward, his great hands clutching for Hoat's throat. The ursanthrope raised his hand to block the charge, but too slowly and Otomos closed his fingers on Hoat's neck. The ursanthrope growled in anger and brought a knee hard up into his opponent's midriff even as Urzon came forward.

'Stop! Now!' the councillor roared.

Neither combatant took the least notice. Grappling, they crashed to the floor, with Otomos uppermost. Zara screamed and ran, disappearing down the passage in a flurry of bouncing breasts and wobbling bottom. Urzon gripped the back of Otomos' cloak and pulled, but to no avail.

'What is this?' a new voice cut in.

For an instant Otomos looked up, and Hoat rolled quickly to the side, disengaging. In the passage stood Ilarion, his face set in a hard frown and every contour of his tall, slim body radiating disapproval.

'I am insulted,' Otomos grunted and gestured angrily at Hoat. 'This piece of bear's dung wiped his prick on my cloak as if it were a courtesan's slop rag!'

'Its best use,' Hoat growled.

Once more Otomos started forward, but the combined efforts of Urzon's strength and Ilarion's glare held him back.

'Then I challenge him,' Otomos spat, 'although he'd be better put in his place here and now.'

'Otomos . . .' Urzon broke in.

'Accepted,' Hoat growled. 'Tomorrow dawn, naked, with neither weapons nor armour.'

'At least try and behave like a man,' Otomos snapped. 'Choose swords, or clubs, pikes even.'

'Naked,' Hoat repeated.

Otomos spat on the ground in response.

'This is not to be!' Urzon cut in. 'Otomos, this challenge is no accident!'

'What of it?' Otomos demanded. 'Do you suppose this hulking outlander moron seeks to challenge for the Lordship?'

'I suspect a less simple scheme,' Urzon stated. 'Withdraw your challenge Otomos.'

'I fight,' Otomos grated. 'Bear witness, Urzon, and you also, Master Ilarion. I have set a challenge and will accept no apology.'

'There'll be no apology,' Hoat growled.

'Otomos,' Urzon spoke soothingly, 'as Lord Presumptive you have the right to appoint a proxy. Is that not so, Ilarion?'

'By the law, yes,' Ilarion answered. 'Yet Otomos would lose face. If, as seems likely, this is the outcome of some scheme, then that may be its intention. No, it would be better if we four agreed to put this aside. Otomos, restrain your anger. Hoat, in return for the rank of Mentor, will you apologise?'

'No,' Hoat answered coldly.

'Nor would I accept,' Otomos snarled.

'Besides,' Urzon added, 'Zara was here, indeed she was part of the cause of this. Even now news of the clash will have reached the hall of courtesans. We cannot hope to keep this quiet.'

'So be it,' Ilarion sighed.

* * *

Zara ran, heedless of her nudity, heedless of the stares of those she passed. Ilana, she knew, would be waiting in a remote corridor in the lower city to hear her report. Yet it was towards the male citadel that she ran, only stopping at an ornate door. Ignoring the gong, she burst inside. Within, the councillor Lomas sat on a couch within easy reach of a tray of sweetmeats and a flask of wine. At Zara's appearance he looked up in surprise.

'Master,' she panted, 'swear I may speak for you alone.'

'What?' Lomas demanded 'Why?'

'Swear it, Master, please!'

'So be it, I swear it. What is it?'

'Listen closely. The ursanthrope Hoat has goaded Otomos to a duel. It is Rufina's doing and she has used me as her tool. I knew nothing of her intent, I swear it. Please bear this visit as proof of my goodwill, and for the sake of all the pleasure I have given you, do not say I was here to Rufina, nor her sisters.'

'What!?' Lomas roared but Zara had already taken to her heels.

Running at frantic speed, she made for her meeting with Ilana.

Rufina waited in her chambers. Before her knelt Jasiel, the Mistress of Courtesans, entirely naked with her glorious coat of yellow and black fur brushed and glossy. Her face was between Rufina's thighs, lapping gently at the true-girl's labia as she had been ordered. Rufina tried to focus on this, stroking Jasiel's fur and occasionally giving a little start or half closing her eyes. Despite this her eyes were on the door and her ears alert for the gong. Zirina, who had her eyes on her sister and was watching as Jasiel's expert tongue did its work, also showed less than complete attention.

When the gong did sound, both women turned quickly to the door, although Jasiel continued her licking with all the insouciance of her training. Ilana entered the chamber, smiling broadly.

'Is it done?' Rufina asked.

'Perfectly,' Ilana replied.

'A moment then. Jasiel, finish me.'

Jasiel's tongue moved from labia to clitoris, working on the little bud with rapid flicks. Immediately Rufina tensed as the muscles of her sex began to contract. Jasiel's lips pressed to Rufina's vulva, sucking to create a maddening pressure in addition to the touch of her tongue. Rufina came, a long, drawn-out orgasm that rose and fell in her head as her body arched out in bliss. At the very peak Jasiel's teeth met on Rufina's clitoris, making her scream and kick out in an unexpected pang of ecstasy. She cursed Jasiel aloud the instant she found breath, but the courtesan simply returned a knowing smile.

'You say it is done?' Rufina asked her sister as soon as the spasms of her climax had subsided.

'Perfectly,' Ilana replied. 'Hoat took Zara and came in her as Otomos approached. Otomos stopped, intent on Zara's pleasure and Hoat wiped his cock on Otomos' cloak. Otomos sprang at Hoat but Ilarion arrived and they separated, otherwise the populace might have missed the spectacle of a duel. As it was, a challenge ensued and Hoat followed the course you ordered.'

'What is this?' Jasiel asked. 'Have you moved to deny Otomos the Lordship?'

'Just so,' Rufina stated as she adjusted her dress, 'Otomos has issued a challenge to Hoat, and Hoat has chosen to fight without arms. Naturally not even Otomos can hope to stand against a full grown ursanthrope.'

'And when Hoat is victorious?'

'The populace will either kill him or chase him from Suza. The suans will then blame the true-men or felians for the intrigue. During the ensuing chaos we alone will retain our senses and may promote a Lord suitable to our needs. A moderately youthful true-man I would imagine, someone sensuous yet pliable. I am told by Eomaea that the old fool Xerinus is to stand down from the male council and seek election for Comus, the essencier, immediately upon the death of the Lord. Comus is a possibility.'

'Comus is not weak, Mistress,' Jasiel objected, 'nor easy to manipulate. He is also greatly addicted to sodomy.'

'Yet I feel we might train him,' Rufina pronounced. 'He is a man, with all the faults inherent in men, and also with all their weaknesses. The current male councillors have no respect for me. They are too old, too dull to see that I alone can bring strength and order to Suza. Comus may prove different; it is simply a question of making him understand that the true route to pleasure lies only at my hands. As to his addiction to sodomy, perhaps the insertion of my fine ebony phallus into his own anus may change his opinion.'

'I rather think it would boost his delight in the practice, Mistress,' Jasiel answered.

As each apple flew towards him Otomos would remain perfectly still. Then, when it seemed that the fruit must pass him, his head would jerk around and his jaws would snap shut around it. After each success he would briefly display the apple between his tusks and then swallow it whole. This was a practised game, and one often used among suans to display the speed of their reactions. Otomos excelled at the sport, and had already caught over a dozen apples.

Immediately on challenging Hoat he had made for the Uhlan barracks and ordered food to be served and wine casks to be broached. It was a gesture of deliberate bravado, the formal response to a challenge, and also the one to which Otomos' nature was most inclined. His

Uhlans had responded quickly, cheering the news of the duel as if it were no more than light amusement. If any felt misgivings, then none voiced them. As the news had spread, other suans, non-suan soldiers and the whole gamut of Otomos' supporters had began to gather, eager to join in the feasting and indulge in the pleasures of wine and sex. Now the hall rang with sound, the harsh blare of brass instruments, laughter, squeals and raucous conversation. Into this atmosphere came Lomas, his serious expression and hurried pace entirely at odds with the general gaiety. Otomos raised his hand to signal a halt to the apple thrower.

'Ah, Lomas, father,' he roared. 'We have wine, food and cunt. Join us.'

'I am not here for debauchery,' Lomas answered, yelling above the roar of the crowd. 'This challenge is the result of an intrigue!'

'Naturally, what else would it be?' Otomos roared back.

'We must outlaw it, or you must appoint a proxy,' Lomas stated as he drew level with his son's chair.

'And lose the respect of my men? Never!' Otomos replied. 'Do not concern yourself, father. Hoat is a shambling beast. He knows nothing of martial combat. What is more his weight advantage is no more than a third piece. I will win, and have the bare-handed defeat of a full-grown ursanthrope added to my role of honour!'

'If you win!'

'I will win.'

Otomos scruffed a passing girl and pulled her up on to his lap, then effectively shut off the conversation by burying his face in-between her plump breasts. Her squeal of delight cut off Lomas' answering remark and the elderly suanthrope was left to shake his head in despair and reach for a comforting flagon of wine.

* * *

Beneath a ledge of rock on the hills that surrounded Suza, Tian-Sha and Xerafina lay on a patch of yellowing grass. The light had began to fade and carried a curious yellow cast. Throughout the day tall clouds had been piling up to the south and west and the air was still and humid, presaging a storm.

'We must act faster than news might travel from Alaban,' Tian-Sha stated. 'Wains take four to five days by the river road, but it would be wise not to hesitate. Yet we should wait for dark before entering the city. Your scent is distinctive, but redolent of Shiraz. If you drink some and spill more on your fur you should pass any but the most suspicious of felians.'

'With luck it will rain and my scent will not be a cause for concern,' Xerafina replied.

Tian-Sha gave a shiver of distaste but nodded agreement.

'You seem uneasy,' Xerafina said. 'Surely it is a small thing to scale a wall and hide. You have prepared a place, I trust?'

'Everything is as it should be,' Tian-Sha answered. 'No, my heat is rising with the approach of night. I need a cock inside me, badly, yet you are right to advise patience.'

'I would gladly help ease your heat,' Xerafina offered, 'and although I have no cock, I know a device that may add to your pleasure. With my tail tip thrust forward between my thighs, I may seek to imitate a male.'

'Thank you,' Tian-Sha said, 'take me kneeling, so that I may best imagine you as a man inside me.'

Xerafina nodded in response and Tian-Sha turned, suddenly urgent for sex now that she no longer had the need to restrain herself. Kneeling on all fours, she presented Xerafina with her bottom, the tail raised to allow access to her vulva. Xerafina also knelt and, as Tian-Sha watched slid her tail up between her legs, then closed them to leave the tip protruding from her groin

147

as if it were a large, black-furred cock. Turning her face down, Tian-Sha anticipated entry and tried to imagine Xerafina as her male counterpart. The tail tip touched her vulva, moving up and down in quick motions that tickled and brought an urgent need to her vagina. Then the tip found her hole and started to ease inside, drawing a long hiss of satisfaction from between her lips. Xerafina's hands closed on Tian-Sha's hips and they began to fuck, moving together in a smooth rocking motion.

With her eyes closed, Tian-Sha did her best to imagine the tail in her vagina as a fat, stiff cock. It was impossible – not only did the fur tickle the mouth of her vagina but Xerafina continuously moved it to create a delicious, but most uncock-like, wiggling motion. Nevertheless it was certainly stimulating, and not unlike the feeling of masturbating with her own tail inserted into her vagina. Soon the pleasure had risen to the point where she wanted to masturbate as she was fucked, and she reached a hand back to find her vulva.

'Let me,' Xerafina offered, 'you may play with your breasts.'

Xerafina's hand slid under Tian-Sha's belly, finding the fleshy quim and searching for the clitoris. Then Tian-Sha's tail was gripped and pulled sharply up, forcing her to raise her bottom and producing a sharp twinge of pleasure. Xerafina began to masturbate Tian-Sha and tug at her tail at the same time, quickly producing a breathless ecstasy. Tian-Sha let her upper breasts into her hands, feeling the full, firm globes as she was teased towards orgasm. A claw tip had found her clitoris, while the tail tip in her vagina had began to push deeper and harder even as the tugs at her own tail strengthened. With her nipples hard between her fingers she allowed herself to be manipulated towards her climax. When it hit it came with a rush and was accompanied by a peculiar feeling of vulnerability, as if presenting her vagina for penetration by another girl somehow reduced her control over her actions. It also brought an overwhelming feeling of satisfaction, and she was purring even as the tail was pulled slowly out. Then she was slumping down on to the dry grass, happy and fulfilled and with a new sense of intimacy with Xerafina.

'You are kind,' she sighed as she propped herself on to an elbow. 'Now I am sated, at least for an hour or so. Can I return the pleasure?'

'If you wish. How?'

'A tongue bath?' Tian-Sha offered.

Xerafina responded with a purr of delight. The offer was intimate, more so than the simple licking of her breasts and vulva, indeed more normally an act between siblings than lovers.

'Lie back then,' Tian-Sha continued, 'and open yourself to me. I do not intend to stint you.'

With a pleased purr, Xerafina spread herself on the grass, allowing her thighs to rise and part to make an open offer of her sex. Tian-Sha moved between her lover's legs, pausing to admire the pretty yellow down of chest and belly, the triple line of black smudges that ran from shoulders to waist and the enticing black oval that surrounded the white furred vulva to make a target of Xerafina's sex. Xerafina was beautiful, also small and strangely vulnerable, and Tian-Sha found the desire to clean her lover more than the simple obligation of returning a favour. Coming forward, Tian-Sha began to lick, moving her tongue across Xerafina's facial fur, first against the grain to fluff up the short, fine undercoat, and then with it to smooth the washed fur back down. Without haste she cleaned Xerafina's face, then her neck and shoulders, tonguing every inch of the soft yellow and black fur. Xerafina had began to moan softly before Tian-Sha even reached her upper breasts, and her moans turned to mewls of unconcealed bliss when the

149

first dab of wet tongue tip found a bare nipple. Tian-Sha took her time, tonguing all six small, rounded breasts, cleaning each with slow, circular motions that ended at the nipple, which she would tweak erect with a gentle nip of her teeth. Xerafina had quickly begun to arch her back, and one arm had gone around Tian-Sha's shoulders.

Leaving Xerafina's breasts with all six nipples standing stiffly upright, Tian-Sha moved down. Tracing slow patterns in Xerafina's belly fur, she cleaned with methodical care and teasing skill. First she washed the low swell of the girl's belly, then burrowed her tongue deep into the tightness of the navel. With that Xerafina began to orgasm, small shuddering peaks that ran through her whole body. Tian-Sha took no notice, but continued to lick out Xerafina's navel until she was satisfied, only then tracing a slow line of kisses down the mid-line of the girl's belly and on to her sex. Two quick dabs of the tongue to the clitoris took Xerafina over the edge of her pleasure to full orgasm, holding Tian-Sha's head and mewing loudly as her thighs locked and her body rose to meet the pressure of the tongue.

When Xerafina's orgasm had run its course Tian-Sha transferred her attention to the girl's thighs. With long, unhurried licks she cleaned each part of the elegant legs, then the arms, with Xerafina purring softly all the while. Only when every inch of the girl's upper fur was clean did Tian-Sha roll her over, apply her tongue to the soft nape of her neck and once more begin to clean. Again Xerafina responded with purrs and mews that rose slowly in urgency as the tongue moved down her back. Tian-Sha reached the twin dimples that marked the start of Xerafina's bottom. She then switched her attention to the girl's legs, even as Xerafina raised her buttocks in anticipation.

With ever more loving attention, Tian-Sha sucked each of Xerafina's toes, then began to work slowly up the backs of her legs, teasing calves, inner knees and finally thighs until the girl was once more mewling openly. Placing a last kiss on the soft crease between bottom and thigh, Tian-Sha turned her attention to the pert buttocks. These formed two balls of rounded flesh, high and firm and covered with fur in rich yellow and glossy black spots. Tian-Sha cleaned each, working from the top downward until only the crease remained. Xerafina was clearly approaching another climax, and as Tian-Sha's tongue began to burrow down between the firm young buttocks, the mewls of pleasure became broken and rapid.

Lifting her hips, Xerafina pressed her bottom into Tian-Sha's face, offering her anus. Without hesitation Tian-Sha began to clean it, working her tongue tip across the little patch of hairless flesh and then into the hole itself, licking at every tiny fold and crevice while Xerafina moaned and shivered in response. With Xerafina's bottom hole a glistening pink dimple, Tian-Sha moved her tongue still lower, to the narrow bridge of pure white fur on the girl's perineum. Xerafina pushed her bottom yet higher, showing eagerness for her sex to be licked again. Tian-Sha responded, teasing first the soft grooves where Xerafina's sex lips met her thighs, then the actual lips, tracing the pattern of the black oval of fur that marked the girl's sex. Xerafina cried out and Tian-Sha put her tongue to the girl's clitoris, then her teeth, nipping the hard bud with a precise, yet gentle movement. Xerafina gasped and her thighs locked around Tian-Sha's head. Pressing her face into the girl's sex, Tian-Sha licked hard, letting Xerafina come and then taking her over into a hissing, mewling climax.

As Xerafina's body relaxed slowly from the orgasm the first heavy drops of rain began to fall. During their love play the clouds had come up overhead and Suza showed as no more than a dim smudge through the sheeting rain, black on slate grey. Tian-Sha stood and began to move down the hill in a slow, easy lope, with Xerafina following. The hill levelled out, giving way to a field of corn and then to a flat rice paddy. Tian-Sha made for a dyke, running along its crest until once more the ground rose and they were on the clear ground that ringed the city. Ahead the wall loomed black against the sky, the sheeting rain obliterating all detail and all scent. Crouching low, the two girls ran for the wall of Suza.

On reaching it the stone proved slick with rain, but their claws still managed to find purchase on the ancient rock and they quickly reached the parapet. No guards were in evidence, and the two girls swiftly descended the inner wall and entered the warren of the lower city. Ducking through a low-set window, Tian-Sha brought them into a wide passage. Now clear of the rain, both girls stopped to shake their fur and apply a few precise licks to the wettest areas of their bodies. The act was brief, an instinctive reaction very different from the leisurely tongue bath Tian-Sha had given Xerafina. Once satisfied, Tian-Sha signalled Xerafina to follow and ducked into a side passage of polished stone. This was set with doors but windowless and followed neither the slopes nor the curves natural to the city. The polished stone of the walls gave way to crude blocks and those in turn to raw rock. The passage narrowed and the floor became less even, until they were no longer walking in a man-made passage but in a natural cave. In absolute blackness Tian-Sha led Xerafina to a shallow pocket in the rock. After a brief and whispered conversation, she left.

Threading her way from the caves, Tian-Sha made for the chambers of Urzon. His voice answered the gong and she stepped inside, not finding him indulging a courtesan as she had expected, but standing at a window and staring out into the rain and blackness.

'Tian-Sha,' he greeted her. 'Still in season?'

'My need fades, Master,' she answered, 'but slowly. I also allowed myself to be lured into the tombyard by a group of boys, both suan and true-men. They tied me to keep my claws from their skin and mated me one by one. Between matings they forced wine down my throat – muscat laced with laudanum. I only woke when the rain began. A day is now missing from my life. How is Suza?'

'Not well,' Urzon answered. 'Otomos has allowed himself to be goaded into a challenge by that ursanthrope from the Baluchi stables. Otomos has the skill to win despite the bear's power, but he is unlikely to come away unscathed.'

'A challenge? Goaded to a challenge?'

'Just so. I suspect some intrigue lies behind it, but what? Hoat would never be accepted as Lord. If he did kill Otomos the populace would rise as one . . .'

'When is the duel?' Tian-Sha interrupted.

'Tomorrow, dawn.'

'Can you not dissuade Otomos?'

'Ridiculous!'

'I mate with Hoat now and again. I will go and try to prevent this, or at the least to discover who is behind it, and why.'

'Good girl, your enthusiasm does you credit.'

Tian-Sha ran from Urzon's chambers and directly to the stables. Hoat was seated on a pile of bales in one of the stalls, filing his claws.

'Not tonight, Tian-Sha,' he greeted her. 'I wish to conserve my energy. I am to fight a duel.'

'Rufina has tricked you,' Tian-Sha answered. 'You must leave or be dead by tomorrow!'

'Not so, I will be a hero,' Hoat boasted. 'The man who slew Otomos, the strongest of Suza, the natural leader. I will be Lord!'

'Not so!' Tian-Sha urged. 'You are alone, with no clique! Kill Otomos and every suan in Suza will rise against you, and others besides. They'll come with arbalests and pikes, trained warriors who have stood charges by Baluchi and elephants!'

'Yet as victor in a duel . . .'

'The mob cares nothing for such niceties. Yes, if Otomos challenged another soldier and lost, then that soldier would be deemed a hero. You would be seen only as an interloper, an outsider bent on power!'

'Then why did Rufina urge me to goad Otomos? She wishes me to be her consort.'

'She wishes only your death! Do you not see? She knows that Alla-Sha will step down. She then will be voted to the Ladyship but must endure Otomos as mate. This is intolerable to her, as would you be. The only Lord she would accept would be a weakling, some feeble male who she could control.'

'Yet she coupled with me in a fashion, and promised more.'

'She coupled with you? Rufina?'

'She masturbated me as proof of her devotion.'

'Only that! I mount you each full moon, yet I ask no more than your sperm! Did she return for more? No, she gave you Zara, not herself. I was there, on the ledge!'

'Yet . . .'

'Listen, Hoat, and believe what I say, for I have nothing to gain from this. Rufina plans that you kill Otomos. Once he is dead the mob will rise against you, thus ridding her of you as well as him. Then, with the male citadel in disarray, she will engineer a weak candidate to succeed as Lord, some male who has been entrapped by her erotic skills.'

'I must speak with her.'

'No, do not. Take a Baluchi and escape tonight by the sally gate. The rain will hide your scent and by morning you will be too far gone to catch. Go north to your homeland. Go anywhere, but do not fight Otomos!'

154

'I have honour, Tian-Sha.'

'Honour! Where is the honour in being manipulated by Rufina?'

'Yet a challenge is a challenge.'

'Let Rufina challenge Otomos then. She has created the quarrel. Also, do not imagine that it will be easy to kill Otomos. Certainly you are larger and have more power. Hand to hand – as I assume you intend to choose – you would seem to have the advantage. You do not. He is a trained warrior with some twenty battles behind him. You run a stable!'

'I will beat him.'

'And die under a hail of arrows within a ring of pikes – magnificent! Run, Hoat, run now.'

The ursanthrope made no response but turned away, seemingly unable to meet Tian-Sha's eyes.

Rufina sat at ease in her chambers, her mouth curved up into a smile of deep satisfaction. In her hand she held a small goblet of blown glass in which a puddle of deep brown wine reflected the red gleams of the torchlight. Her sisters sat opposite, also sipping the rich brown muscat and equally self-satisfied. The door gong sounded and an instant later Zara appeared. Rufina's instant annoyance at the unannounced entry faded immediately to concern at the sight of Zara's face.

'What is it, girl?' She demanded.

'I went to the stable as you ordered me,' Zara gasped out. 'Hoat is not there! He is gone!'

'Then he is probably somewhere in the lower city,' Rufina answered. 'Swilling mead no doubt.'

'No, Mistress, he is gone. A Baluchi is missing and there was a rumour of the sally gate being found open!'

'Stupid brat!' Rufina spat and grabbed Zara by the hair.

'Mistress! No! It's no fault of mine!' Zara squealed as she was wrenched down across Rufina's knee.

155

Zara's protest was ignored and her culottes torn down to expose the plump swell of her bottom, wriggling in desperation as she kicked helplessly in Rufina's grip. With her teeth clenched and her eyes blazing, Rufina began to vent her rage on Zara's bottom, slapping and slapping until the girl's large, soft cheeks danced in the torchlight and the chamber rang with squeaks of pain and protest. Only when the unfortunate girl's cries had begun to turn to whimpers of pleasure did Rufina stop smacking the now scarlet cheeks and shove her victim from her lap.

'Stupid beast!' Rufina swore as the red-bottomed Zara tumbled to the floor. 'Now I will be forced to bed down with that gross pig Otomos, or else surrender my hopes of the Ladyship!'

'Not so, sister,' Ilana put in. 'Alla-Sha has made an error. By setting the election to the Ladyship immediately before that for the Lordship, she has allowed you a new opening. The election to Lord is intended as no more than a formality, yet with your vote against Otomos, you need only two votes to ensure a stalemate. The suans are impossible, Khian-Shu also, but Ilarion is debauched and Comus, as you say, may be subject to our will.'

'Perhaps,' Rufina answered, 'although it is a gamble, and at best buys time.'

'Invaluable time,' Ilana responded.

'What other choice do we have in any case?' Zirina asked.

'Very little,' Rufina answered, 'certainly we dare not move against Otomos except within the law. Very well, let us waste no time. Comus will be first – who knows what he might give in return for a taste of our skills.'

Making their way to the hall of essences, they found Comus seated at his bench. A small knife was clasped in one hand, which Rufina noticed was not bronze but appeared to be silver. Before him a large chunk of

156

Judaswood had begun to take on shape, that of a pig, a pig that bore more than a passing resemblance to Otomos.

'Do you tire of life?' Rufina asked.

'To the contrary,' Comus answered. 'I exalt in life. I am planning it as a present to Otomos to celebrate his elevation to Lord Presumptive.'

'He will make you eat it, in all likelihood,' Zirina responded.

'Not so,' Comus said. 'He will be the first to appreciate its humour. But no matter. How can I help? Fresh Azure balm? Oil of urtica? An emetic?'

'We are not here for essences,' Rufina answered. 'We wish to ensure that as a true-man you support the clique with sufficient will to wish to back the true-girl clique within the female citadel.'

'In the broad sense, yes,' Comus admitted. 'In so far as my support carries weight. Can you be more specific?'

'We are told,' Rufina spoke easily, 'that you seek election to the council.'

'News doubtless taken at the tip of a whip,' Comus replied lightly, 'I am a Mentor and of some seniority and repute. With the coming of a new Lord the council is certain to undergo changes. But let me expedite your explanation. When the Ladyship election is held you will be chosen and so gain a vote on the male council. Thus, when the formal vote to elect Otomos as Lord is taken you will be able to present a token vote against him. Yet if you manage to subvert but two councillors you will be able to create an unexpected stalemate. Lomas and Urzon are hardly suitable targets for your scheme, nor Khian-Shu.'

'Precisely,' Rufina answered. 'You are wise, Comus.'

'A simple exercise in logic,' Comus responded. 'Yes, I will support you – at a price.'

'Naturally,' Rufina said. 'You are known for the subtlety and refinement of your sexual tastes. My sisters

157

and I can offer the most exquisite erotic tortures. Perhaps the turtle's head while my sisters apply their tongues to your cock and balls?'

'A kind offer,' Comus replied, 'but not entirely to my taste.'

'The Apian torture then,' Zirina offered. 'I myself will strip.'

'More generous still, but I find the bees tickle in the most distracting manner.'

'We might swell your scrotum out?' Ilana offered. 'Have you a syringe?'

'No, you are kind, but I have a simpler suggestion. You, all three that is, are to bend across my workbench, expose your prim little bottoms and accept a simple whip and cunt stimulation delivered by Ciriel and myself.'

'Me? Whipped and masturbated like some common slut!' Rufina exclaimed. 'How dare you!'

'For that,' Comus replied coolly, 'I shall finger your anus while I lick you. Now what is your answer?'

Rufina said nothing, managing only to glare at Comus while she balanced the prospect of being made to come under his cane against the prospect of being mated by Otomos every night. Then, with her lips set tight, she moved to the workbench and draped herself across it with as much dignity as she could muster. Zirina and Ilana followed, assuming identical positions beside their sister. With her eyes set firmly to the front, she reached back and tugged up her skirt, then, with even greater reluctance, she eased her silk culottes down over her bottom. A glance to either side showed that Zirina and Ilana were also bare bottomed. Comus stood behind, admiring the row of naked female behinds with an amused grin. He appeared in no hurry, but seemed content to inspect the details of their bottoms and the quims that Rufina knew would peep out from between their thighs. Comus' attention was lascivious even by the normal standards of a male inspecting the sex of a girl he was about to beat, and this quickly began to fluster her.

'Call your apprentice then,' she finally snapped. 'Tell her we're ready for her tongue.'

'Her tongue?' Comus queried. 'No, no, you mistake me. I will be licking, Ciriel will wield the cane.'

'Ciriel?' Rufina demanded. 'Come now, Comus, if we must be beaten let it be by a man of rank, not some stripling apprentice girl!'

'Not so, Ciriel must do the beating.' Comus answered. 'How else would I be able to insert my finger into that haughty little bottom? Ciriel! Come here, and bring a cane.'

'Am I to be beaten, Mentor?' Ciriel's voice came back and then trailed off as she came into the room.

'No, my little one,' Comus answered. 'Your sweet bottom will be remaining pure and white, at least barring the odd lingering bruise from your last punishment. The cane is for these pert little backsides, which you are to beat while I lick their cunts. Beat the Mistress Zirina first, then her twin, that the Mistress Rufina may better appreciate what is coming to her.'

'But, Mentor . . .' Ciriel objected.

'No buts,' Comus cut in, 'or there will shortly be four bare female bottoms in the line and I will fetch a Warden of guards to do the beating. Would you prefer that, Rufina?'

'No I would not,' she answered hotly.

'Then assure me that Ciriel is to be spared your requital?'

'I swear it,' Rufina answered. 'Now do what you must. If I am to be treated like a slut I prefer it to be done quickly.'

'Now, now,' Comus chided. 'Where is your gratitude? It is you who will achieve climax, after all.'

'I prefer to climax with more dignity,' she answered.

159

'Not with my bottom stuck out for some chit to beat while I'm licked.'

'Then you should broaden your understanding of erotic pleasure,' Comus answered. 'To work then. Mistress Zirina, perhaps if you would be good enough to part your so-elegant legs?'

Rufina, unable to hold herself back, turned to watch her sister beaten. As Zirina parted her legs Comus sank down between her and the bench, then her eyes opened abruptly in pleasure as his lips found her quim.

'Try to show some restraint,' Rufina ordered as her sister gave a low moan.

'Call when you need it,' Comus said, briefly pulling her head back. 'Ciriel is skilled and may be relied upon neither to strike your thighs nor back, nor to allow the cane tip to curl on to your hip.'

Again he began to kiss Zirina's quim, while Ciriel came to stand behind her and measured her stroke with the long golden brown cane in her hand. Zirina flinched as it tapped her bottom, then gave a little cry as Comus' tongue found its mark. Ciriel pulled back her arm, then abruptly brought the cane round to land with a sharp smack on the target of naked flesh. Zirina yelped and pulled her bottom in as her feet danced briefly in her pain. Then Comus took her thighs and eased her back into readiness. Her cry was louder at the second stroke, but of a different timbre and followed by a sob. At the third she barely flinched and didn't dance her feet at all, and after the fourth she was pushing her bottom out eagerly. After two more she began to beg, and at the seventh she came, crying out her shame and pleasure to the hall despite Rufina's angry hiss.

'That was quick,' Comus announced as he pulled his face from between Zirina's thighs. 'You are a slut at heart, Mistress Zirina, but then I suppose your sister beats you often enough. No, no, stay still, I wish to have three pretty bottoms decorating my hall for as long as I may.'

Zirina made no response, but stayed in place, contenting herself with putting a hand back to feel the seven long welts that now criss-crossed her bottom. Rufina turned, to find Ilana wide-eyed and expectant with her legs already well parted. Catching her sister's eye, she received a resigned shrug.

'Slatterns, both of you,' she snapped. 'Have I taught you nothing?'

Ilana's only response was a soft sob as Comus buried his face in the soft curls of her underbelly. Like her twin sister, she made no real effort to retain her dignity, allowing her responses to both pain and pleasure to show freely. With a great deal of kicking and squirming of her bottom, she took nine strokes of Ciriel's cane; at the tenth stroke she tugged her dress down to expose her breasts; and at the eleventh she came, squeezing her breasts with the erect nipples poked out from between her fingers. Rufina watched her sister's wanton display with a mixture of disgust at its weakness and relief that she herself would not have to try too hard to show a greater level of reserve. Comus stood, nodded politely to the girl who had just come under his tongue and then stepped back to admire the three naked bottoms, two well whipped, one still pristine. Then he reached out and Rufina felt his finger trace a slow line up the crease of her bottom.

'Wait with this one, Ciriel,' Comus instructed. 'Do not apply the cane until she asks for it.'

Rufina steeled herself as Comus sank down beneath her. She felt his hands slide up the backs of her thighs to cup her bottom cheeks, and then his mouth had found her vulva. As Comus began to lick, a dizzy pleasure built in her head. His tongue was less skilled than Jasiel's but not by a great margin, and the careful tracing of her labia without ever touching the actual clitoris quickly had her wanting badly to call for the cane. Determined not to cry out, she gritted her teeth and steeled herself against the pleasure. His tongue had begun to explore the entrance to her vagina, and his hands had moved to grip her bottom, squeezing the cheeks and pulling them open. Knowing what was coming, she braced herself, yet could not prevent a sigh escaping her lips as his fingers found her vagina and anus at the same time. Comus transferred the attention of his tongue to her labia as a finger slid up her vagina, while the other began to tickle her anus. Her muscles tensed as the little ring was teased slowly open, first enough to take the top joint of his finger, then the second and finally its full length. The one in her vagina had began to rotate, then the two pinched closed on the soft membrane between vagina and rectum. At that moment his tongue found her clitoris and the words she had been holding back burst from her lips.

'Now,' Rufina begged. 'Do it. Beat me, beat me hard, but make me come!'

The response was instantaneous, a biting pain across the very crest of her bottom which pushed her sex into Comus' face and tugged her holes against his fingers. A wash of ecstasy followed the pain, the heat going straight to her sex as she had known it would. Comus' licking immediately became firmer and his fingers pushed deeper into the moist cavities between her legs.

Rufina gasped as the second cane stroke bit into her bottom, then again as the third was applied in quick succession. As if understanding her need, Ciriel made no pause, but continued to apply the cane to Rufina's bottom, striking again and again. Despite trying to hold herself back, Rufina found herself screaming out loud as her legs started an involuntary dance and the muscles of her sex began to spasm. As the climax hit her Comus pushed a thumb into her vagina and a second finger up her bottom, then abruptly pulled the two holes wide at the exact moment her bottom leapt to a furious stroke of Ciriel's cane. The effect was to make her lose all control at the very peak of her climax. Only when she began to come down did she realise that she had been screaming and thrashing in a display less dignified even than those made by her sisters. Zirina was regarding her wide-eyed; Ilana was giggling behind her hand. Swallowing hard, Rufina gave each a dirty look. She rose, tugged up her culottes and smoothed down her dress as her mind struggled to regain composure.

'I see you enjoyed the experience,' Comus said and then pointedly wiped the thin moustache of her cream from his upper lip.

'I respond as any woman would,' she snapped, 'and now that you have enjoyed us may I take it that on the resignation of Xerinus you will become our supporter in the male council?' Rufina said.

'Xerinus? Resign?' Comus queried. 'I have no knowledge of this. I assumed you wished me to influence him, nothing more. No, my plans to achieve council status are more of a long-term nature. Had I thought that you wished to buy my supposed vote my price would have been higher by far.'

The tone of Comus' voice showed nothing of falsehood, and as the implications of what he was saying began to sink in Rufina's mind started to boil with fury. She had been tricked, fed false information along who knew what complex channels? Perhaps it had even been for the sole purpose of arranging the caning she had just taken. With her teeth set she turned on Comus, only to be met with a polite smile.

'Oh, and do have a little cream,' Comus said, reaching up to a shelf. 'It is prepared from a complex recipe of soothing balms and is strongly recommended for beaten girls. This jar should be sufficient for three bottoms of modest proportions, but be sure to rub it well in.'

Angrily snatching the jar, Rufina made for the door, closely followed by Ilana and Zirina.

'Consider,' Comus called after them, 'as you soothe each other's bottoms, that Ilarion's price will doubtless be to sodomise you – frequently!'

6

The Coercion of the Powerful

Comus emerged from the great gate of Suza to stand at
the centre of the broad road that led away to the south.
His eyes scanned the river bank, looking out over the
fields in an attempt to identify Pomina. The night's rain
had left the air clear and the ditches brimming with
water, providing agrarians with more than their normal
load of work. Pomina, he knew, was somewhere
checking to see what losses might have occurred from
the carp ponds.

Several times he glimpsed suan girls of similar build
to her, but rejected each and finally set off across the
fields in the general direction of the carp ponds. Pomina
proved to be on the dyke that separated the ponds from
the main body of the river. Comus hailed her and was
greeted with an excited wave. Picking his way delicately
around the still fresh puddles, he made his way to her
and greeted her with a kiss. Pomina responded warmly
but then pulled back with a nervous glance towards a
group of agrarians who were working on a nearby
sluice.

'I came out to gather water hyacinth,' he explained,
'but on seeing you realised that I had an opportunity for
yet more beautiful company. Besides, I have something
for you.'

Pomina giggled, watching as he extracted a glass vial
from his shirt pocket.

'This is yours – a supply of musk apple essence,' Comus said, and tossed the vial towards Pomina.

It fell short, missing Pomina's outstretched hand to shatter on a rock. Immediately the rich scent of musk and apples filled the air.

'Oh, Comus!' Pomina gasped. 'Oh, I am sorry!'

'No matter,' Comus replied, 'the fault was mine. Put it from your mind. Come, sit with me on the river bank.'

'I have tasks to complete,' Pomina objected.

'If the carp are here,' Comus replied, 'then they will remain here. If they have gone, then they will now be some part of the way to Alaban and so beyond your reach. Estimate a loss of, say, one carp in twenty-four, and both your mother and Zirina will be impressed by your diligence. Meanwhile, do I not provide better company than fish?'

'Yes,' Pomina answered, 'but . . .'

'Come,' Comus insisted. 'Who would dare report the favourite of the terrible Otomos?'

Pomina shrugged in response, but glanced around before allowing Comus to help her on to the ridge of the dyke so that they could sit and look out over the river and its fringe of reed beds. The day was warm and still, yet with a distinct freshness to the air. For a space they sat in silence, both watching the slow progress of a string of pack camels on the far bank of the river.

'When we made love,' Pomina said, finally breaking the silence, 'you gave me a higher pleasure than I have known before.'

'Thank you,' Comus replied, 'you are kind to say so. Yet surely I seem a poor substitute for the power and virility of Otomos?'

'Otomos satisfies my body like no other. When I play with girl friends I achieve a very different pleasure, which is largely in the mind. With you the two came together.'

'And therein lies the secret, my little one. In order to

166

gain a full appreciation of pleasure, it is vital that the
responses of mind and body be in balance. To indulge
one or the other alone provides a measure of pleasure,
to indulge both together provides not twice that
pleasure, but an ecstasy many times their sum.'

'Perhaps I understand.'

'Do you enjoy honey cakes?'

'Certainly.'

'Do you enjoy muscat wine?'

'Of course.'

'What of honey cakes and muscat wine?'

'It is the classic meal of lovers. Who does not enjoy
it?'

'When possible then, you would always have the two
side by side?'

'Myself and every other citizen.'

'Exactly. Physical pleasure is the same. Your girl
friends tie your hands and tease your clitoris with apple
oil, bringing to your mind wonderful feelings of
helplessness and of being subject to another's will.
Otomos fills you with cock and makes you come by
sheer virility.'

'Yes, but there is the pleasure of touch with the girls
and also helplessness in Otomos' grip.'

'Certainly the two are seldom entirely separate, but it
is possible to take the idea to more elevated levels.'

'How so?'

'What did you feel when I kissed your pretty bottom?'

'Excited.'

'And when I kissed your equally delectable anus? Be
truthful, only I can hear your answer.'

Pomina paused and a flush rose to her cheeks before
she replied.

'Excited, but also ... bad, I suppose. It gave me
pleasure; a feeling similar to having my cunt kissed. Yet
it is the most debauched of acts!'

'Exactly. You did it and took pleasure in it, but your

knowledge of the debauchery it represents gave a new dimension to your pleasure. When you were little I imagine you used to run across the rooftops, although I have no doubt that Soumea forbade it.'

'Yes, often.'

'The pleasure came more from your mother's disapproval than from the running, I'd imagine?'

'Yes.'

'It is the same feeling. You perform an act and your mind thrills at the thought of your disobedience. As my tongue searched your little hole all of Suza was in your mind, aghast at your act. Yet it pleased you.'

'And you also?'

'Immensely, myself and a select few of the more refined citizens – even one among the council – enjoy such acts. The secret lies between us, and the very act of keeping that secret gives yet more pleasure.'

'You might do it again, if you wish.'

'A delightful offer. Yet think, if a kiss provides such exquisite pleasure, how would it feel with my cock up your bottom?'

'Comus!'

'Ciriel enjoys the experience.'

'Ciriel!?'

'She takes it, almost nightly. Indeed she craves it. I am often exhausted before she has had her fill and must send for another.'

'But she is so small! So delicate!'

'She accepts me with a certain degree of exertion but no pain. A fair quantity of lubrication is required to ease her passage, usually oil of urtica, which we find adds an exquisite tingling sensation.'

Pomina gave a shiver and turned to look out over the broad, placid expanse of the river. Comus held his peace, understanding the desires and uncertainties that would be going through her head and also allowing the effect of the musk to build up.

'Perhaps ...' Pomina began, speaking slowly and with both tension and uncertainty in her voice. 'Perhaps one night, after a lengthy period of teasing and with a good measure of the musk apple oil. It makes me feel so open, so receptive. Perhaps you could scent a candle with it and let it burn while we make love. Then, when I was strongly aroused, you might do as you wished.'

'You paint a beautiful picture,' Comus answered, 'and render my cock stiff in my breeches. You tempt me beyond endurance. Pomina, I need you now, I need to fill your exquisite bottom with cock, I ...'

'Here?' Pomina demanded. 'Out in the fields! We'd be seen!'

'Not so,' Comus responded. 'Down among the reeds not only will your body be hidden, but you will have plenty of lovely cool mud to kneel in. I will be able to keep watch, and even if somebody is to walk out along the dyke the worst case would be for them to think I am enjoying your vagina.'

'What of lubricant?' Pomina objected. 'You said Ciriel's passage needs greasing. So will mine.'

'As it happens,' Comus answered, 'I have another vial of essence of musk apple.'

Pomina sighed, as if sensing the inevitability of buggery. Comus rose, and, taking Pomina's hand, scrambled down to the edge of the reed bed. Suddenly they were alone, standing between bank and reeds with no more company than a lone bird high above them.

'We had best strip,' Comus remarked. 'It would be a shame to soil our clothes.'

Pomina nodded and began to work on the fastenings of her kirtle. It was a simple work garment and came off quickly, leaving her in chemise and fancy culottes. Comus watched as these followed, revealing the soft, girlish curves of Pomina's body. Only when she was nude did he begin to undress himself. When his erection sprang free of restraint she gave a delighted squeal and

169

seized it, tugging quickly even as she glanced nervously up to the dyke.

'Patience, my little one,' Comus said, 'that will be inside you soon enough. Come now, into the reeds.'

He took Pomina's hand and led her in among the tall reeds, walking until an area of smooth mud provided space for their coupling. Pomina knelt down, her knees sinking deep into the soft mud. Comus watched in delight as she raised the plump sphere of her bottom and pulled her back in to make the cheeks spread and display her anus. He put his hand to his cock, nursing his erection as he made a quick check of the surrounding area. Two fishing skiffs were visible, some way up river, while he could here the noises of the gang working on the sluice. Far down the dyke a group of girls was visible, performing some task the nature of which was not obvious. Smiling to himself, he returned his attention to the gloriously naked girl at his feet.

Kneeling in the mud, Comus put his cock to the mouth of Pomina's vagina. It slid in easily, twisting to the left and drawing a pleased squeak from her. He fucked her swiftly, enjoying the wet, loose embrace of her vagina until his cock began to give twinges of approaching orgasm. Pomina squealed her way through it, becoming ever more noisy and ever less nervous as her pleasure rose. Comus stopped, but kept his cock inside her as he opened the vial of oil. Then, spreading her lush buttocks with his fingers, he poured the viscous fluid into her crease. Pomina gave a resigned sigh as the oil pooled in the dimple of her anus, but pulled her back in yet further to give Comus the best possible access to her bottom. Carefully, as if performing the most delicate of tasks, Comus pressed the tip of his penis to the puckered hole of Pomina's anus. She gave a small squeal at the touch, then sighed as he began to rub the firm meat of his glans over the minute valleys and bulges of her ring, smearing the oil well in.

With each rub he pressed a little harder, gradually opening Pomina's anus. She had begun to shake, and to make curious little whimpering noises, but made no move to stop him. Placing the underside of his knob against the damp hole, he pressed. Slowly the knob disappeared within her anus, bit by bit, until only the upper rim showed. Then it was in, the head stretching out her hole so that Comus could feel the ring of muscle squeezing the fleshy head of his cock, trying to eject him. Pomina grunted and pushed back, easing the head up her bottom so that her ring closed fractionally on the neck of his penis.

'Good girl,' Comus sighed and began to push his shaft up her bottom.

It went in slowly, push by push, each small withdrawal allowing another segment to slide in as Pomina wriggled her toes and panted in response. With most of it in his front met her chubby buttocks, which he spread to allow himself deeper penetration. Two more pushes left his balls pressed to her empty quim and his pubic hair against the soft flesh of her crease. She groaned deeply as he began to move in her bottom. For a moment Comus indulged himself, buggering her with slow, deep strokes that drew out deep sighs and little, abandoned squeals.

'Think, little one,' he said softly. 'Think of the full length of my penis, hard in your rectum. Think of how your anus is stretched, of how you have permitted yourself to be sodomised, of how good it feels and how dirty an act it is.'

Pomina responded with a sob of helpless pleasure.

'Good girl,' Comus went on, 'now enjoy the feeling while I bring you to your first climax.'

He slid his hand beneath Pomina's belly to masturbate her, quickly finding her large clitoris. She squealed at the touch, then again, louder, as he began to run his fingers over the firm bud. Buggering her with short, hard pushes, he worked on her clitoris, bringing her rapidly towards her climax. Her squeals grew louder and less restrained, then her anus tightened suddenly on his shaft. A desperate piping burst from her lips and her anus went into spasm as she bucked her bottom about on his penis. Abruptly he took his hand from her clitoris, leaving her on a plateau of pleasure as he returned to making long, even strokes up her bottom.

Pomina had put her face in the mud towards the start of her climax and now kept it there, wallowing as she stroked her breasts and only occasionally surfacing to gasp in air or to squeal in response to a particularly deep stroke. Comus – seeing that she was too far gone to pay attention to her surroundings – continued to ride her at an even pace, taking pleasure in the feel of her hot rectal flesh around his penis but never allowing his pleasure to take him towards his own climax. Occasionally he would look up to the bank, only to quickly turn his attention back to Pomina's shivering body and the junction between her cock and her bottom-hole.

Only when the group of girls along the dyke began to walk towards them did he increase the pace of his thrusts. Once more curling his hand beneath her belly, he found her clitoris and gave it a gentle tap. Pomina shuddered, then began to buck her bottom on his intruding penis. Comus, his eyes on the approaching girls, began to tease her vulva. Her squeals became louder, more eager. He began to rub her clitoris, running his fingers back and forth over the hard bud yet concentrating on the feel of his cock in her bottom. Pomina's anal ring began to go into spasm around his cock and Comus felt his climax approaching. Her squeals rose in pitch, then broke and changed to a frantic piping noise of even greater volume. She came, her anus clamping tight on his cock again and again, bringing him to the very edge of climax as the clamour of her orgasm rang out across the river. The working of her muscles made it seem as if his cock was being sucked by her bottom-hole, a feeling that was impossible to resist. As the demented piping of Pomina's orgasm began to die away Comus gave a flurry of short, hard pushes, rubbing the fleshy part of his shaft in the tight embrace of her still pulsing anus. His cock spasmed inside her and he pushed it hard in. Pomina squealed as the full length of his penis slid suddenly up her. Gritting his teeth in ecstasy, Comus came, his cock erupting to fill her rectum with rich, thick come.

For a long moment he stayed still, his mind focused entirely on the delicious sensation of draining his sperm up a girl's bottom. Only when he felt his cock begin to slacken did he allow himself to become aware of the world beyond their two bodies. Thanking her, he spread her buttocks and began to pull his cock slowly from her hole, taking his time to avoid hurting her and watching as the thick shaft eased slowly from the everted ring of her anus. As he did so he looked around. On the dyke, no more than twenty paces distant, stood the group of girls, every one staring open-mouthed. Further away an agrarian workgang watched with equal interest, and in the river two fisherman were stood up in their boats.

Comus smiled and nodded politely. Tamina, the foremost of the girls, responded with a squeal and by pointing a finger to where it was quite obvious that Comus was in the process of withdrawing from Pomina's anus. Hearing the squeal, Pomina looked up, raising her head above the reeds.

'Pomina!' Tamina exclaimed, then looked to Comus with her cheeks flaming red and her mouth wide. 'You were in her bottom! You debaucher! You beast! Otomos will learn of this!'

'Tamina, sister, please!' Pomina responded, but Tamina had already began to run towards the city.

Comus gave a polite nod of his head to the remaining girls, who ran after Tamina.

'What have we done!' Pomina exclaimed. 'Otomos will kill you, and all for a moment of pleasure! You must flee!'

'Certainly not,' Comus replied, 'one must always be prepared to reap when one has sown.'

In the map room of the great barracks Otomos stood over a great model of Suza and the surrounding plains. Khian-Shu stood opposite, with Urzon, Lomas and two senior Wardens also present. All eyes were focused on the model, which bore simulacra of a ring of proposed defensive forts.

'A costly exercise,' Lomas was saying, 'although undoubtedly of value.'

'We could use agrarians in the winter months,' Urzon suggested and then stopped abruptly as the door flew open.

Tamina entered the room, panting and dishevelled.

'My Lord, my Lord,' she gasped to Otomos. 'Comus has sodomised Pomina! By the river, not a glass ago!'

'Sodomised!' Otomos roared, 'By the river!'

'Yes, Lord,' Tamina went on, 'in full view, with thirty or more agrarians looking on! Also fishermen, the other girls who were with us and . . .'

'Enough!' Otomos screamed.

He stormed from the room, ignoring the entreaties of Urzon and Lomas not to rise to what was in all probability bait. The Wardens followed, and Tamina, leaving Khian-Shu alone. Between the barracks and the hall of essences he never once broke his pace, nor answered his companions. Then, on arrival, he marched through the door and into the main chamber. Comus sat at his bench, holding his wooden pig as he demonstrated to Ciriel the technique for applying polish. The apprentice took one look at Otomos and scampered into a corner. Her Mentor remained seated, following her rapid departure with a puzzled frown.

'There you are!' Otomos roared, then stopped as he focused on the pig. 'What is that!?'

His face, already a rich red, turned slowly to purple.

'A pig,' Comus replied. 'Done in Judaswood.'

Otomos produced an incoherent spluttering of rage.

'Do you like it?' Comus asked. 'When polished, I always feel that Judaswood has the very finest of patinas.'

Otomos lurched forward, snatched at the carving and sent it sailing out of the window. Comus watched as the pig performed a lazy arc out over the city and shattered against a parapet far below.

'You seem perturbed,' Comus remarked. 'Was the last batch of tusk oil not to your liking?'

'To the pit with tusk oil!' Otomos roared. 'You have debauched my Pomina, you vile beast!'

'Not at all,' Comus replied soothingly. 'I think you'll find her in excellent fettle. A little sore in the anal area perhaps . . .'

Otomos sprang forward as Comus moved swiftly to the side. With Urzon, Lomas and both Wardens clinging to his arms, he was eventually pulled back to stand grunting and glaring down at Comus.

'I challenge you,' he snarled, 'although I should crush you into pulp with my bare hands!'

'So be it,' Comus answered.

'Dawn then!' Otomos roared, 'and none of your coward's weapons!'

'The choice of weapons I leave open,' Comus replied airily. 'As to dawn, I really must object. The customary revels are likely to last some time and I do so detest lack of sleep. Let us say four glasses before noon; a more refined hour that will allow us to lunch following our exertions.'

'For you there will be no lunch!' Otomos grated and stamped from the hall.

* * *

As evening began to settle over Suza, Rufina strode through a long, ill-lit corridor. Her brain still seethed with anger and the desire for revenge. Yet it was impossible for her to find a focus for her fury other than Hoat, and Hoat was gone. She was in no doubt that she had been tricked. The ursanthrope had been hers, mind and body, willing to risk death for her promised rewards. Someone, some opponent to her in the schemes, had anticipated her move and destroyed her plans. Zara alone had known of her association with Hoat, and Zara was likely to have been the source from which her plans had been leaked. Yet Zara was no more than a puppet, and certainly incapable of working her own intrigues. More likely was Alla-Sha, who could hardly be expected to sit by and allow Rufina to move unchallenged. Yet the death of Otomos would have been to Alla-Sha's advantage, and Rufina had been expecting a different move from the ex-Lady.

It seemed impossible that Zara had forewarned the suan clique, or else Otomos need never have risen to the challenge in the first place. Any other element within the male citadel should have welcomed the death of Otomos, so they also might be dismissed. That left a rival female element that was not suan, and given that the information must have spilt from Zara, it seemed most likely that Jasiel, the Mistress of Courtesans, had turned traitor. Yet Jasiel also, by any reason, should have welcomed the death of Otomos. What was needed was clearly a long period in a deep cell with Zara, a whip and a selection of devices of torment. Then the truth would quickly come out. Unfortunately with both the suan clique and the male council alert for any suspicious move on her part, it was not practical to seek out Zara, nor Jasiel.

Perhaps more galling still had been Comus' treatment of her bottom, along with those of her sisters. The cane marks still stung, but less so than the memory of how she had whimpered with pleasure under his tongue while Ciriel beat her. Comus had also guessed correctly. There was no doubt that should Ilarion allow himself to be subverted, then the price would be to sodomise her. Many, both male and female, had writhed in the pleasure of anal penetration on her fingers or carved phalli, including her sisters, but she herself was anally virgin. The thought of submitting to sodomy made her burn with humiliation, yet it seemed likely to be exactly what she would have to do to avoid the yet worse fate of becoming the mate of Otomos. Taking Comus' finger in her anus had been bad enough, but a cock represented a level of degradation a hundred times more intense. Then she was also faced with the task of coaxing Xerinus, who might be expected to make yet more extravagant demands.

Faced with the necessity of feigning innocence and indifference, yet burning with the need to vent her pent-up fury, Rufina had chosen to descend into the lower city to find a substitute on whom her skills could be put to good use. Yet the passages and stairwells seemed close to desertion, with only guards and the occasional lone warrior or group of agrarians abroad.

She had begun the descent of a stairwell when she heard it, the soft pad of felian feet on stone. Rufina stopped, and around the turn of the stairs below her a figure appeared. The dim light revealed the yellow and black markings of an acyonthrope, while the triple-paired breasts showed her as a female.

'Jasiel?' Rufina queried, but the girl made no answer.

For a moment Rufina felt the bite of fear. For all Jasiel's small size and love of erotic torture, she was an acyonthrope with the claws and teeth of her cheetah-derived genotype. Alone in a deep stairwell, Jasiel might not prove the meek, obedient girl she had always seemed, especially if she was the traitor. Rufina's grip tightened on the handle of her whip and her other hand began to steal towards the knife at her belt, then stopped as she realised that the acyonthrope was not Jasiel. Her markings were subtly different, and she also showed a touch more height and rather less curve at the hip. Yet if the girl was not Jasiel, she was certain to share the sensitivities that marked the genotype and made it an ideal target for Rufina's pleasure.

'Mistress,' the acyonthrope addressed Rufina as they came close.

'Say who I am, girl,' Rufina answered.

'Rufina, Mistress of Castigation.'

'Yes, Rufina, who is shortly to be Lady. What is your work?'

'I locate nests of vermin in the lower levels.'

'Hardly an elevated task. It is no surprise that I have not seen you.'

'No, Mistress.'

'And what of your season.'

'I am approaching heat, Mistress.'

'Aside from simple coupling and the biting of your neck, what erotic refinements do you practise?'

'I suck the cocks of the work gang for which I locate, Mistress. I have also been beaten in order to create a false heat.'

'Crude, simple pleasures. I referred to more subtle delights.'

'You are famed for your skill, Mistress.'

'Do you wish to sample that skill?'

'As it pleases you, Mistress.'

'A good answer – the one that Jasiel gives. So, come behind me, and who can say, soon you may find that the scent of rat no longer features so prominently in your daily experience.'

Rufina turned on her heel and walked back up the stairwell. The girl followed, keeping meekly to the rear and never speaking as they threaded their way through corridors and up stairs until at last they reached

Rufina's private chambers. Here the girl was ordered to strip and bags of leather were tied over her hands and feet to cover her claws. Rufina then laid her on a leather swing and hauled her into the air, fixing all four limbs to the swing's ropes to render the girl helpless, with her bottom projecting over the edge of the swing and her legs held wide to display every detail of her sex. With the girl tied firmly in place and entirely helpless, Rufina stood back to admire her victim's pursed quim and trembling breasts.

'Beautiful,' Rufina stated. 'I shall enjoy torturing you. Now, I wish to take my time with you, and so that there will be no unseemly noise that might bring an interruption, I shall gag you. Loosely though, as I do not wish to be altogether deprived of the pleasure of your mewling.'

With a brisk motion Rufina reached up beneath her dress and pulled down her underwear, a small pair of black silk culottes.

'You can also taste me as I take my pleasure,' she continued, 'which is a privilege I do not always bestow. Come girl, open wide.'

The yellow-furred girl opened her mouth in meek acceptance of the gag. Balling the culottes, Rufina stuffed them into her victim's mouth and tied them off. She then stepped away and selected a whip from a rack of instruments of punishment. Her choice was a short cane bound with braided silk and ending in a vicious adder-tongued snap. Twice she flicked it against the girl's quim, drawing sharp mewls and faster breathing.

'Erotic torture is an art,' Rufina pronounced. 'As the finest xenomavro exceeds a coarse agrarian muscat so does my skill exceed the crude spankings you will be familiar with. There are innumerable subtle permutations to this art, by no means all of them physical. Indeed, it is within the area of mental torture that the finest pleasures and most subtle refinements are to be found. Take, for example, imprinting. You are a felian, with all your genotype's dislike of damp and filth, yet given time I could build in your mind a link between sexual pleasure and being immersed in the foulest of slurries. When I had finished you would be unable to climax without first being rolled in river mud, or even beast dung if I so chose. Watching as you struggled between the need for climax and your revulsion at the act would be my pleasure. As you reached orgasm in the filth I would also climax, naked before you, sweet, clean and so, so far above you.'

Rufina paused to place a painted talon beneath her victim's chin. The girl lifted her head in response to the pressure, turning large, liquid eyes to her tormentress.

'An exquisite torture for you, or indeed for any felian and many true-girls,' Rufina continued. 'Yet to inflict such a device on a suan would be meaningless. All day they dream only of their evening visit to the bathhouse and immersion in warm mud. To link that to sex in their minds would be no torture but an act of kindness. Thus hardly satisfying for me. Beating works well for true-girls. They lack the resilience of felians and the thick skin of suans. Also they become more agitated by the public exposure of their cunts. For suans binding is best, then the careful application of the whip and irritant oils. Helplessness affects them strongly. Thus you see that for each genotype certain tortures are appropriate. The same works for individuals and also for the sexes.'

The fingernail began a slow course along the girl's body, down her neck, between her breasts and on to her belly, stopping where the dark oval of her labial fur began.

'For you,' Rufina stated, 'sadly I lack the time to make your pleasure dependent on being strapped to the cock of a Baluchi or to give you a yearning for hot oil in your vagina. Yet I do have something for you,

180

something more subtle but no less effective in its way. Indeed, it expresses what is perhaps the highest facet of the art of erotic torture: to bring a victim to ecstasy in a fashion that breaks her most deep-seated taboos. It is a trick I sometimes practise on Jasiel, and to which your genotype is especially sensitive. She loathes every instant of it, yet her screams at climax are enough to frighten the Baluchis, and she always returns for more. I intend to shave certain areas of your fur, most especially that pretty cunt.'

Despite her helpless position, the girl's eyes betrayed her shock.

'Think!' Rufina laughed. 'Think how you will look! The populace will see your beauty, your elegance, the pretty yellow of your fur, the charming black markings. Then they'll see your cunt, as bald as an egg!'

The girl shivered in her straps.

'Then,' Rufina continued, 'as you sway past on your beautiful legs – so young, so poised – they will turn to admire the shape of your back and bottom, the patterns of your fur, the way you tail swishes over that tempting little rear . . . They'll be expecting sweetly furred little globes, sleek and lovely, with perhaps a tiny, teasing glimpse of fluff down between your cheeks. Yet that is not what they'll get, is it, my pleasure? No, they'll see two fat pink orbs like a pair of bald men sharing a secret!'

Rufina laughed and once more flicked her quirt against her victim's sex. The girl's vulva had begun to juice and open, and the swollen tip of her clitoris was now protruding from beneath its hood. Rufina reached out and touched the little bud with a long, scarlet painted fingernail, drawing a mewl of helpless pleasure from her victim. Again the quirt lashed out, this time to strike the girl's lowest pair of breasts and leave one pale nipple crossed by a darker line. Then Rufina continued.

'The effect would be wasted in the sewers, so you

181

must ensure your preferment. I will elevate you, to, let me see, yes, to herald for the female council. That is a wonderfully public task. As long as you keep your cunt and bottom shaved and work nude you may retain the rank! Otherwise, back to the sewers! Yes, that is a fine jest!'

Turning away, Rufina placed the quirt back in its place and lifted another object, a slim tube of ebony bound with silver. The girl's eyes became rounder still as she recognised the shape of a razor, her response drawing an amused chuckle from Rufina. With a single, abrupt motion she flicked the blade out, then twisted it to show her victim the tiny coruscations of freshly sharpened bronze. The girl was trembling hard, with her eyes locked on the razor, watching as her tormentress moved it slowly down towards the defenceless lips of her vulva.

'Terrible, isn't it?' Rufina smirked. 'An unbearable thought for you. Yet within less than the space of a glass you will be begging me for it.'

The bound girl responded only with a wide-eyed stare of helpless submission. Briefly, Rufina touched the flat edge of the blade to the girl's clitoris, drawing out a long, low mewl. Rufina responded with a smile and replaced the razor, taking up in its stead a vial of thick, dull orange liquid.

'Three parts oil of urtica, two parts oil of pimento,' Rufina announced. 'We are fortunate in having an essencier who understands the pleasures of erotic pain. Applied to a girl's clitoris this oil will induce a climax of quite remarkable force – eventually.'

The girl laid back her head and mewed but pushed out her sex to leave her clitoris projecting from the centre of her vulva.

'What an obedient little slattern you are,' Rufina purred. 'I suppose you imagine that I will simply use it to bring you close to climax until you beg to be shaved.

That, my little one, would be too simple. You will beg to be shaved. You will offer me your pretty fur, but it will not be solely in response to the urgency of your clitoris. I intend to oil your fur and use that to ease the path of the razor. Imagine how the oil will feel on your freshly shaved skin.'

A shiver passed through the girl's body, but she kept her sex thrust out.

'When you want it to start, just slap your tail on the floor,' Rufina stated.

With the girl watching in horrified fascination Rufina pulled on gloves of fine leather, then poured a good measure of oil into one palm. Slipping her hand beneath the girl's bottom, she slapped the oil on to one cheek and began to rub it in. At first the girl produced only a faint mewling as her fur was oiled, then, as it began to penetrate her skin, she set up a low whimpering sound and her breathing became deeper and less regular. Rufina continued to work the oil in, smoothing it over one furry buttock and then the other until her victim's mewls had risen to a frenzied whimpering.

Rufina laughed softly, then took up the vial of oil and poised it over the girl's sex. Slowly she poured, watching the girl's eyes as the heavy liquid reached the lip of the vial. The meniscus broke. Oil trickled over the edge, landing in the pink groove at the very top of the girl's vulva, then on the fur of her pubic mound and outer lips as Rufina began to move the vial around.

The girl began to gasp, then hiss through her gag as the oil ran down the most sensitive parts of her sex, touching her inner lips and pooling in the mouth of her vagina. A drop formed on the bar of her perineum, then tipped over, filling her anus and coursing down the groove of her bottom. Only her clitoris remained unoiled, and she was pushing her crotch out to meet the oil and writhing under its heat.

Rufina watched her victim's response, smiling as the

muscles began to pulse. The girl's vagina had opened, revealing a dark, fleshy pink hole from which ran a trickle of white juice. Her anus was contracting rhythmically, tightening and then exposing a centre of bright pink flesh with each expansion. Leaning forward once more, Rufina tipped the vial with great care, applying a single drop of oil to the helpless girl's clitoris.

As it soaked in the girl started to writhe, squirming her hips and pushing her belly up with increasing urgency. Rufina laughed at the sight and replaced the vial, then, moving with a slow deliberation, she picked up the razor and opened it. The girl pushed her sex out and held it there, offering herself as she began to slap her tail tip frantically on the ground. Rufina, moving the blade slowly down on to the soft swell of the girl's lower belly, pressed and scraped until the first tufts of fur began to come away from the pink skin beneath. Slowly she was denuded, her beautiful fur scraped away from her lower belly, then from her buttocks, leaving only a roughly triangular patch on her sex and a little in the cleft of her bottom. As it was done her reaction became ever more intense, her breathing heavier, her pulse faster. Tears had quickly begun to pool in her eyes, and these Rufina kissed away before standing back to admire her work.

The girl's buttocks and belly were nude and pink, the skin fresh with a somewhat angry shade to it. The ragged remains of fur around the swollen vulva and between the buttocks added to her ridiculous and humiliating condition. For a moment Rufina considered leaving them like that, then bent down and spread open the girl's bottom. Within, the anus was already pulsing, a wet pink ring in a bed of yellow-white fur. Rufina applied the razor, carefully flicking away each piece of fur to expose the sensitive pink flesh, like that of a baby mouse. The girl had begun to cry out loud by the time her crease was clear, then she began a desperate mewling as Rufina started to work on the soft bulge of her sex.

The black sexual oval was cleared slowly away, an act that Rufina knew would be the most intense of all, an act that to the girl represented the removal of her womanhood, for the characteristic shape only appeared with maturity.

It was done, leaving the girl sobbing in her bonds and thrusting her sex in wanton response to what had been done to her. Rufina responded by once more taking up the vial of oil and beginning to drip it slowly on to her victim's clitoris. The girl was shaking, always close to the edge of orgasm, but never attaining it. Each time her mewls began to soften Rufina would apply another drop of oil to the swollen clitoris, bringing her victim back to a new heat. The girl begged, then began to scream, but only when the screams had taken on a demented quality did Rufina finally take mercy and apply her knuckle to the swollen clitoris. As she came, the girl's loss of control was absolute, a screaming, writhing ecstasy that bordered on madness. Rufina laughed as she finished her victim with a cruel twist of her knuckle directly on to the clitoris, then she pulled back to leave the girl mewling, shivering and only half aware of her surroundings. The girl's eyes were glazed, and Rufina waited until they had cleared before speaking.

'Beautiful,' she remarked, looking down at the denuded buttocks and sex, 'and now for a final reminder of your place.'

With a few, deft motion of her fingers, Rufina worked the gag loose and pulled it free, then set her sodden culottes carefully to one side. An adjustment of the swing laid the girl down on the floor and Rufina came to stand directly over her.

'You have had your pleasure, so now I shall have mine,' she announced. 'I shall think of your humiliation as I masturbate, but first, a little extra touch. Keep your mouth open.'

Rufina tugged up the tight leather sheath of her skirt,

exposing her vulva to her victim. Then Rufina let go and urine erupted into the girl's face. Even as the stream was gushing out, she put her hand to her sex and began to masturbate. Rubbing hard in between spurts, Rufina watched as the girl's mouth filled with urine.

On the summit of a malachite dome Tian-Sha sniffed the air, searching for a combination of azure balm and the salty musk of female arousal that would allow her to locate Rufina. The scent was quickly found, coming from the tall oval windows of the councillor's chambers and mixed with the ammoniac tang of urine. Tian-Sha sprang from her perch and made for a row of bright windows directly below the looming bulk of the male citadel. Leaping from wall to walkway, crossing roof gardens and dodging among clusters of gables and chimneys, she quickly reached her goal. Sliding smoothly between the columns of a long window, she entered the chambers of Ilarion.

The master was standing, naked, the muscles of his tall, spare frame tensed. In his hand he held his erect penis and on the couch before him knelt Zara, her full buttocks held wide and her open anus glistening with oil and sperm. Ignoring the freshly buggered Zara, Tian-Sha made a quick gesture of apology to Ilarion and cut off his remonstrance as to her manners.

'There is no time for manners, Master,' she announced. 'There is a girl of Alaban in the Mistress Rufina's chambers, an assassin. I smelt her from the roof tops.'

Ilarion paused only to wipe his cock on Zara's discarded culottes, then began to dress hastily while he demanded details from Tian-Sha. He then ordered her to visit the chambers of the other male councillors and assemble in the passage. Tian-Sha left by the window and presently a group of herself, Ilarion, Lomas, Khian-Shu and Zara had assembled in the passage. A brief run brought them to Rufina's door, and, bursting within, they found her sprawled on a couch with a naked acyonthrope kneeling before her with shaved buttocks stuck out to the room. At the group's entrance the girl sprang for the window, only to be caught in Khian-Shu's powerful grip and pushed on to the couch by Rufina. The mistress herself rose with an expression of outrage on her face, only for her angry demand to be cut off by Tian-Sha.

'There, Masters, as I said!' Tian-Sha declared, pointing to the cowering yellow-furred girl. 'Smell her, Khian-Shu, she is not of Suza! She is an assassin!'

'Assassin!?' Rufina demanded, suddenly nonplussed. 'She is no assassin. She is a locator of vermin!'

'She is an assassin, from Alaban,' Tian-Sha insisted. 'The smell of wine still clings to her fur, and I can smell knife oil, also fresh leaves of the Shiraz vines, which is how I knew her. There is also a sharp tang, perhaps a poison.'

'She smells of Alaban,' Khian-Shu agreed.

'She is of Suza!' Rufina insisted. 'I met her in the north city, on a stairwell. Tell them, girl!'

'I am of Alaban,' the girl sighed. 'To say otherwise is useless. Their senses are too keen.'

'What!?' Rufina demanded.

'Spare me and I will confess every detail,' the girl went on. 'I am rated skilled in Alaban. I will work for you.'

'Enough of this!' Rufina demanded, 'If she is an assassin, why have I shaved her cunt and bottom? Is this wise behaviour towards one who kills for her work?'

'A simple bluff,' Ilarion said tiredly, 'too simple for one of my years, Rufina.'

'No,' Rufina swore, 'this is not just. I demand the judgement of the full council!'

'A request easily granted,' Ilarion answered. 'Zara, my pleasure, run to fetch the remaining members of both councils.'

187

Zara left and Ilarion turned to the acyonthrope, who had curled into a protective ball and placed a cushion to cover her bare nates.

'What then were you to do?' he demanded.

'To kill your Captain of Uhlans, Otomos,' the girl answered. 'It was to be by means of a dagger loaded with the venom of cowries from the gulf of Liramir. A scratch would have been enough. I was to come hooded, pretending to be your Mistress of Courtesans, one Jasiel, and so enter his chamber late tonight. I would have been on the road to Alaban before his body was found, and no one the wiser.'

'What is this?' Rufina demanded. 'I made no such plan. I know nothing of this! This is some intrigue to discredit me!'

'The girl's knowledge is remarkably detailed,' Tian-Sha put in. 'Also this is a poison I know nothing of, nor even recognise the scent of.'

'Nor I,' Khian-Shu agreed.

'Comus alone might know it,' Tian-Sha continued, 'perhaps Ciriel.'

'That is it!' Rufina cried. 'Do you not see? Comus seeks my downfall and has constructed this entire elaborate charade. He will have her kill Otomos but make me seem responsible! Is it not typical of his style?'

'Comus?' Ilarion questioned. 'Tomorrow Comus duels with Otomos. Why should he be concerned with your downfall? Why duel if he had an assassin coming to Otomos?'

'As a bluff!' Rufina stated. 'As to my downfall, who knows who he is leagued with.'

'More likely you yourself engineered the scheme,' Khian-Shu put in. 'Also, I do not smell Comus. His reek of spice and weird herbs is impossible to hide. The girl would be bound to have at least a hint of it on her fur. I smell none, only Rufina's perfume, both natural and artificial.'

Ilarion laughed, drawing a glare of pure hatred from Rufina. Moving close to the girl, Tian-Sha put her nose into the sleek yellow fur and sniffed, then withdrew.

'Nothing of Comus,' she stated, ' just her own scent, those of her horrible trade, those of Rufina and a hint like my own, perhaps from Khian-Shu when he grappled her.'

'Do you still deny this?' Ilarion demanded of Rufina.

'Absolutely!' Rufina spat back. 'It is none of my doing. What do I gain from the death of Otomos? I have a clear majority in the female council and will be Lady!'

'Exactly,' Lomas cut in, 'and Otomos will be Lord. He is not one to be manipulated to your ends, nor will he forgo his right to be your mate. Thus you seek to kill him.'

'There is more,' Tian-Sha put in, 'before my misfortune in the tombyard I had thought to visit Hoat the ursanthrope for my pleasure. From the ledge above the Baluchi stable I observed Rufina make a present of Zara to Hoat. At the time I thought it merely one of her cruel erotic jokes, but when I heard of Hoat's goading of Otomos I realised the truth. Rufina sought to have Hoat kill Otomos. The mob would then have disposed of Hoat and Rufina would have been free to further her aims. It was I who persuaded Hoat to flee.'

'She-demon!' Rufina hissed.

'Why did you not report this to Urzon or myself?' Lomas demanded.

'And have Rufina deny it?' Tian-Sha retorted. 'I had no proof, and did not wish to spend a day strapped out for whipping and public ridicule.'

Lomas grunted and nodded his head.

'And Zara?' Ilarion demanded. 'It was she who Hoat was coupling with before he insulted Otomos.'

'She was left in a stall while Rufina spoke with Hoat,' Tian-Sha answered. 'That is all I know.'

'She is a courtesan and a natural slut,' Lomas stated, 'also in thrall to Rufina. However, she came to me after the incident to absolve herself and to explain the true cause of the challenge. Otomos would take no notice and I had sworn to preserve Zara's secret against Rufina. Her blame is minimal.'

Rufina gave a furious hiss but said nothing.

'What of the assassin?' Xerinus asked. 'She is Tian-Sha's by right.'

'She has skill and knowledge,' Khian-Shu put in. 'We should not waste these.'

'What of her loyalty?' Lomas objected.

'How could we ever trust her?' Tian-Sha added. 'She is mine, Masters, let me have her.'

The men exchanged glances, ending with Ilarion giving a faint nod. Lifting the girl easily across her shoulder, Tian-Sha left the room. The passages of Suza were quiet, and scent or sound allowed her to avoid those few still abroad. After numerous detours on a path that always tended to go down, she reached a dark passage that disappeared into the native rock. Here she set Xerafina down, untied her and sent her off with a kiss and a pat on her denuded bottom. For an instant one claw pricked the bare skin, and a single drop of blood welled out and on to Tian-Sha's claw.

Moving at a slow lope, she made her way back to Rufina's chambers, arriving to find the full quota of both councils assembled. Khian-Shu's eyes met hers as she entered and a brief prickling showed in his fur as he responded to the scent of Xerafina's blood. Alla-Sha and Jasiel also wrinkled their noses before turning back to the discussion that Tian-Sha had interrupted. Rufina had gone, along with her sisters.

'Rufina is to be banished!' Zara hissed excitedly into Tian-Sha's ear. 'So too are Ilana and Zirina. It is only by a majority vote that Jasiel is not going with them.'

'Banished?' Tian-Sha whispered back.

'So it has been decided. They left with a squad of guards and are to be given a boat and provisions and set loose on the river. They will have to travel far to find a friendly reception; neither our allies nor enemies would take them in.'

'So true,' Tian-sha answered. 'What is happening now?'

'They discuss how to keep the repercussions of this to a minimum,' Zara stated.

As Zara fell silent Tian-Sha turned her attention to the debate, which focused on Ilarion.

'With no Lady and the Lord dying, we cannot wait on ceremony,' Ilarion was saying. 'Mistress Alla-Sha, who do you propose to bring the female council to strength?'

'Tian-Sha,' Alla-Sha responded. 'She is my niece and will be the third felian on the female council, thus somewhat balancing the suan supremacy.'

'She is young,' Ilarion responded cautiously, 'and not even a Mentor.'

'She is capable,' Alla-Sha insisted, 'as we have seen tonight. She is also well suited to take Ilana's place as Mistress of Tomes. Do you wish it, Tian-Sha?'

'Yes, I will accept,' Tian-Sha answered. 'I believe I will serve Suza well.'

'You have shown support for the suan clique before,' Lomas stated. 'Would you support Pomina's claim to the Ladyship?'

'I would,' Tian-Sha responded, 'yet you must accept that I act as a check against an excess of suan power in the female citadel.'

'This is natural,' Urzon put in. 'Soumea?'

'She is intelligent, and a realist,' Soumea answered. 'I support her election if Pomina is brought up in tandem. Jasiel?'

Jasiel nodded nervously.

'Then so be it,' Ilarion said. 'As to Pomina, you know

191

that I feel she lacks the maturity, yet I suppose she may be Mistress of Agrarians as well as any other. Besides, with Otomos as Lord, who will deny her?'

'A wise decision,' Lomas put in. 'Do any object?'

'I support her,' Tian-Sha replied.

'I cannot,' Alla-Sha objected. 'She is barely more than a child and follows Otomos' will blindly.'

'As you followed that of Lord Pallus,' Soumea put in. 'She has will, albeit a perverse will. Why else did she couple so rudely with Comus?'

Alla-Sha gave a sniff, then responded.

'Jasiel has a vote, for all her near disgrace.'

'It seems fated,' Jasiel answered. 'I support her as Mistress of Agrarians.'

'Then we need only a new Mistress of Castigation,' Ilarion said. 'It must be a true-girl to maintain balance between the cliques. Which female Mentors did not support Rufina?'

'None dared otherwise,' Lomas answered. 'What of Igalia?'

'Another suan? Otomos' sister?' Alla-Sha answered. 'No.'

'Eomaea?'

'She is in the sanitorium with her baby and was always an easy tool for Rufina. Hardly suitable.'

'Me,' a small but firm voice spoke from the back of the chamber.

'You?' Lomas laughed, turning to look at Zara.

'I came to you despite Rufina,' Zara responded. 'I am well liked. I am of an age with Tian-Sha.'

'You are well liked because you are the most debauched slut in Suza,' Alla-Sha answered her. 'As for your being Mistress of Castigation, that is a fine joke when you've had to be put up for whipping yourself more times than I can remember.'

'Exactly,' Zara answered. 'Who knows the art better?'

'Elect her,' Lomas laughed. 'At least she has spirit!'

192

'She will ensure Pomina's vote to Lady,' Soumea put in. 'I support her.'

'I support her, she is the finest of my courtesans,' Jasiel said.

'I also,' Tian-Sha added.

The Uhlan barracks rang with noise. The great hall was thronged, and not only with soldiers. All those who supported, or wished to be seen to support, Otomos had gathered, meaning that the revelry was not confined to the hall but spilt out into the corridors and nearby chambers. At the centre of it all was Otomos. The giant suanthrope had set up a curious game, and was now indulging himself in it. With a great flagon of wine in one hand, the other was closed on the scruff of a small, fat suan girl, her culottes already pulled down over her chubby, squirming buttocks in preparation for entry. Another girl was sucking his cock, or at least close to half of it, also masturbating while she did it.

The game was simple. The male players were to catch the females and enter them, keeping their cocks in vagina or mouth while the girl masturbated. When she had come her captor scored a point and could continue to the next girl as long as he had not come himself, in which case he was obliged to retire. Once fucked, a girl was to be stripped, and those nude no longer counted towards the contest. Otomos was winning by the simple expedient of holding a girl in one hand while he serviced another. They also seemed to reach orgasm particularly easily with his outsize member in either their mouth or vagina.

The girl whose mouth was around his cock was his seventeenth, and as she came under her fingers he immediately pushed her away and lifted the one in his grip on to his ready erection. She squealed as it slid up her and again as he began to fuck her, then a third time as his hand found her vulva and began to rub at her clitoris. Across the room an Uhlan Warden groaned as he lost control and came into his eighth girl's mouth. Another Uhlan, mounted on his fifth, gave a despairing look at Otomos and surrendered himself to climax, spraying come over the upturned bottom of the girl. Otomos roared with laughter and glanced around, finding himself the winner. His flagon struck the floor with a crash as he seized the plump suan girl's hips and thrust hard into her, coming on the instant with an explosion of come bursting from the mouth of her vagina.

The revelry in the hall of essences was quieter, if no less debauched. Not wishing to show support for one so obviously doomed, few citizens had dared attend, and most of those had simply drunk a hasty toast and left. Now only Ciriel, Tian-Sha and Zara remained, the girls attempting to show a merriment that in Comus seemed entirely genuine. Tian-Sha, eager to lift the mood, had offered Comus any pleasure he cared to name.

'The answer to that,' Comus replied suavely, 'I am sure you know. Yet it is not something I would seek unless I am certain that the girl is willing. Indeed, in your case I am unsure if I would dare to suggest it.'

'Tell me,' Tian-Sha insisted.

'Why, to sodomise you of course,' Comus replied. 'You have an exquisite bottom, high and firm, soft-furred and glossy. To slide my penis between those magnificent cheeks would be heaven for me, yet I realise that you the consider the act unacceptable.'

'Perhaps,' Tian-Sha answered, 'yet if it is just the view of my bottom you enjoy, have me kneeling.'

'It is more than that, much more,' Comus answered. 'The feeling is different in a girl's rectum to her vagina for one thing. Not better, as such, but different. More importantly, it is the girl's knowledge that my cock is up her bottom that provides the true spur to my lust. For

194

a girl of your pride and strength to kneel and pant out her feelings as I sodomise her would be an exquisite experience.'

'It would be no less strong for me,' Tian-Sha answered, 'and in the circumstances it would be churlish to refuse.'

'Are you certain?' Comus inquired.

'Entirely,' Tian-Sha answered. 'Yet it would be wise to tether me, and to tie my hands and feet. I might lose control.'

'Will it be your first?' Zara asked.

'Yes,' Tian-Sha lied.

'Then I'll hold you,' Zara said, 'you'll find it easier to take with your head in the comfort of my breasts.'

'Thank you,' Tian-Sha answered. 'That would be pleasant. May I suckle you?'

'Of course,' Zara giggled.

'Then I shall let you do it,' Tian-Sha announced to Comus. 'Be slow and careful, and use plenty of oil.'

'Naturally,' Comus replied, 'and be assured that you will not lightly forget the experience. Now, you may lie on your back with your legs curled up or kneel. I confess a preference for the kneeling position, it displays your bottom to good advantage.'

'Then I shall kneel,' Tian-Sha answered.

Tian-Sha knelt on the couch, intensely aware of just how debauched an act she was to perform, but intent on seeing it through. Crossing her hands behind her back, she allowed Zara to bind her wrists with a silk rope. This was then tied off around her belly, rendering her arms useless and constricting her waist in order to bring her buttocks and hips into full prominence. Ciriel then leashed her, attaching a cord to her neck and passing it beneath the couch. Zara took it and pulled gently, easing Tian-Sha's head down to the level of the couch, which in turn forced her to raise her bottom. As she complied she felt the cheeks of her bottom part and a touch of cool air on her anus. With the hole that was about to be entered exposed, her feelings of rudeness and excitement rose higher and she felt herself start to shiver.

To Tian-Sha the thought of surrendering her anus, even her supposed anal virginity, to Comus was powerful in the extreme. Her quim had begun to swell and juice at the thought, a condition noticed by the giggling Zara as Tian-Sha's bondage was completed. The neck tether now led under the couch and had been tied off on the loop of cord that constricted her waist, rendering her entirely helpless and forcing her to keep her bottom well up in the air. The position produced an intense feeling of vulnerability, which was heightened by the playful giggling of Zara and Ciriel.

Tian-Sha watched over her shoulder as Comus stripped and then placed his penis in Ciriel's mouth. As it stiffened Zara came behind her and began to tongue her sex, licking her labia and clitoris until she was shivering with pleasure. With Comus' cock erect in his apprentice's mouth, Zara transferred her attention to Tian-Sha's anus, licking the little hole until it was slick with saliva and had begun to relax. The insertion of a finger followed, opening Tian-Sha's sphincter and rendering her ready for buggery. Zara then stopped and Comus came behind Tian-Sha, took her tail and lifted it, uncovering the crease of her bottom and the target for his penis. She tensed involuntarily, acutely aware of the exposure of her anus and also that her vagina was moist and open. She felt the head of his penis slide in among the soft fur of her bottom crease, tickling her and making her anal ring twinge in anticipation. Then it was touching, making her tighten her ring in an involuntary and indignant response.

'Relax, my pleasure,' Comus instructed, addressing her as if she were a courtesan, 'the art is to push out, fooling your little ring into thinking she is about to emit something when in fact she is about to admit something.'

Tian-Sha obeyed, felt a curious popping sensation as her anus surrendered to the pressure, then gasped as the head of his penis was pushed past her ring. Zara giggled and hugged Tian-Sha's head tighter into the soft flesh of her ample breasts. Comus paused and Tian-Sha felt her sphincter clamp down on the neck of his penis. With her bottom-hole plugged by the head of his cock her awareness of the act of being sodomised rose steeply. Moving her head to take one of Zara's prominent nipples into her mouth, she began to suckle, soothing herself on her friend's teat to ease her sense of shame. Zara sighed deeply and began to stroke the fine hair at the nape of Tian-Sha's neck, then Comus took her hips and began to push.

As her rectum filled bit by bit with thick, solid penis, Tian-Sha could only gasp out her emotion on to Zara's breast. As it had with the cynocephalid, the cock up her bottom seemed to fill her to the top of her head. Yet Comus' penis was a great deal larger and as it squeezed slowly inside her she found her senses spinning with reaction. She was vaguely aware that Zara had began to whisper soothing words to her, but they seemed to be coming from a great distance. Comus grunted faintly. Tian-Sha felt his pubic hair touch between her buttocks and knew he was in her to the hilt. Then his balls slapped on to her empty quim and he started to move inside her.

As she was buggered, Tian-Sha's eyes began to water, gently at first and then in streams as the overpowering sensation of having Comus' erect penis moving in her rectum built in her head. It was stronger even than when the cynocephalid had buggered her, a breathless ecstasy built of the bigger cock, the greater intimacy and the two giggling girls who were watching her sodomised with such obvious pleasure. Then Zara sank down and

197

cradled Tian-Sha's head in between her big, fleshy breasts to soothe and excite. Ciriel's hands found her breasts and she sank into their embrace, enjoying the full pleasure of being helplessly buggered yet stroked and soothed at the same time. For a long space Comus rode his cock in and out of her bottom, placing her on a plateau of pleasure. Then he began to speed up and push deeper into her bowels, destroying her sense of equilibrium.

'I'm going to come in you, Tian-Sha,' he said through gritted teeth. 'I'm going to have my orgasm up your bottom. I'm going to fill your bowels with sperm, and then you'll come on my cock like fifty other dirty little slatterns before you.'

Then his thrusts were knocking the air from her lungs even as the shame of knowing she was about to have her rectum come in built in her head. Suddenly it was unbearable and she was screaming into Zara's breasts, begging him to stop even as his cock jerked and the sperm erupted into her body. The it had stopped, the pain vanishing to be replaced by an exquisite sense of being owned by the man whose penis was stretching out her bottom-hole, and at that instant she knew she had to come. Divining her need, Ciriel put a finger to her clitoris. Then, focusing on the feel of the thick cock trunk in her rectum, Tian-Sha allowed herself to be masturbated to orgasm. Comus held himself inside her, keeping her full in awareness of her need. Zara's grip tightened and as Ciriel rubbed harder Tian-Sha was thinking the same word over and over in her head: buggered, buggered, buggered . . .

Her climax hit her and she felt her anus tighten on his penis and her empty vagina squeeze on air. She screamed, only for a big nipple to be thrust into her mouth. Comus began to pull back and she came again, her bottom-hole clamping on his cock once more, then on nothing as her gaping anus flooded with cool air. She felt it close and the trickle of hot come flooding her vagina. A third orgasm hit her, then a last, smaller peak and she was slumping into the girl's arms and the tight cords that held her.

With Tian-Sha buggered, Zara and Ciriel sat back to masturbate each other over the sight, only untying her when both had come. What was intended as a pause followed, in which they washed and refreshed themselves, but afterwards the mood proved impossible to recapture. Finally Comus declared his intention to rest and would not be dissuaded. Pressing two couches together, they formed a wide bed. This allowed Comus to lied full length with a girl snuggled to either side, and Zara at the edge, a position which they quickly adopted. Pulling herself tight into Comus' embrace, Tian-Sha realised that he was already asleep and wondered at his ability to remain so detached when faced with what seemed the certain prospect of death in the morning.

7

Duel

Tian-Sha awoke to bright sunlight and an urgent thirst. Beside her Comus still slept, his easy, humorous features beautiful in repose. Zara was up, also Ciriel, both girls being seated on the bench and speaking together in quiet, tense whispers. Seeing Tian-Sha awake, they gave her wan smiles, Zara then indicating that they should leave. Sensing the suddenly oppressive atmosphere and nodding her understanding, Tian-Sha followed Zara from the hall of essences.

In the corridors beyond there were few people, and those present seemed hurried, also merry, as if pushing to complete their work before what was evidently viewed as high entertainment. Tian-Sha and Zara received several curious stares at first, citizens surprised at their choice of open support for Comus. Further off the interest died somewhat, until it became limited to passing interest that might typically have been due to two newly elected councillors. In Tian-Sha's chambers they bathed and breakfasted, then fell to a somewhat strained discussion of politics until they could no longer hold themselves back from starting for the hall of contest, only to become separated in the crush.

The hall of contest was crowded, with citizens occupying every seat and vying for what remained of the standing room at the back. Tian-Sha gave one look at the heaving mass of humanity and shook her head in distaste. Across the heads of the crowd she could see the row of high-back chairs that were reserved for the council, with the twin thrones for Lord and Lady at their centre. Neither throne was occupied, but all five of the female council members were present – Soumea and Pomina looking nervous, Jasiel and Zara excited, Alla-Sha tense. Rather than create a problem by demanding a council seat, she used her strength and agility to scale a pillar and pull herself up among the rafters. Seated on a thick beam, she found that she had an unparalleled view of the duelling ground.

The centre of the hall was an open square, paved with wide flags and strewn with sand. Doors opened at either end, leading to the two arming chambers, while seating flanked the remaining sides, broken only by the public entrance doors. Almost every place was taken, with many standing at the rear and a few of the more athletic up among the eaves. Every single person seemed to be talking at once, an excited drone that seemed to swell and fall, then swell again to a new intensity. Then the chatter of voices died slowly and every head turned to look at the arena door.

Otomos had stepped into the hall. The giant suanthrope stood four-square, his massive legs planted apart and his arms folded across his chest. He wore full armour: polished bronze over a coat of crimson silk. A morion covered his head. Despite being gold-chased silver and decorated with a tall crest of scarlet ibis feathers, it was no mere ornament but designed to give full protection to the wearer. His great chest was protected by a breastplate, while gauntlets, greaves and other plates protected all but a tiny proportion of his body. Two scabbards hung at his sides, each the length of a man's forearm and with the bronze hilt of a knife standing from the top. A third knife rested in a sheath attached to one boot.

At Otomos' side was the senior Warden of Uhlans,

his second and an arms-bearer. This was a heavily built suanthrope, yet dwarfed by Otomos. He carried an enormous mace of bronze studded wood that reached from the floor to his chin, also a round shield of wood, bronze and crimson-stained bull's hide with a long spike protruding from the boss. As Otomos raised his head to survey the hall the crowd found its voice, cheering until the room echoed and re-echoed with the noise. Rather than listen, Tian-Sha watched their faces from her vantage among the eaves and sniffed the air. The overwhelming sensation was of excitement, an atmosphere of public merriment, with few of the sharper undertones that would have marked serious concern, and nothing to indicate hostility save what came from Otomos himself.

Comus then emerged, followed by Ciriel, and the crowd roared again, still hearty but with a new, mocking tone. Tian-Sha watched as Comus glanced around, focusing first on Otomos and then taking in the crowd. The contrast between Otomos and the true-man was absolute. The essencier wore no armour whatever. His clothing was his normal combination of immaculate white silk shirt and breeches of fine scarlet leather. His only concession to the martial nature of the event seemed to be his boots, which were of his favourite soft black leather, but showed only a thumb's breadth of heel rather than his customary four. Stepping forward, Comus made a polite inclination of his head to the empty thrones and then to the councillors on either side.

For a long moment the crowd was silent, and then came a roar of salute, even Otomos clashing his mace against his shield in grudging recognition of his opponent's courage. Comus acknowledged them with a smile and the slightest of nods, then turned to where Ciriel had entered behind him. She held a cushion, on which lay three pieces of armament. One was a bronze knife not dissimilar to those carried by Otomos, the second a small bronze shield. It was the third that attracted Tian-Sha's attention. This was a sword, not remarkable in size, but of a longer, thinner design than was normal in Suza. More strangely still, instead of the honeyed lustre of bronze, it was black except for the edges and these gleamed bright silver.

As she watched, Comus went through a series of motions with the air of a magician performing a new and remarkable trick. First he took up the bronze knife and passed it to a burly suanthrope in the crowd, instructing him to test it. The suan peered at the knife as if expecting it to bite him, then tried to bend it, without success. Comus then retrieved the knife, spun on his heel and threw, embedding it deeply in a pillar. Then, taking up his curious sword, he struck the knife. The crowd gasped as the black metal sheared through the bronze, snapping the knife as if it had been made of wood.

Otomos had watched the entire display with indifference and now gave a disdainful snort, then demanded that the duel begin. Comus nodded politely in response and removed the knife hilt from the ground. The seconds withdrew to stand by the doors, the big Warden confident and smirking, Ciriel large-eyed and afraid.

The two combatants faced each other, Otomos dwarfing Comus despite the true-man's height. Tian-Sha saw the look on Comus' face; one of wary caution, of precise calculation, not at all that of a man facing what most saw as suicide. Then Otomos lunged with his mace. Comus parried easily, only for Otomos to swing his shield around. The spiked boss missed Comus' side by inches, forcing him to dance back. Before Comus could find his balance Otomos had leapt forward and brought his mace down with all his power. It rang loud on the floor even as Comus rolled away and struck out. Otomos parried with his shield, which caught Comus'

204

blade for an instant. The great mace came round, whistling through the air to catch Comus' sword and pluck it from his grip to fly, arrow-straight, into a pillar. For an instant Comus stood, staring aghast at his empty sword hand, then ran.

Otomos followed with a roar of rage, swinging his mace to narrowly miss Comus. Then Comus was at the door, and through, with Otomos in pursuit. The crowd roared, then seemed to swell as every citizen at once began to push towards the exit through which the duellists had fled. Tian-Sha pulled herself swiftly up among the eaves and through a skylight on to the rooftops of Suza. Outside the air seemed oddly still, with the clamour from below a distant, irrelevant noise.

Above her the hall roof rose to a sharp ridge, with a great head of carved stone projecting from each gable end. She climbed to the nearest of these and looked out, trying to judge where Comus' flight was likely to have led him. Directly below her was a jumble of small gables and flat roofs, beyond that the high wall of the great corridor that led from the citadels to the city gates. Numerous windows opened into the wall, and from these she heard the clash of armour and then scented the rank smell of the giant suanthrope's anger.

A leap took her from the stone head to a lower gable, a second to the summit of a dome and a third to a crumbling section of parapet that seemed to grow from the high wall. Scrabbling at the stones with her claws, she pulled herself up to a window and peered within. The corridor ran below her, tall enough to accommodate a Baluchitherium, wide enough for two of the beasts to ride abreast. Comus was directly below her, running down the centre of the corridor and well clear of Otomos.

Yet even as she watched he faltered, then stopped and turned. Otomos gave a roar of triumph and swung his mace, only for Comus to dart away at the last moment.

Again the manoeuvre was repeated, and again. Each time Otomos came forward Comus would dance back, always seeming to risk the great mace but never coming close enough to be struck. Rather than allow himself to be goaded, Otomos remained calm, keeping the mace poised and ready, not wasting his energy but always waiting for the moment Comus would make an error and come in too close. Then the crowd began to spill from doors and once more Comus ran, moving up the slope towards the citadels.

Tian-Sha scrambled the last few feet up the wall. Pulling herself on to the flat roof of the corridor, she ran light-footed, confident in overtaking Comus yet with her senses alert to the sounds coming from beneath her.

Otomos followed Comus at a lumbering trot. That Comus' lighter clothing and sparser frame gave an advantage in speed he realised, yet it did not concern him. Eventually he would catch up, or Comus would turn at bay in his despair – there were no other alternatives. Comus' taunts and feints he ignored, intent on keeping his concentration as the duel moved from passage to chamber and from roof to hall. The sound of the crowd, the cheers of support and the rush of feet were mere background noise, of no more concern than the sounds of battle with which he was so familiar.

Ahead, Comus darted into a corridor. Otomos followed, keen to finish the duel but hoping that Comus would find another weapon and thus allow him the full honour of victory. Comus dodged into a right-hand corridor, then again, bringing him back to the main aisle. Otomos gave a grim smile as he realised Comus' manoeuvre. By circling, the essencier could return to the hall of contest and so retrieve his weapon. Yet the corridor was thronged with spectators, blocking Comus' path despite their best efforts to get clear. Otomos sprang forward, intent on finishing the duel, only for Comus to dart into a side passage.

Now Comus ran in earnest, with Otomos thundering behind him. Together they ran, along darkened corridors and past long ranks of arches open to the bright sun, up broad, marble-flagged slopes and tight, winding spiral stairs, through public halls and private chambers. Twice Otomos came close to catching his prey, once at a sharp angle in a passage when Comus collided with two men, once on a roof garden from which Comus was forced to leap, only to vanish through a window below.

Tian-Sha paused, momentarily puzzled as to the location of the combatants and then recognising Otomos' roar from a colonnade some way up a slope. Changing her direction, she scrambled from roof to roof, running along wall tops and up slopes with her senses straining to keep in touch. Her path took her up the city slope, until at last she came out on to the roof below the hall of essences itself and realised that Comus had retreated to his own chambers. Extending her claws, she scrambled up the rough stone and pulled herself on to the ledge of a window.

Comus stood at the end of the hall, his back set against a bench. His shirt was gone, and two long rips showed in the scarlet leather of his breeches. His face was white and set, his neck taut with the veins standing high from the skin. Fear burned in his eyes, and he gave no sign of awareness of Tian-Sha's presence but stared dead forward in terror at the advancing Otomos.

The giant suanthrope stood four-square in the centre of the hall, his great arms spread to prevent all possible means of escape. He had dropped his shield and mace, but held a dagger in each hand, their fresh sharpened bronze blades glittering in the sunlight. Slowly he advanced, one step at a time, his eyes set on Comus. To Tian-Sha he gave but a single glance, his lip curling briefly down to expose the full length of a tusk in warning.

Knowing that to move against him was to die, Tian-Sha made a quick gesture of submission and drew back, but stayed on the ledge, unable to look away. Otomos was halfway along the hall, crouched low, intent on his prey. Comus could retreat no further and, as Tian-Sha watched, his fingers scrabbled on the bench behind him, seeking anything that he might use as a weapon.

She saw his hand close on an apple and felt a pang of sorrow at the pathetic, hopeless gesture. He threw, his arm moving with the strength of terror, only for Otomos to snatch the fruit in his mouth with a single, contemptuous motion. Tian-Sha heard the pulp crush in the great jaws and saw Otomos' mouth curl into a grim smile. Then once more he began to advance on Comus.

Tian-Sha turned to Comus, crying out to her friend as her muscles tensed to perform a leap that she knew could only result in her own death as well as his. But Comus was no longer pressed back against the bench, nor was his face set in terror. Instead he had his arms folded casually across his chest while his face showed only a smile of dark humour.

Otomos had frozen, his great eyes locked on his intended victim and every limb held exactly still. Then, moving with a slow inevitability, he toppled forward to crash on to the floor, inert, the apple still wedged between his tusks. Otomos lay dead.

Alla-Sha touched a tear from the white fur of her cheek. Before her lay Lord Pallus, now still in death.

For a long while she stayed kneeling, her thoughts running back over their years as Lord and Lady, aware of nothing beyond the still, noble figure on the couch. Only when the thin strips of sunlight that came through the shuttered windows had faded to old gold did she rise and walk slowly to the stairs, wishing to gaze out over the city and remember things as they had been. As she came on to the roof she became aware of a sound, a distant humming, somehow urgent and somehow angry. No, it was not anger, but another adrenaline-charged emotion, or rather a blend of determination, excitement and expectation. As she shifted the focus of her senses from scent to sound she caught a rhythm to it, a rhythm that rose and fell to one name – Comus.

8

Lady

Comus walked boldly across the high span that joined male and female citadels, heedless of the drop beneath him. His face was wreathed in smiles, yet expressed only a fraction of the elation that he felt at having succeeded in his intrigue. Each detail of his scheme had fallen out to perfection. From the long years of establishing his popularity among the populace and impressing his qualities on his father to the bluff with the iron sword, each careful move and calculated risk had fallen out as intended. The duel had been his most hazardous gamble, goading Otomos to a challenge and so risking death. Yet he had known that Otomos could never match him for pace, especially when in full armour, and also that the giant suanthrope would never be able to resist showing off by catching the apple that had been laced with enough poison of ashwort to fell a Baluchi. Less uncertain had been the response of the populace. He had slain a hero in fair combat, and if he had used a trick, then that only magnified his skill. He had also judged correctly that much of Otomos' popularity was born of fear, while his own came from genuine liking and the saving of many lives with his skills. Led by Ilarion, Xerinus and those others who had dreaded the ascension of Otomos, the demand for his appointment to the Lordship had risen quickly until any other choice would have led to a riot.

When the council voted Ilarion and Xerinus had given him unqualified support, as they had promised. Urzon and Lomas, with their plans in disarray, had nevertheless stood against him, suggesting that Lomas should become Lord and Comus a councillor. Khian-Shu had objected to the true-man majority that either option would result in, at which Comus had made his final move. Turning to Xerinus, he had nodded and called him father. As arranged, Xerinus had stepped forward and offered his resignation in favour of a male felian of Khian-Shu's choice, the same ploy the suans had used to gain a majority for Otomos. Khian-Shu had smiled and given the faintest of nods and Comus had become Lord.

An added pleasure was the inability of the female councillors to choose a Lady, which had led to the postponement of the election to after he had been made Lord and so gained a vote on their council. This also meant that all six of them were eager to please him, a situation that could only be to his advantage, although he knew that his vote would ultimately go not to she who proved most erotically enticing, but to she who seemed most suitable to rule. Pausing briefly on the centre of the span, he looked down on his city and his grin briefly became as broad as that of a young man after his first virgin.

Quickly adopting a more noble demeanour, he crossed the span. The roof garden of the female citadel was empty, as was the Lady Chamber beneath. The council chamber on the next level down was anything but, as all six female councillors were present. Comus nodded to each and took his place in the high-backed wooden throne that was reserved for the Lord. For an instant he felt that he was doing something profoundly wrong, as if an outraged Lord Pallus was likely to appear at any instant. Then it had passed, replaced by the sense of his own worth.

212

'Mistresses,' he greeted them, and gave a brief glance at their faces.

Alla-Sha sat to his right, a place beyond the throne she had occupied as Lady, her expression proud but somewhat drawn. Jasiel was next, nervous and eager, then Tian-Sha, poised and cool. Soumea was to his left, with Pomina beside her, their shared lineage evident in all but age. Finally there was Zara, bright-eyed and excited.

'So,' he said, 'have you reached a decision?'

'No,' Alla-Sha answered.

'Then it seems we must vote formally,' Comus went on. 'Who wishes to stand for Lady?'

'I was to be Lady,' Pomina declared proudly, 'and still may. Moreover, you, Comus, have shown me special favour. Tian-Sha, Zara, do I still have your support?'

'I fear you never did,' Tian-Sha answered. 'My support of the suan clique was simply a device to ensure my election to the council.'

'I too was playing less openly that it might have seemed,' Zara added. 'As to Comus, it is true that he finds you appealing, but he and I have coupled a hundred times for each time he has visited you. Yet I cannot claim to be his favourite. That is Ciriel and always will be.'

'This is true,' Comus admitted.

'What of you, Soumea, mother?' Pomina asked.

'Now that Otomos is no longer to be Lord, my little one,' Soumea answered. 'I doubt you have the experience to be Lady. I myself, as senior female suan, would be more suitable.'

'Senior female suan,' Alla-Sha cut in, 'but not senior female. Let us make this simple. I will accept re-election to Lady and all will be as before.'

'Not so,' Jasiel retorted, 'by your resignation you showed yourself as unfit. You have lost the trust of the felian clique. I would be better suited to be Lady.'

'Why another felian?' Soumea demanded. 'I am the only choice. Who would back me if they themselves could muster no supporters?'

'I would, mother,' Pomina answered reluctantly.

'I might,' Zara added, 'but what of you, Comus? You have a vote, to which of us would it go?'

'The question is by no means simple,' Comus answered. 'Alla-Sha and Soumea have the experience, yet for a mate I equally enjoy the prospect of any of you younger three. Zara, you are exquisite and perhaps have more of a mind than we are apt to credit. Pomina, you too would make a fine mate, and your appointment would go far to soothe the tattered nerves of the suan clique. Tian-Sha, you are the most beautiful of all . . .'

'I make no claims,' Tian-Sha announced. 'I believe intelligence to be the foremost virtue of a Lady, then experience. I would back Alla-Sha, or Soumea subject to certain conditions.'

'The choice is far from easy then,' Comus continued. 'Each of you has virtues. I am prepared to give a casting vote to any who can muster the support of three others.'

Each woman looked to the others, none ready to relinquish her chances in favour of a rival. It quickly became clear to Comus that none was prepared to make a commitment.

'I wish to make a suggestion,' Tian-Sha stated. 'There is much room for the building of animosity here if each knows who has stood for and against them. There has been too much of this in Suza of late.'

'True,' Alla-Sha agreed. 'What do you propose?'

'That instead of being held openly the election be conducted by secret vote. Thus whoever wins will have no specific antagonisms.'

'How is this possible?' Soumea demanded.

'Simple,' Tian-Sha stated, 'We take six clay vessels, each marked clearly with the name of one of us. We then place discs in the vessels, silver if the vessel's owner

214

could have our support, bronze if not. The vessels will stand in a private chamber so that no other may see how we vote. Whoever commands the most support is elected as the Lady. The discs must be distinctive, like the coins of Alaban.'

'What are those?' Pomina asked.

'Metal discs used in barter,' Tian-Sha answered. 'Each bears a complex symbol so that they may not be copied, a camel on those of bronze, an elephant on those of silver and a crown on those of gold. Thus they may not be copied.'

'A most elegant device,' Comus put in. 'I for one support its use.'

'There is a problem,' Alla-Sha said. 'Everyone will place a bronze disc in all the vessels save their own, thus continuing the stalemate.'

'Not so,' Tian-Sha answered, 'each of us will have three silver and three bronze discs. The silver go in to those three we are most able to support.'

'Yet there is still a high chance of a stalemate,' Soumea objected.

'Not so,' Tian-Sha continued. 'If two or more among us gain the same number of votes, they go together into a second draw, with each of us now holding as many discs as there are candidates. If necessary, a third draw is possible. Thus a stalemate is avoided.'

'What is to prevent us tampering with the vessels when we go in to vote?' Zara asked.

'They will be designed with only a narrow slit in the top,' Tian-Sha answered. 'Thus discs may be put in but not removed save with great effort. To count the vote they will need to be broken open, one by one in clear view of us all.'

'A thin blade might extract these discs,' Pomina objected.

'Each of us may be searched, or we may go in naked if you insist,' Tian-Sha countered. 'Besides, such a process would be slow and leave marks on the vessels.'

'It seems a fair and clever device,' Alla-Sha agreed. 'Yet the process must be carefully governed. Will you compete, Tian-Sha?'

'I feel I must,' Tian-Sha answered. 'I suggest that Alla-Sha and Soumea and Zara oversee the disc production, while Comus, Pomina and myself arrange the construction of the vessels, making extra in case of breakages or should we need more than one vote. Thus the cliques are balanced. Male councillors may oversee the draw.'

'Reasonable,' Soumea said. 'We would seem to need six discs each of two distinct types, to a total of forty-two. What of the symbols?'

'As a calligrapher I will provide them,' Tian-Sha offered, 'and as I am not overseeing the coin-making there can be no question of infidelity. Orthodox capitals will serve, an S on silver for support, and O for objection. The symmetry of the two letters allows for no confusion.'

Tian-Sha glanced to the other councillors. Alla-Sha and Soumea gave guarded nods, Comus a more enthusiastic approval, Jasiel, Zara and Pomina apathetic shrugs.

'So be it,' Alla-Sha declared. 'We meet again in three days to allow the artisans to complete the necessary work.'

Outside the hall of potters Tian-Sha stood with Comus and Pomina. Within, a number of identical vessels had just been withdrawn from a kiln, work which the three of them had overseen.

'Take them to my chambers,' Tian-Sha instructed as a potter emerged with the vessels on a tray.

'Yes, Mistress,' he responded and promptly left.

'I will paint our names on later,' Tian-Sha addressed Pomina, 'they may be collected before the vote.'

'I see no difficulty with that,' Pomina agreed. 'Now I

216

must leave, I have to discuss harvesting with my Mentors.'

'Doubtless in a warm mud bath with a good helping of cock to follow,' Comus remarked as Pomina left. 'Her erotic appetite has become voracious since the death of Otomos.'

'It must be hard to suffer the jealous attentions of such as he,' Tian-Sha responded. 'Now, it is a pleasant day, bright but not unduly hot, perhaps you would care to walk with me down towards the river? Also I am in what will be the last or second last day of my season, a fact of which you might wish to take advantage.'

'I realise that you wish to gain my support,' Comus replied, 'but I give you fair warning, you are not alone.'

'Naturally not,' Tian-Sha answered.

'Zara, for instance came to me last night,' he continued. 'She took my cock in her bottom and worked her anus with a muscular precision more like that of a mouth. Three times she milked me of sperm before I was forced to call a halt to proceedings.'

'Only three times?' Tian-Sha asked.

'Just so,' Comus answered, 'for she arrived shortly after the departure of Jasiel, who had licked me from sphincter to cock tip with an oral skill she alone possesses. Twice I came, the first time across her face, the second in her mouth.'

'Exquisite, no doubt,' Tian-Sha answered. 'I cannot compete with the skill of courtesans, nor can I offer you any virgin pleasures as you have already buggered me. Yet you are of refined tastes, and I am aware that a level of competition exists between you and certain other skilled eroticists.'

'True,' Comus said as they turned into the high-roofed corridor that led to the great gate.

Tian-Sha waited until there was no chance of being overheard before continuing.

'Would witnessing unusual couplings gain you prestige?' she enquired.

'Certainly,' Comus answered, 'although such as Master Ilarion are unlikely to be impressed by mere orgies.'

'What of watching me put to an alpha-male cynocephalid?' Tian-Sha asked coolly.

Comus gave a choking cough before regaining his composure.

'But they are more baboon than man!' he eventually stammered. 'Ferocious to say the least, and as to the size of their cocks! You speak in jest, surely?'

'I am in earnest,' Tian-Sha continued. 'They have a certain primal lust that I find appealing. As a female on heat I doubt I have much to fear from their ferocity, besides which I am not powerless myself. As to cock size, I used to take a good half of Hoat's organ. Indeed I rather miss coupling with him.'

'Well, if you are certain,' Comus answered, 'then I accept with both enthusiasm and anticipation. I take it you mean to do it now?'

'Certainly,' Tian-Sha answered, 'come, let us walk up into the hills and I will scent out a troupe.'

The cynocephalid troupe was gathered by a pool. Perhaps as many as three dozen females clustered together, drinking at the water's edge, grooming each other's fur or simply enjoying the warmth of the sun. These were small creatures, perfectly human in form but with pale, sky-blue bottoms and labia. Despite their vacuous expressions, they had a certain beauty and Tian-Sha could see why some men enjoyed mating them.

The one other cynocephalid was a creature of very different appearance. This was the alpha-male, a great, brutish thing that was stalking suspiciously around the edges of the troupe. He, or it, as Tian-Sha found it hard to accept such a savage-looking beast as of human lineage, resembled the beta-males who had taken her in the hills only in the way a bull resembles a calf. So massive was the development of its upper body that instead of frequent shifts to an upright posture it remained almost permanently on all fours. The face and buttocks were a startling turquoise, the former ferocious, the latter frankly obscene.

Bearing her intentions in mind, Tian-Sha found her eyes drawn irresistibly to the genitals. These were huge, dangling blue and wrinkled beneath the hairy belly, the scrotum bulging with its burden of testes larger than balled fists, the penis long and thick, with the very tip of the scarlet glans showing where the foreskin had drawn back.

As they watched, the male's penis began to swell, the head emerging fully from the foreskin and the shaft swelling and elongating until it formed a rigid pole that extended some three spans below the creature's belly. Tian-Sha swallowed hard, thinking of how the big cock would feel in her vagina. Then it squatted down and took hold of its penis, then began to pull slowly at the shaft, still with its eyes searching the surrounding landscape.

Then, with alarming speed, it had grabbed a female and rolled her beneath it, bottom up. All Tian-Sha could see was the girl's kicking legs as she was mounted and fucked, that and the male's frantically bobbing buttocks and huge scrotum. Then the huge cock was being pulled from the girl's vagina and laid between her bottom cheeks, glistening with juice and sperm.

For a moment the male paused, rubbing its cock idly along the crease of the female's bottom. Then it dismounted and shambled away, leaving the fucked female on the ground. Tian-Sha expected her to rise, but instead she only pushed her bottom up and it quickly became evident that she was masturbating. Comus chuckled, at which Tian-Sha turned to him with a questioning look.

'She reminds me of Zara,' he explained. 'Not that Zara has a blue bottom, but their behaviour is certainly similar.'

Tian-Sha laughed but with a nervous edge. Together they watched the cynocephalid girl bring herself to orgasm, a noisy process that the other members of the troupe ignored entirely. The alpha-male, meanwhile, climbed on to a large boulder and sat scratching its balls in a meditative fashion.

'No doubt the experience will be exciting,' Comus remarked, 'but are you sure this is wise?'

'Yes,' Tian-Sha answered, 'but beat me first to make the best of what remains of my heat, otherwise I may not smell right. Besides, the stimulation will do me good.'

'With pleasure,' Comus said. 'Come, let us retreat a little way. Would my belt suffice, or would you prefer to search out a clump of bamboo?'

'I prefer bamboo,' she answered. 'It stings and brings the blood to my bottom more quickly, producing a sharper flush of pleasure.'

Withdrawing from the ridge from which they had been watching, Tian-Sha and Comus found a clump of bamboo in the shade of a great rock. Choosing a suitable piece of shade, Tian-Sha pulled out the back of her culottes and drew her tail out of the slit designed to accommodate it. The act produced an immediate feeling of vulnerability, its effect being to simplify the act of striping her bottom.

'Ready?' Comus enquired.

Tian-Sha nodded and bent at the waist, pushing her bottom out towards him. Comus smiled at her action, accepting his right as chastiser to pull down his victim's most intimate garment. Taking hold of her culottes, he lowered them with an unhurried motion, never once taking his eyes from her bottom as it was revealed. The garment was left at the level of her thighs, Comus then choosing a bamboo and cutting its stem to leave himself with a length some half of his height. Tian-Sha poised herself, taking hold of her ankles and raising her tail to leave her bottom fully exposed. Looking back, she watched Comus as he gave the bamboo an experimental swish through the air.

'A hand's worth, I think,' he stated. 'Enough to let you know you have been beaten, but not so many as to in any way overshadow your coming experience.'

'As you please,' Tian-Sha answered as he raised the bamboo.

Immediately it came whistling down, landing across her cheeks to produce a sharp, stinging pain and draw a hiss of shock from her lips. The second came lower, jamming her buttocks up and sending her forward on to her toes before she could regain her stance. The third struck lower still, under the curve of her cheeks to jar her sex and immediately increase the open feeling of her vagina. Comus was grinning and squeezed his crotch as he applied the fourth to cross the three existing lines. Tian-Sha gasped at the impact but pushed her bottom further out to catch the fifth high on her now flaming cheeks. Again she gasped and now hung her head as the effect began to work, only for Comus to add an unexpected sixth stroke full across the sensitive flesh of her upper thighs. At this she yelped, yet knew at once that it had been done to add a piquant sense of injustice to her feelings. As the sting of the stroke faded to leave her bottom with a dull, overall ache, Tian-Sha found herself breathing hard and badly in need of a stiff penis in her now heavily lubricated vagina.

'A pretty view,' Comus stated. 'I have always found something exquisite about a female who is clothed above the waist but naked below, especially when she has had her bottom beaten. It is only a shame that your fur hides what would otherwise undoubtedly be the prettiest of welts, yet the way your buttocks and tail

221

peep out from beneath the hem of the chemise is exquisite. Still, our eager male is unlikely to appreciate such fine distinctions. He is simply likely to tear your pretty chemise in his urgency to get at your breasts. I suggest you strip.'

Tian-Sha responded by peeling her chemise over her head and kicking off her sandals. Naked, and with her bottom burning from the five hard cuts, she started back towards the cynocephalids. The alpha-male was still on his rock, playing idly with his genitals and surveying his harem. He caught Tian-Sha's scent before he saw her and stiffened, then turned with his hackles rising and his teeth bared. She dropped quickly to all fours, then made a turn to display her bottom and allow him to catch the rich scent of her arousal. He had reared to his full height, but now sank back a little, seemingly puzzled and by no means unaggressive but with his cock twitching instinctively. She wriggled her bottom, then pushed it up, making it blatantly clear that her cunt was on offer. Still he hesitated, then jumped down from the rock and she once more began to approach. He put a hand to his cock and peeled the thick blue foreskin down over the scarlet glans, then gave a flurry of jerks that brought it to erection. Tian-Sha found her eyes glued to its bulk and found her eagerness increasing at the thought that it was about to be put inside her.

He edged towards her. She turned and raised her tail again, presenting a full view of her bottom. Suddenly all restraint was gone and he came rushing forward on his knuckles. A hand grabbed her hair, another a leg and she was pushed to the ground. One muscular arm came under her belly, lifting her bottom up to meet the hard jut of his cock. Then it was in her, forcing entry to her vagina without the least preliminary. She gasped as she took the thick shaft, then began to mewl as he began a frantic humping motion on top of her bottom. He was grunting loudly with each stroke and his balls were slapping against her quim, touching her clitoris in a way that quickly had her scrabbling at the ground and hissing in ecstasy. Yet it was not enough for her orgasm, even when he took his hand from her hair and began to tug at her tail to improve his purchase inside her.

She reached beneath her belly, groping for her quim even as she was shaken like a doll by the ferocity of the fucking. Even as she found her clitoris he changed his grip, taking her by the thighs and sinking into a squat above her body. Gripped hard, she was jerked back and forth on his cock, leaving her legs and arms flying and making it impossible to masturbate. Then he came, erupting sperm deep inside her and then holding his erect cock deep within her as the come drained out. She was dropped and the thick cock pulled abruptly from her vagina. He made to dismount as she found her sex and began to rub herself, then stopped and squatted down on her legs.

Tian-Sha found herself trapped beneath him, with her hand still on her vulva. His balls were resting between her thighs and his cock in the crease of her bottom. Her cheeks opened as she lifted her bottom in pleasure, then closed, catching his shaft and squeezing into the deep, furry furrow. A hand closed on her tail and pulled it up, bringing her to the edge of orgasm. She started to come, then gasped in shock as a new sensation reached her, a warm, wet feeling in the crease of her bottom and around the base of her tail. She screamed in ecstasy, her brain filled with delight at the impropriety of what she was doing and the realisation that she was being urinated over to mark her as one of his troupe. Her climax lasted as the warm pee ran down over her sex and dripped from her fingers, her screams ringing out loud. It irritated her cane stripes too, bringing back the memory of her so recent beating and the fact that Comus was watching what was happening to her.

Finally it ended and her body relaxed, prone on the

ground as he emptied his bladder across her buttocks and back. Only when he had shaken out the last drops did he dismount and leave her, his interest waning as rapidly as it had waxed. Shaking with reaction, she crawled to the edge of the pool and quickly washed herself. The male took no notice whatever, clearly no longer regarding her as a possible threat but simply as another female, marked and there to be fucked at leisure. Nor did he attempt to herd her back to the troupe and, as she climbed the slope back to where Comus waited, she speculated wryly that the group of females might in fact stay together out of a desire for each other's companionship rather than anything to do with the male.

Comus was among the rocks where they had concealed themselves before, his breeches undone and his erect penis in his hand. His expression registered excitement and not a little awe, and Tian-Sha smiled as she closed with him and took hold of his member. It felt hard in her hand, and the tip was wet with fluid. Evidently the sight of her being taken by the big male had brought him to the edge of orgasm, yet he had held back to finish with her. She pulled at his cock, kissing him as his arms came around her body to take her by back and bottom. She hissed as his fingers dug into one smarting buttock, then sank down to place the head of his cock in her mouth. She started to nibble gently as she masturbated him into her mouth, nipping his swollen glans with her teeth. He gave a sharp grunt, then his cock jerked and her mouth was full of hot, salty come. As he erupted into her mouth she took his cock right in, swallowing the sperm and then sucking him clean and swallowing once more. He gave a long, satisfied sigh and pulled slowly out to sit down on a convenient boulder. She also seated herself but on the highest point of the rocks, then, raising one elegant leg, Tian-Sha began to lick her fur. From the corner of her eye she could see the upper slopes of Suza, with the twin citadels at the peak. Both showed a hot sienna tone with a cap of green to mark the roof gardens. As she watched, a flash of yellow showed on the bridge that joined the citadels. Tian-Sha allowed herself a brief smile.

In Suza, Jasiel sat in Alla-Sha's chambers, sipping arabica and discussing the coming election.

'You plan something?' Jasiel asked.

'I have planned something from the beginning,' Alla-Sha answered.

'I had expected you to move against Otomos,' Jasiel said.

'You mistake me,' Alla-Sha replied. 'I objected to Otomos as Lord, but more to an overall suan supremacy or to Rufina as Lady. It was within the female citadel that I intended to move. To manoeuvre Pomina to the Ladyship Otomos needed to persuade you and me to vote for her, thus thwarting Rufina. For me to move against Otomos would have been to play into Rufina's hands.'

'So I understand,' Jasiel stated.

'Thus my move was against Rufina; also Ilana and Zirina, for without their support Rufina's power would have been limited.'

'Just so.'

'By setting the vote for Lady immediately before that for Lord, I thought to ensure that there was no Lord to vote on our council, thus leaving only we six female councillors. I had then intended to drug the three sisters with a cocktail of laudanum and essence of mnemosyne; they would then be taken to the lower city by certain male associates. On waking they would have discovered themselves to have indulged in an orgy of debauched practices and also that the crucial vote had taken place.'

'And if I had sided with Soumea?' Jasiel asked.

'Then Pomina would have been Lady,' Alla-Sha answered. 'No, my pleasure, my intention was not to seek re-election, else why resign in the first place? My intention was to offer to support you, thus providing a majority. Would you have accepted?'

'Yes,' Jasiel answered.

'And your skill as a courtesan would have allowed you to accept Otomos as mate. Thus my situation would have been optimal, if not ideal, while Suza would have been saved from a period of suan supremacy.'

'True, but I see certain weaknesses in the scheme. The responses of Rufina and her sisters on waking, for instance.'

'It would have been too late. Besides, on waking to find they had indulged in sodomy with an unknown number of men, do you think they would have dared speak out? Also, they could not have forced a re-election without the support of the male council, who might have supported Pomina against us but would have delighted in Rufina's downfall. She could have done nothing.'

'Perhaps, perhaps not.'

'I confess to a degree of desperation when hatching the scheme,' Alla-Sha admitted. 'Not that it matters now. What is significant is that I still have the cocktail and that if we now drug a single female councillor we have assured that one of us will be elected Lady.'

'How so?' Jasiel demanded.

'I am right, so long as Tian-Sha accepts the pact. Thus we may guarantee that each of us receives three silver discs. With only two female non-felians voting, neither can gain four, while Comus must vote for one of us, maybe all three. Thus either one of us will win or there will be a second vote with only felian candidates.'

'As you say,' Jasiel answered, 'but who should we drug? Not Comus, that gains nothing.'

'Just so,' Alla-Sha agreed, 'and Soumea is too wily for

the device to be practical. Zara might serve our purpose, but her votes might go our way in any case. Pomina is the best choice.'

'Let it be Pomina then,' Jasiel said, 'and we take our chances as to which of us triumphs.'

'Indeed,' Alla-Sha answered, 'but to ensure a minimum of risk, let us stay together tonight.'

'What of Tian-Sha? Should she not be party to this?'

'There is too much of honour and not enough of duplicity to Tian-Sha for this scheme. Still, I have sent for her and will tell her what we intend – roughly. I have also sent for the others of the female council, the idea being that if we are together then there is no room for mischief. We are to meet in the Lady Chamber.'

'A good suggestion,' Jasiel agreed, 'but how are we to drug Pomina?'

'She will be cautious of wine and arabica,' Alla-Sha answered, 'also food. Rather than use such simple techniques, I have sought to exploit the love of her kind for a stuffed cunt. I have ordered sweetmeats and will place a certain copper vessel among these. It contains dumplings laced with my elixir. We will play with Pomina, and you may suggest the use of the dumplings as an erotic device. No suan could resist such an offer, while the drug will be quickly absorbed through the walls of her vagina.'

'A cunning device,' Jasiel stated. 'Yet how are we to distract her mother and Zara?'

'She will need to wash after her stuffing. My basin is empty, so she will need to leave the chamber and they will think nothing of it. One of us must go with her, and I have ordered certain males to collect her at a glass after midnight. If questioned, we must say that she was desperate for cock and left to explore the erotic freedom that the death of Otomos has given her.'

On returning to her chambers Tian-Sha found a messenger in the corridor outside. This was a young male oncanthrope, black furred and magnificent, which added to her pleasure as he greeted her with a deferential nod.

'The Mistress Alla-Sha requests your company, Mistress,' he intoned as Tian-Sha approached. 'In the Lady Chamber.'

'Tell her she shall have it,' Tian-Sha answered. 'I have been in the hills, hunting, and need to change my dress.'

'Indeed, Mistress,' he answered, his eyes taking a tour of her naked body. 'If I may remark, Mistress' scent suggests that she is close to the end of her season.'

Tian-Sha smiled and closed with him, sliding a hand beneath his wrap to find the sleek fur of his scrotum. His cock was erect, standing proud in response to her scent. Unsheathing her claws, she ran them through the fur that covered his balls, then abruptly squeezed. He was on her in an instant, pressing her to the floor even as her thighs came apart. She felt his cock nudge her vagina, then find the hole and slip inside with the short barbs grazing her tender flesh. Their mouths met and her arms locked on to his back, her claws digging into his flesh even as he fucked her with a frantic flurry of pushes that ended in the eruption of his cock deep inside her. Tian-Sha clutched him tight to her chest, rubbing her erect nipples into his fur. Her excitement was high, the last flush of her season having brought her close to orgasm. Yet it was not close enough, and as he dismounted she found herself desperate for the touch of his tongue to her quim.

'Lick me,' she demanded.

'Mistress, I must go', he protested, but her hand had locked in his hair and was pulling his head down towards her sex.

'Lick me!' she ordered, and pulled his face hard into her sperm-wet quim.

He began to lap, leaving her to wonder at her own forcefulness. Then his tongue found her clitoris and nothing else mattered. The climax was quick, an explosion of ecstasy that began in her sex and moved through the muscles of her belly and bottom, up her spine to her head. Only when he rose did she see the peculiar expression on his face and realise that he must have tasted the big cynocephalid on her. With an odd mixture of satisfaction and embarrassment she dismissed him and entered her chambers.

After washing thoroughly and putting on a loose camisole of deep-blue silk, she made her way to Alla-Sha in the Lady Chamber, finding Jasiel already there. Both felians greeted Tian-Sha, and Alla-Sha poured her a vessel of Shiraz of Alaban. Tian-Sha sniffed carefully before taking a sip.

'Your suspicion is unfounded, niece,' Alla-Sha stated. 'You are the last person I would wish harm to.'

'Merely an instinctive reaction,' Tian-Sha answered. 'Is this a council meeting?'

'No,' Alla-Sha stated, 'it is purely for we three, yet it concerns tomorrow's vote.'

'How so?' Tian-Sha asked.

'If the felian clique is to retain more than peripheral influence,' Alla-Sha stated, 'we three must work together.'

'So much is evident,' Tian-Sha answered cautiously.

'Jasiel and I have a compact,' Alla-Sha went on. 'We will each vote for the other, and ourselves, naturally. If you wish to join this compact then each of us is guaranteed three silver discs.'

'Certainly I will join,' Tian-Sha agreed, 'but this device does not ensure victory for any one of us.'

'It would were a councillor to fail to make tomorrow's vote,' Jasiel put in.

'And who is this luckless individual?' Tian-Sha answered.

'Pomina,' Alla-Sha answered. 'She will be joining us shortly for an evening intended to provide mutual reassurance. I expect that she will overindulge and go off in search of cock. After her stuffing she will doubtless wish to wash. There is inadequate water here and so she will have to go down to a lower level. One of you must go with her, the rest I have arranged. She should be back at some time during the following night, quite healthy if perhaps a little sore.'

'A risky device,' Tian-Sha stated. 'Have you no concern for the anger of the suan clique?'

'Personally, none,' Alla-Sha answered. 'She will have been seen with three true-men, and during the course of the evening she might well take in a little essence of mnemosyne. If she remembers anything, then the blame will come to rest on Zara.'

'And how is this to be done?'

'By a simple device designed to suit suan tastes. Be advised, eat only from the buffet and above all do not interfere with the little game I have planned to keep us entertained.'

Tian-Sha nodded in response and curled herself on to a couch as she attempted an assessment of Alla-Sha and Jasiel's intent. Both had a right to expect her support as a fellow felian, neither regarded her as intent on the Ladyship. It seemed likely that the assurance of her vote would counteract any intent they might have had to destroy her chances, either together or separately. Also, if Pomina was to be taken out of the game, then it would be unwise to double the same device. No, if either woman intended to improve her chances then it would not be at Tian-Sha's expense, more likely each other's the following day.

'The device is this,' Alla-Sha was saying. 'We shall select six erotic torments and draw lots for who may choose each. Thus whoever draws the first lot will have the choice most suited to their temperament. I shall ensure that Jasiel wins first, then Pomina. Undoubtedly she will choose to have her cunt stuffed.'

'Just so,' Tian-Sha agreed. 'What are the other torments?'

'They must be ones disagreeable to Pomina,' Alla-Sha answered. 'Yet not unbearable as we ourselves must enjoy them.'

'Then we had best choose carefully,' Jasiel added. 'Perhaps something anal? Pomina enjoyed being sodomised by Comus, yet is still embarrassed by such play.'

'As she should be!' Alla-Sha answered. 'Zara enjoys her anus used, the slut, and I have a fine ivory phallus that will serve well. What else?'

'Before now Pomina has remarked on the excess vigour with which Otomos spanked her,' Jasiel answered. 'A really firm beating would probably not be to her taste.'

'A strapping then,' Alla-Sha said, 'with the belt that holds back the window drape.'

'What of the Apian torture?' Tian-Sha suggested.

'Cruel yet exquisite,' Alla-Sha answered. 'It is likely to be the fate of whoever draws last. What do you wish for yourself, Jasiel?'

'Rufina always liked to shave me, as she did the Alaban spy,' Jasiel answered. 'It is exquisite, more so even than the Apian torture. Yet we are likely to be made to vote nude tomorrow in order to guard against devices. No, I will choose oil of pimento and a slow tongue, probably from Zara.'

'So that is four . . .' Alla-Sha stated.

The door gong interrupted her. Pomina, Soumea and Zara appeared at her call, each greeting the three felians with cautious nods. Alla-Sha explained her reasons for summoning them and the entertainment that was planned. Each agreed but not without cautious glances to the wine and food.

'Do not be concerned,' she assured them. 'If any of you have doubts then I will be happy to sample

231

anything you choose, or to drink from any vessel or eat from any plate.'

'I have no doubt of it,' Soumea chuckled, 'yet I recall how you first achieved favour with Lord Pallus and will be cautious.'

'I would be insulted were you not,' Alla-Sha replied.

'Just so,' Soumea answered.

'We are six,' Alla-Sha continued, 'and we have selected four erotic torments so far. What of the fifth and sixth? Jasiel, Zara, you are the experts?'

'Is there anything that might be used as forcemeat among the sweetmeats?' Jasiel asked.

'Dumplings perhaps?' Alla-Sha answered as Pomina gave an audible sigh of anticipation.

'Ideal,' Jasiel replied. 'Zara, do you have a suggestion?'

'Indeed so,' Zara answered enthusiastically, 'masturbating while smothered beneath a honey-smeared bottom!'

'Light, but fine,' Alla-Sha answered. 'So, in addition to vaginal cramming and smothering we have chosen oil of pimento and tongue, a severe strapping, sodomy with an ivory phallus and the Apian torture. I have everything we need except for a girl's bee chamber and someone will have to go to the hives for bees and honey. Preferably someone furry, we do not want anyone stung prematurely.'

'I will go,' Tian-Sha volunteered hastily and rose to her feet before anyone else could volunteer.

Taking a vase glazed in cobalt blue and a decorative tile, she made her way quickly to the roof garden of the female citadel. Pale moonlight illuminated the scene, showing the high arch that led to the male citadel, the carefully tended beds and the squat domes of the beehives. A sniff of the air revealed the myriad scents of the city, with a hint of Shiraz of Alaban that brought a faint smile to her lips.

'All is well,' she announced, seemingly to the night, then crossed swiftly to the beehives.

Having captured an adequate number of bees and taken a good measure of honey, she returned below to find Alla-Sha laying out a number of coloured wooden chips on a table. A fat-bellied, thin-necked copper pot stood by them.

'Choose one,' Alla-Sha was saying, 'and break it in half and place half in the pot. Retain the other half. I will draw, but if my own comes out first or second I undertake to replace it.'

'That is reasonable, generous even,' Jasiel answered and reached out for the yellow chip.

Each of the others made their choice, leaving Tian-Sha with the black chip. She dropped it into the pot and went to select wine and sweetmeats, then curled herself on to a couch as Alla-Sha dipped her hand into the copper pot. The yellow chip was withdrawn and Jasiel gave a mew of pleasure as all eyes turned towards her.

'It is not an easy choice,' she said excitedly. 'The pimento is tempting, while I'm not sure I dare the Apian torture. To be stuffed would be pleasant, more so than a strapping perhaps, while I prefer to avoid sodomy. No, it must be the honey smothering, it is too great a pleasure to be missed!'

'I had hoped for that!' Zara called out. 'So at least choose me to sit on your face!'

'If I'm to be smothered I like the bottom to be as big as possible,' Jasiel retorted. 'Nobody could call your behind slim, Zara, but Soumea has the most magnificent bottom among us. Soumea it must be, if she will. I'm sorry, Zara.'

'Then kiss my anus to show it!' Zara demanded.

As she spoke she turned on her couch and presented her bottom to the room with the two fat cheeks straining out the silk of her kirtle. Jasiel laughed, shuffled a little way on her knees, pulled Zara's kirtle aside and planted a firm kiss on the girl's anus. Zara giggled in response and sat back down, now visibly flushed. Soumea, meanwhile, had risen and was working on the complex fastenings of her skirt. Her face showed unconcealed pleasure at having been chosen.

'I will strip,' she announced as her skirt fell away to reveal the lower part of a tightly laced leather corset and an ample pair of culottes. 'I have no wish to ruin my clothes with honey and I suspect we will all be nude before too long in any case.'

Tian-Sha watched Soumea strip, idly playing with herself as the big suan exposed a corset carefully designed to cup all twelve of her ample breasts. This fell away to expose a silk chemise of elaborate design, which in turn was removed to expose naked breasts, each a fat handful of flesh though no one quite as large as Zara's pair. The culottes came last, exposing the plump swell of Soumea's sex and then, as she turned, the broad expanse of her bottom. Nude, Soumea was certainly impressive: big, powerful and mature, her flesh was set in opulent curves and heavy rolls that never sagged. Looking at the huge bottom, Tian-Sha found herself imagining what it would be like to be smothered beneath it. The prospect was both daunting and enticing, the more so when the big woman bent forward and pulled open her cheeks to reveal a big, fleshy vulva and the puckered hole of her anus.

While Soumea stripped, Alla-Sha had been preparing the honey, first tempting the bees into another jar and then extracting a good measure with a spoon. This she applied to the top of Soumea's bottom crease. The big suan sighed as the honey ran down between her buttocks to coat her sex, then reached back between her thighs to smear it over her vulva and around her anus. Jasiel, meanwhile, had stripped naked and laid herself on the floor, from which she looked up at Soumea's bottom with wide, excited eyes.

Soumea spread her bottom and lowered it on to
Jasiel's head, then wiggled it into place. Jasiel's face was
immediately lost beneath the enormous buttocks, yet
Tian-Sha could hear the lapping sound as Soumea's
quim and anus were licked. Breathing, she knew, would
be impossible, the only option being to lick and
masturbate with the sure knowledge that the bottom
would remain pressed into her face until she came.
Jasiel's hands were on her vulva, with the lips spread
wide and a finger rubbing hard at the clitoris. Soumea's
face was also set in increasing bliss as the tongue worked
frantically between her thighs. Then suddenly both were
coming, Soumea squealing in passion, Jasiel lifting her
bottom from the floor as her body tensed in ecstasy.
Soumea finished, but Jasiel did not, coming again with
her face still smothered full between Soumea's buttocks.
As Jasiel squirmed in her second climax all eyes were
locked on her body. Moving quickly, Tian-Sha reached
out and took a vial of aromatic bitters from a tray of
condiments. This she slid into her vagina, then returned
to her leisurely masturbation as Jasiel's climax ran its
course. Finally Jasiel began to thump her tail on the
floor. Soumea raised her bottom, revealing the gasping
Jasiel with the yellow and black fur of her face liberally
smeared with honey and come.

'A fine display,' Alla-Sha remarked as she withdrew
her hand from the front of her culottes. 'I could almost
wish I myself had been the victim.'

'At any time you wish,' Soumea answered.

Alla-Sha made no reply but placed her hand into the
pot and drew out a blue chip, the sight of which drew a
pleased squeal from Pomina.

'I'll be stuffed!' Pomina exclaimed before she could be
offered a choice. 'Who will do it?'

'I will,' Tian-Sha volunteered. 'I have yet to have the
pleasure of you.'

Alla-Sha responded with a faint smile, the others

simply nodding acquiescence. Tian-Sha rose to fetch the dumpling pot while Pomina began to fiddle with the fastenings of her clothing. As with her mother, and typically suan, she wore elaborate, flounced garments that enhanced her waist and emphasised the plump swell of her bottom and hips. Nude, she climbed on to a table and lay back, pulling her knees up and spreading her thighs as she did so to leave her sex open. She was wet, with her clitoris a hard bud of glossy skin and her vagina an open, fleshy mouth from which white fluid trickled down to the puckered spot of her anus and dripped to the table.

'I am ready,' she sighed as she began to stroke her top pair of breasts.

Tian-Sha reached into the dumpling jar and felt among the soft, squashy shapes for a large specimen. The reek of laudanum and oil of mnemosyne was strong, even among the previous overwhelming aromas of female musk, wine and spiced food. Yet neither Soumea nor Zara showed the least unease, while Pomina herself was panting and flexing her thighs in anticipation. Tian-Sha pulled a fat dumpling from the jar and held it up for Pomina to see, then pressed it to the gaping hole. Pomina giggled as the big dumpling was pushed firmly up her vagina, then grunted as Tian-Sha's fist briefly followed. A second dumpling followed, and a third, until Pomina's vagina was bulging with suet. Tian-Sha stopped and raised questioning eyes to Pomina's face.

'More,' Pomina sighed, 'much more.'

Amazed at Pomina's capacity, Tian-Sha selected another dumpling. It went in, Pomina groaning as the walls of her vagina stretched to accommodate it. Another followed, squashed in until Pomina's vaginal mouth was a gaping pink ring stuffed by a thick plug of moist suet.

'Enough,' Pomina sighed. 'I am so full, so full. Let me feel it, Tian-Sha, let me squeeze it.'

Tian-Sha drew back and watched as the head of the suet pushed out of Pomina's gaping vagina, then broke off and fell to the table with a soggy slap.

'Make me come,' Pomina begged and arched her belly high to present Tian-Sha with her straining sex.

Tian-Sha obliged, leaning forward and applying her tongue to the swollen knob of Pomina's clitoris. As she began to lick she scooped up the fallen suet and pushed it back into Pomina's vagina, then forced her fist in as well. Pomina squealed and took hold of Tian-Sha's hair to improve the contact between tongue and clitoris.

Pomina's squeals rose in volume and pitch as Tian-Sha licked, then abruptly changed to the frantic piping of orgasm. At that instant Tian-Sha puckered her lips and sucked the bud of Pomina's clitoris into her mouth as if it were the head of a cock. Pomina's piping rose to a crescendo and then broke into a long, high screech of pleasure that carried far more of the pig than the human. Her thighs locked around Tian-Sha's head, squeezing hard as her vagina clamped tight around its load. Tian-Sha felt the suet squash out around her wrist, then suck back in, only to be forced out once more. Then Pomina's muscles were relaxing and her bestial noises dying to a pleased moaning noise, then to silence as the climax finished.

'Good, I trust,' Tian-Sha stated as she pulled back from the mess of Pomina's sex.

'Good indeed,' Pomina answered. 'In fact so powerful that I feel faint. I must wash, and perhaps walk a little.'

'I fear the basin is empty,' Alla-Sha said. 'The roof tank will be full, or you could go down to the public aquaria.'

'I shall use the aquaria,' Pomina replied.

'I shall join you,' Tian-Sha stated. 'I am still somewhat on heat and licking you has left me too much in need to wait my turn with dignity. A little cold water will do me good. If you could wait until we return before drawing the next chip?'

'Certainly,' Alla-Sha responded.

Tian-Sha took Pomina's weight on her shoulder and helped her towards the stairwell, then down it and down two more flights to the public level of the citadel. As they descended Pomina's sense of balance deteriorated and Tian-Sha was carrying her full weight when they reached the audience chambers. The aquaria were to one side, and as she approached Tian-Sha caught the scent of male true-men. Pulling the vial quickly from her vagina, she pushed the cork out and poured the contents out over Pomina's hair. The girl took no notice whatever and a moment later three hooded figures stepped from the shadows.

'Look, Pomina, some ready cock for us,' Tian-Sha said.

'Lovely,' Pomina answered groggily. 'Lift me up you men, fuck me, two in my hole at a time . . . then you can bugger me, I like that, I like that so much . . .'

'Keep her amused,' Tian-Sha addressed the men as they took Pomina.

'Won't you play too?' Pomina asked.

'I'll come down later,' Tian-Sha promised. 'Remember, I've yet to be tortured.'

'Choose to be buggered if you can,' Pomina advised. 'It's nice, so nice.'

'I shall,' Tian-Sha answered and stepped away.

As they helped Pomina from the room Tian-Sha saw the suan girl burrow her hand down the front of one man's breeches, then they were gone, with only the girl's giggling to signal their departure, that and the lingering scent of aromatic bitters. Satisfied with her work, Tian-Sha made a brief visit to the aquaria, splashing her face and sex to clear her senses and quiet her heat, although her urgency for sex had now dulled to a faint echo of what it had been. Back in the Lady Chamber, she found the other female councillors relaxed and drinking wine.

'Where is Pomina?' Soumea asked, her voice slurring somewhat.

'The stuffing put her in need of cock,' Tian-Sha stated. 'We met three men who at this moment will be attempting to fill her. She promises to return when she has had her fill. Let us continue.'

'She was always wayward,' Soumea stated, 'and Otomos was too jealous by far. She has a great deal of cock to make up, poor thing. Come, Alla-Sha, choose a chip, I am eager to see what I shall have to suffer.'

Alla-Sha gave a light laugh and stretched her hand out for the copper vessel to withdraw a green chip.

'Me!' Zara cried eagerly. 'I want the beating!'

'I would dearly enjoy giving Zara her thrashing,' Soumea declared. 'Also, it is between Tian-Sha and I as to who has the strongest arm and she has just had the pleasure of stuffing Pomina. I claim my right.'

'Just so,' Tian-Sha agreed. 'I would not wish to appear greedy.'

'I licked you!' Jasiel protested to Soumea. 'Alla-Sha or I should do the beating!'

'You lack strength,' Soumea answered, flexing one brawny forearm. 'Yet who is it Zara prefers?'

'I wish to know I've been punished,' Zara answered. 'Let Soumea do it.'

Jasiel answered with a shrug. Zara readied herself, shivering slightly but far from reluctant as she pulled down her kirtle from her shoulders and over her broad bottom, then bent over a table, then took a firm grip on the far edge. Alla-Sha had already begun to detach the thick leather strap from her window drape and now handed it to Soumea who gave it an experimental slap on the palm of her hand. Zara's bottom was well displayed – two plump, quivering globes of girl flesh with the lips of her quim and a froth of dark hair peeping out from below. With her kirtle down her breasts were also bare – two fat pillows of flesh that squashed out beneath her chest. She was looking back, her eyes wide and her lip trembling as she watched Soumea heft the thick strap over her naked bottom.

The strap came down, whistling through the air and landing with a meaty smack across Zara's bottom. The girl's buttocks bounced under the impact, the soft flesh spreading and wobbling back into form as she gasped with the shock. Soumea was grinning, and applied the second stroke without allowing Zara time to fully recover. Again the fat buttocks bounced and again the victim yelped, only to give out a full-blooded scream as the third stroke caught the plump tuck of her cheeks. Soumea took no notice, but applied a fourth stroke high on Zara's cheeks.

Tian-Sha slipped a finger into her vagina as she watched Zara beaten. The girl was quickly kicking her legs and thrashing her head about, also yelling out her pain without thought for her dignity. The big buttocks quickly became red, then purple as smack after powerful smack was applied to their surfaces. Then suddenly Zara grabbed her breasts and began to knead desperately. Soumea abruptly changed her angle, bringing the strap up between Zara's spread legs to smack directly on to the meaty sex lips.

Zara screamed and then slumped to the floor as Soumea quickly pulled the coming stroke. Rolling her legs up to display her reddened buttocks to the room, Zara began to masturbate, alternately rubbing at her clitoris and slipping a finger into her well-juiced vagina while her other hand curled around to caress one well-beaten bottom-cheek. She came, screaming out her climax but not stopping. Instead she rolled on to her knees, sticking her bottom high as if determined to have the others inspect the state she was in.

'Beat me, Soumea,' she begged and once more began to play with herself.

Soumea obliged, bringing the strap down hard across

the already severely punished behind. Zara merely gasped, then screamed as a second, harder stroke caught her. Yet it was not a scream of pain, but of ecstasy as she hit her second climax. A choking mew from Jasiel signalled that she too had come, and Tian-Sha turned to see her with her thighs spread wide and a finger working the centre of her sex. Only then did Tian-Sha realise how close she herself was to the edge of a climax. Three quick touches completed it and she came with her eyes locked on to the purple mess of Zara's welts.

As she came down she shared glances of pleasure with the others. Her need for sex had now risen, but not with the desperate need to have her vagina filled that came when she was on heat but with a desire for exposure and to have the sight of her naked body produce the same reactions in others as Zara's had in herself. Three chips remained in the pot, and each carried an obligation to accept an erotic torture that would not only hurt but would also strip all dignity from her as she came under its power. Both Alla-Sha and Soumea evidently shared her feelings, for their expressions showed tension, nervousness and deep excitement. Yet both of them would have the option of three choices, and the oil of pimento represented the obvious choice. For Tian-Sha only two choices remained.

Once more Alla-Sha dipped her hand into the pot. The expression of concern on her face deepened as she drew out a red chip and Soumea held up the matching half.

'The choice is hard,' the big suan girl announced, 'harder, indeed, than it would seem. I would have liked to be stuffed, also the beating, but both have gone. As to the sodomy, I would never allow a male to practise so degraded an act on me, yet in my younger days I was occasionally put to the enjoyment of anal penetration by the then Mistress of Castigation. Yet to accept it would rob me of the chance of watching either Alla-Sha or Tian-Sha buggered in what is still a most ignominious fashion. No, that is too good to resist and the Apian torture has never been to my taste. I will take the oil of pimento, from Zara if she will oblige.'

'Certainly,' Zara answered.

Without fuss Soumea positioned herself on the table and readied herself with her plump thighs spread to expose a moist vulva and her hands on her breasts. Zara came forward with the vial of oil and carefully applied it, first to Soumea's outer labia, then the inner and the vaginal passage. Soumea's clitoris was done last, Zara rubbing in a single drop of oil and then corking the vial. At first nothing happened, then Soumea started to squirm as the heat of the oil began to have its effect, rubbing her nipples erect and grunting with mounting excitement. Zara waited, watching the plump sex lips redden and swell with the heat of the oil while the clitoris pushed up from its hood to stand proud and shiny in a ring of pale, rosy flesh. Only when Soumea had begun to squeal and clutch at the table was she given relief, Zara leaning quickly forward to apply her lips. The climax came fast, Soumea tensing and screaming out as her sex was kissed, then going into a frantic piping similar to her daughter's as Zara took her clitoris between her teeth and nipped.

When Soumea had regained her composure and had the oil cleaned from her sex, attention was once more turned to the game. Tian-Sha's anus twitched in anticipation of entry as Alla-Sha reached for the final chip. It came out white. Tian-Sha swallowed hard. Alla-Sha was anally virgin, notoriously so. It seemed certain that Tian-Sha's two anal experiences were about to be added to and in the most public fashion. Yet there was no denying the thrill of the prospect. Then, with an odd mixture of relief and disappointment she realised that if Alla-Sha had been able to pick Pomina for the second torment then she would undoubtedly have been able to select herself for the third. Alla-Sha was not the luckless victim she made out, but intent on being buggered in a way that made it seem the choice of honour and sense.

Yet if it was an act it was well played. Alla-Sha held the white chip up, looking at it in what seemed an agony of indecision and biting her lower lip. The pattern of her thoughts appeared obvious, an agonising choice between the shame and degradation of breaking the taboo against anal sex balanced against the prospect of the far greater pain of the Apian torture. Finally she spoke.

'It seems I must at last surrender myself anally,' she sighed. 'When I think of how many practised debauchers I have refused, both male and female, yet now it seems I must submit. Still, at least it is not to some triumphant, grunting male. Who wishes to sodomise me?'

'I do,' Soumea answered quickly, 'for many years I have been your subordinate and you can only imagine the satisfaction I will feel from filling that proud backside with thick, ivory dildo.'

Alla-Sha shivered but began to disrobe. She was quickly naked, her compact, white-furred body poised, sensual and elegant, even after she had moved into a kneeling position that flaunted her pert bottom to the room. Soumea had taken up the phallus and was attaching the straps that would hold it in place, a process watched by Alla-Sha with wide-eyed expectation. When ready, the phallus jutted out from the mound of Soumea's sex with all the pride and power of a real male, its rounded head poised to deflower Alla-Sha's anal ring.

'Two of you hold her cheeks wide,' Soumea instructed. 'This I must see.'

Tian-Sha responded, rising at the same instant as Zara. Between them they took hold of Alla-Sha's bottom cheeks and thighs, spreading her until her anus was stretched wide, a puckered pink target in a nest of white fur. Soumea poised the vial of oil above her target, then slowly tipped it, allowing a thick drop of viscous fluid to form on the lip, hang for a moment and tumble over the side to splash in the shallow, furry groove that separated Alla-Sha's bottom cheeks. The second landed actually on the anal ring, which twitched in response, opening a trifle and then closing so that the oil pooled briefly and then oozed forth to trickle on to the bar of the perineum.

She put the head of the phallus to the moist hole, which drew a groan of resignation from Alla-Sha, then began to push. For a moment Alla-Sha's sphincter resisted intrusion, only to suddenly pop under the pressure, admitting the thick, ivory phallus head suddenly into her rectum. The penetration of her anus destroyed her serenity on the instant, drawing a sharp hiss from her and then a long, drawn-out mew that carried all of her ecstasy and all of her self-disgust. The sodomising was slow, Soumea taking full advantage of the opportunity to ensure that Alla-Sha appreciated the full significance of being buggered. Again and again the phallus was withdrawn, only to be once more put to Alla-Sha's anus and thrust within. Each time it would be pushed fully into her cavity, until her anus was stretched taut around the thick base of the shaft. Soumea would then give a series, of firm, deep pushes, sending Alla-Sha into a breathless, mewling panic which would die slowly as the phallus was pulled back, only for the cycle to start once more.

Tian-Sha watched with delight, even though her own anus squirmed in sympathy. Alla-Sha did her best to retain her self-control, but it was a hopeless task and she soon began to play with her breasts, then to masturbate in a flagrant, unconcerned fashion. This drew a satisfied laugh from Soumea as she once more burst through the resistance of Alla-Sha's sphincter. Then Alla-Sha began to beg for deeper, harder thrusts, for her buttocks to be stretched wider and for her tail to be pulled. Tian-Sha obliged, gripping the slender white tail and pulling it hard upwards. Alla-Sha started to come, hissing and writhing her bottom on the intruding phallus while the others watched in delighted silence.

Soumea kept the phallus up Alla-Sha's bottom until the ecstasy of climax had passed and then completed the buggery with more deep, firm thrusts intended to ensure full awareness of the act. She then pulled out, leaving Alla-Sha's bottom hole gaping and red above a wet, swollen vulva. Tian-Sha watched it close, then let the tail fall. She turned to the room to find that all eyes were now on her. Zara smiled and held up the bee chamber. Tian-Sha began to strip, trembling as she did so.

'I will do this,' Jasiel announced when Tian-Sha was nude. 'First, a pillow to raise her bottom.'

Tian-Sha watched as Jasiel selected a plump cushion and placed it at the centre of the table, then patted it to indicate that she should sit on it. Climbing on to the table, she followed Jasiel's instructions and spread herself out, extending her limbs to leave each near a corner. Her hands and feet were taken and stretched further apart, then cords were wound around each and fastened off on the legs of the table, leaving her spread-eagled and helpless with her pudenda thrust up by the pillow that now supported her bottom.

Zara passed Jasiel the bee chamber, a double container of glass designed to fit over the female sex and cup the turn of the buttocks. In the upper part a number of bees buzzed angrily. Tian-Sha found her eyes locked to the thing as it was pushed on to her sex and strapped into place with the rim pressing firmly into her flesh. Then Jasiel placed a hand on the lever that would release the bees, and locked eyes.

'Do it then,' Tian-Sha said.

Jasiel responded immediately, tugging the lever down to expose Tian-Sha's genitals to the bees. She stiffened as they touched her, straining her limbs against the bonds, desperate to keep still despite the knowledge of how great her eventual ecstasy would be. The gesture was useless; angered by their confinement, the bees immediately attacked her, settling on the lips of her vulva to press their stings into her flesh. Her fur provided some protection, but still she hissed at the sharp stabs of pain and was quickly writhing in her bonds. One found the tuck of her bottom, another the bare flesh of her anus, both drawing sharper, more pained hisses from her. As her sex began to throb her mind filled with an agony of anticipation, not from the pain, but from the knowledge that her vulva was swelling and opening to reveal more and yet more of the sensitive flesh at the centre. Already aroused from the evening's debauchery, it was not long before she felt the legs of a bee on her inner labia, tickling as it crawled slowly down towards her vagina. Then the sting went home and she screamed and bucked, only to further enrage the insects. Another stung her sex lips, a third the mouth of her vagina. One seemed to be trying to burrow into her anus, another into her vagina. Legs rasped the skin of her clitoris, gripping it. She felt the sting touch her skin, and then it was driven home and she came, screaming out her ecstasy in the full agony of her bee-stung cunt an instant before her world went black.

Tian-Sha awoke to the insistent throbbing of her sex, but even as she reached down to masturbate a distinctly unfeminine musk caught her attention. Her claws came out automatically as she sat up with a start, to find Ilarion standing in the arch of the Lady chamber and a group of burly guards within.

'Be calm,' Ilarion said quietly, 'this is simply a device to ensure that the election goes smoothly and without incident. These are your honour guard, two to each councillor, who will protect you from any possible harm.'

'And ensure that we inflict none,' Tian-Sha answered wryly, 'yet allow me a moment, Master Ilarion, I am somewhat spoiled from the night's pleasures. Oh, and before you wake the others, send a felian to sniff out Pomina among the lower tunnels. You will find she has a strong scent of aromatic bitters. She has been given laudanum and will also be short of memory, so have her taken to Comus for a restorative – Ciriel rather, my mind is not what it might be at present.'

'Your sense of honour does you credit,' Ilarion answered, with a lift of his eyebrows.

'Perhaps,' Tian-Sha answered, 'yet be sure that she knows, and naturally not the others, that I was responsible for her rescue.'

Ilarion gave a soft laugh and signalled to a tall, black-furred oncanthrope among the guards. He nodded gravely and left. Tian-Sha rose and shook her head, then padded softly to the water trough. The cool, clear fluid went some way to clearing her mind, and also to soothing her vulva, although she knew that she would need to visit Ciriel for ointment as soon as was practical. A brief lick completed her toilet, by which time the other female councillors had been roused. None showed more than mild annoyance at the presence of the guards.

Arrangements for the election were made swiftly. The women were escorted to the female council chamber on the level below and the six earthenware vessels taken into the Lady Chamber by Ilarion after each had been carefully shaken to show that it was empty. Tian-Sha sat and sipped brown muscat with a honey cake while the arrangements were made, watching for any possible stratagems among her rivals. None was evident, although when the oncanthrope guard returned with a deeply groggy Pomina both Alla-Sha and Jasiel showed the briefest flickers of annoyance. Comus was the last to appear, dressed in his full black robes of Lordship and wearing a self-satisfied smile. He nodded to each councillor in turn, then went to stand with his back to the window.

'All is prepared?' he began, addressing Ilarion.

'Every detail, my Lord,' Ilarion answered. 'The vessels stand on a table in the Lady Chamber; each is empty. All six female councillors are present, as you see. I myself have the discs, which I shall count out in plain view once the women are naked.'

'Just so,' Comus answered. 'Mistresses, I would be grateful if you could disrobe. We cannot be too careful.'

None objected. Tian-Sha, still nude as she had guessed the need for it, stayed on the couch as the others stripped. A few subdued chuckles greeted the sight of Zara's heavily welted buttocks, but in general decorum was maintained as the six women stripped naked. Ilarion then asked if a search was felt to be necessary and after some debate it was decided to do so. Zara was searched first, bending over a table with her naked, welted bottom thrust high while first Igalia and then Khian-Shu probed her vaginal and anal recesses. She was declared clean and Ilarion then nodded towards Tian-Sha.

'Be careful,' she requested as Igalia approached her. 'I took the Apian torture last night and am somewhat sore.'

'Of course,' Igalia replied. 'If you could open your legs as much as possible it will hurt less.'

Tian-Sha spread her thighs and Igalia applied one thick finger to her vagina. She winced as it went in and made a brief exploration of her cavity, then again as it was drawn slowly out.

'Clear,' Igalia announced.

'And her anus,' Ilarion instructed.

Tian-Sha rolled herself up and took hold of her legs beneath the knees, presenting a clear view of her bottom-hole to the room. Igalia paused to oil her finger and then pressed it to Tian-Sha's anus. Tian-Sha could not restrain a mew as the inflamed sphincter was penetrated and was gritting her teeth as the thick digit made a thorough and deep investigation of her rectum. Only when it was withdrawn and her anus had closed with a sticky sound did she wonder how it might feel to be buggered while her anus was still bee-stung. Shaking her head to rid herself of the disturbing thought, she returned her attention to the room. Pomina had bent and was holding her bottom open as Igalia inserted a finger, producing on Pomina's face a combination of pleasure and embarrassment. Jasiel followed, taking the intimate inspection without the slightest concern, then Soumea and Alla-Sha, both of whom accepted fingers in their most intimate places with serene composure.

'Excellent,' Comus pronounced when all six women had been searched. 'Now we may proceed.'

'A moment,' Tian-Sha put in. 'My stings are really too painful to allow me to concentrate. Could you send to Ciriel for some suitable ointment?'

'Yes, if no one objects and as long as Igalia applies it in plain view,' Comus replied.

'Let her be soothed,' Alla-Sha answered. 'It cannot be a device, for she received the torture by random chance.'

'Just so,' Comus answered and signalled to a guard who nodded and left the chamber.

'Continue,' Tian-Sha stated, 'I have no objection to voting last.'

'Very well,' Comus stated. 'Master Ilarion, perhaps if you could distribute the discs? Mistress Alla-Sha, I believe you enjoy precedence.'

Ilarion inclined his head and dug into the pocket of his robe, from which he extracted six discs, three of bronze and three of silver. These he gave to Alla-Sha in plain view. Alla-Sha rose, naked and poised, and crossed to the stair that ascended to the Lady Chamber. Presently she returned, her face expressionless, and went back to her couch. The process was repeated for Soumea, then Jasiel and Pomina, at which point the guard returned with Ciriel and a vial of cream.

As Zara ascended the stairs Tian-Sha once more spread her thighs to the caress of Igalia's thick, soft fingers and allowed the soothing ointment to be applied to her bee stings. The effect was rapid: first a delicious coolness, then a warmth as the insistent throbbing and itching began to subside. As Zara returned to the chamber she rose to accept her discs from Ilarion. He counted them out into her palm, three of each as had been agreed. Ascending the steps, she found the six vessels set out in a line on the very table to which she had been strapped the previous night. The room still smelt of sex, honey and the other erotic adjuncts they had used and she wrinkled her nose as she crossed quickly to the window. An upward glance revealed the face of Xerafina, half-hidden among the foliage overhanging the parapet.

The six vessels stood side by side on the table, each clearly marked with the symbol of the candidate. Ilarion stood to the rear, calm and stately as the others took their seats. Tian-Sha alone remained standing, her eyes moving quickly and her nose wrinkling to asses the quality of the others' emotions. Their body movements and scents showed feelings similar to her own; excitement, tension and hope balanced by caution and a measure of mistrust.

Reaching out at random, Ilarion chose Jasiel's jar and pressed down with his thumbs to cave in the thin clay seal. He then threw out the contents on to a high-rimmed tray. Three silver discs lay with four bronze and the acyonthrope gave a sigh of disappointment. Lomas reached out to scoop in the discs. Ares, Xerinus' replacement on the male council, tilted the tray to show that it was empty. Ilarion chose another vessel, that of Alla-Sha, and repeated the process, again revealing three silver discs stamped with the distinctive shape of the orthodox S and four of bronze – each bearing an O. Like Jasiel, Alla-Sha gave a deep, sad sigh. Pomina's vessel followed and gave the same result, as did Soumea's.

Tian-Sha glanced at Zara to find the true-girl counting nervously on her fingers as Ilarion took up the second last vessel. Zara's eyes were wide as Ilarion broke the seal of her vessel and tipped it into the tray. Seven discs rolled out, four of silver, three of bronze. Zara's face broke into a broad smile and her eyes scanned the others with a look of both question and mischief. Only Tian-Sha's vessel remained, and as Ilarion took it up she was already smiling. Soumea turned her a wry look, but the others remained intent on the tray as Ilarion broke the seal and spilt the contents. Two bronze discs lay among five silver.

'Then it seems that I must accept the Ladyship of Suza,' Tian-Sha stated.

9

Epilogue

Tian-Sha stood at the window of the Lady Chamber, looking out over Suza and the land beyond. Bright morning sun illuminated the brilliant colours, making them seem brighter still in contrast to the hot sienna of stone and earth. She had risen and washed, then moved to don the rich black garments that marked her rank, only to have her attention drawn to the city, her city. The door gong sounded from below and she turned, calling out even as her sensitive nose detected the characteristic scent of Ilarion. A moment later his head appeared from the stairwell.

'My Lady,' he greeted her with a respect to which she was only beginning to become accustomed.

'Master Ilarion,' she responded. 'Is there anything of import, or is this merely a casual visit?'

'Casual, no more,' he replied. 'I came to see how you found your new place. The accommodation, the appointments – are all to your liking?'

'By and large,' Tian-Sha answered. 'Mistress Alla-Sha's tastes are largely in accord with my own, although, I thought, perhaps a panel of calligraphy would make the long wall less bare and these deep blue drapes suited her fur colour so much better than my own. Black, or a rich green, would be my choice.'

'Just so,' Ilarion stated. 'Allow me to have a present made of both items.'

'You are generous,' Tian-Sha said.

Ilarion made no immediate answer, but turned to examine an arrangement of poppies and cave fern before speaking again.

'A rumour came to me from Alaban this morning,' he stated easily. 'It is said that one of their newly sentenced criminals was spirited away two nights after the full moon. She was an acyonthrope. It is also said that scents suggest the abductress to have been a young tigranthrope. Furthermore, just such a tigranthrope is known to have been in the city claiming to be an apprentice wine merchant of Suza. This is, needless to say, simply a rumour; or it might even be propaganda designed to increase the tension between our cities. In any case the correct policy is clearly to pay no heed to such gossip.'

'A wise course,' Tian-Sha answered, 'and one which I support without reservation.'

'More absurd still,' Ilarion continued, 'is the rumour that the acyonthrope was a skilled metal-smith convicted of forming copies of the Alaban barter coins.'

'Just so,' Tian-Sha agreed.

'Yet,' Ilarion went on, 'this rumour casts an interesting light on a small experiment I ventured to conduct during the vote for the Ladyship. When placing the jars in the Lady Chamber, I incised a small cross on the base of each. Afterwards these had vanished, which seems remarkable.'

'Remarkable indeed,' Tian-Sha agreed.

'The circumstances of your rescue of Pomina and your being the last to cast her vote are less remarkable,' Ilarion said quietly.

'The simple dictates of honour and necessity,' Tian-Sha answered.

'You play well, my Lady,' Ilarion finished. 'You do credit to Suza.'

Tian-Sha responded with an inclination of her head,

then turned to the window that looked out high above the city. Leaning one elbow on the sill, she put her ankles together and pulled in the small of her back. Swishing her tail to one side she ensured that Ilarion had the best possible view of her bottom and also of the details of vulva and anus that her position revealed. For a long moment she held the pose, then turned her head and spoke.

'I am told, Master Ilarion, that you are among the select few who understand the pleasures of sodomy.'

NEW BOOKS

Coming up from Nexus, Sapphire and Black Lace

Discipline of the Private House by Esme Ombreux
January 2000 £5.99 ISBN: 0 352 33459 2
Jem Darke, Mistress of the secretive organisation known as the
Private House, is bored – and rashly accepts a challenge to submit to
the harsh disciplinary regime at the Chateau, where the Chatelaine
and her depraved minions will delight in administering torments and
humiliations designed to make Jem abandon the wager and relinquish
her supreme authority.

The Order by Nadine Somers
January 2000 £5.99 ISBN: 0 352 33460 6
The Comtessa di Diablo is head of the Order, an organisation
devoted to Mádrofh, demonic Mistress of Lust. Tamara Knight and
Max Creed are agents for Omega, a secret government body charged
with investigating the occult. As they enter the twilight world of
depraved practices and unspeakable rituals, the race is on to prevent
the onset of the Final Chaos, the return of Mádrofh and the ushering
in of a slave society over which the Comtessa and her
debauched acolytes will reign supreme.

A Matter of Possession by G.C. Scott
January 2000 £5.99 ISBN: 0 352 33468 1
Under normal circumstances, no woman as stunning as Barbara
Hilson would have trouble finding a man. But Barbara's
requirements are far from the normal. She needs someone who will
take complete control; someone who will impose himself so strongly
upon her that her will dissolves into his. Fortunately, if she can't find
a man to give her what she wants, Barbara has other options: an
extensive collection of bondage equipment, an imagination that
knows no bounds, and, in Sarah, an obliging and very debauched
friend.

The Bond by Lindsay Gordon
February 2000   £5.99   ISBN: 0 352 33480 0
Hank and Missy are not the same as the rest of us. They're on a ride
that never ends, together forever, joined as much by their increasingly
perverse sexual tastes as by their need to satisfy their special needs.
But they're not alone on their journey. The Preacher's after Hank,
and he'll do anything to Missy to get him. The long-awaited third
novel by the author of *Rites of Obedience* and *The Submission
Gallery*.

The Slave Auction by Lisette Ashton
February 2000   £5.99   ISBN: 0 352 33481 9
Austere, masterful and ruthless, dominatrix Frankie has learnt to
enjoy her new life as mistress of the castle. Her days are a paradise
of endless punishments and her nights are filled with cruel retribution.
But with the return of her arch-enemy McGivern, Frankie's haven is
about to be shattered. He is organising a slave auction in which lives
will be altered forever, and his ultimate plan is to regain control of
the castle. As the dominatrix becomes the dominated, Frankie is left
wondering whether things will ever be the same again.

The Pleasure Principle by Maria del Rey
February 2000   £5.99   ISBN: 0 352 33482 7
Sex is deviant. Disgusting. Depraved. Sex is banned. And yet despite
the law, and the Moral Guardians who police it, a sexual underworld
exists which recognises no rule but that of desire. Into this dark world
of the flesh enters Detective Rey Coover, a man who must struggle
with his own instincts to uncover the truth about those who recognise
no limits. Erotica, science fiction and crime collide in one of Maria
del Rey's most imaginative and explicit novels. A Nexus Classic.

A new imprint of lesbian fiction

Getaway by Suzanne Blaylock
October 1999   Price £6.99   ISBN: 0 352 33443 6
Brilliantly talented Polly Sayers had made two big life shifts
concurrently. She's had her first affair with a woman, and she's also
stolen the code of an important new piece of software and made her
break, doing a runner all the way to a seemingly peaceful coastal
community. But things aren't as tranquil as they appear in the haven,
as Polly becomes immersed in an insular group of mysterious but
very attractive women.

No Angel by Marian Malone
November 1999   £6.99   ISBN 0 352 33462 2
Sally longs to test her limits and sample forbidden pleasures, yet she's
frightened by the depth of her yearnings. Her journey of self-
discovery begins in the fetish clubs of Brighton and ultimately leads
to an encounter with an enigmatic female stranger. And now that
she's tasted freedom, there's no way she's going back.

Doctor's Orders by Deanna Ashford
January 2000   £5.99   ISBN: 0 352 33453 3

When Dr Helen Dawson loses her job at a state-run hospital, she is delighted to be offered a position at a private clinic. The staff at the clinic do far more than simply care for the medical needs of their clients, though – they also cater for their sexual needs. Helen soon discovers that this isn't the only secret – there are other, far darker occurrences.

Shameless by Stella Black
January 2000   £5.99   ISBN: 0 352 33467 3

When Stella Black decides to take a holiday in Arizona she doesn't bargain on having to deal with such a dark and weird crowd: Jim, the master who likes his SM hard; Mel, the professional dominatrix with a background in sleazy movies; Rick, the gun-toting cowboy with cold blue eyes; and his psychotic sidekick Bernie. They're not the safest individuals, but that's not what Stella wants. That's not what she's come for.

Cruel Enchantment by Janine Ashbless
February 2000   £5.99   ISBN: 0 352 33483 5

Here are eleven tales of temptation and desire, of longing and fear and consummation; tales which will carry you to other times and other worlds. Worlds of the imagination where you will encounter men and monsters, women and gods. Worlds in which hermits are visited by succubi and angels; in which dragons steal maidens to sate special hungers; in which deadly duels of magic are fought on the battlefield of the naked body and even the dead do not like to sleep alone.

Tongue in Cheek by Tabitha Flyte
February 2000   £5.99   ISBN: 0 352 33484 3

When Sally's relationship ends everything seems to go wrong for her – she can't meet a new man, she's having a bad time at work and she can't seem to make anything work at all. That is, until she starts hanging out around the local sixth-form college, where she finds the boys more than happy to help out – in every way.

NEXUS BACKLIST

All books are priced £5.99 unless another price is given. If a date is supplied, the book in question will not be available until that month in 1999.

CONTEMPORARY EROTICA

THE ACADEMY	Arabella Knight	
AMANDA IN THE PRIVATE HOUSE	Esme Ombreux	
BAD PENNY	Penny Birch	
THE BLACK MASQUE	Lisette Ashton	
THE BLACK WIDOW	Lisette Ashton	
BOUND TO OBEY	Amanda Ware	
BRAT	Penny Birch	
DANCE OF SUBMISSION	Lisette Ashton	Nov
DARK DELIGHTS	Maria del Rey	
DARK DESIRES	Maria del Rey	
DARLINE DOMINANT	Tania d'Alanis	
DISCIPLES OF SHAME	Stephanie Calvin	
THE DISCIPLINE OF NURSE RIDING	Yolanda Celbridge	
DISPLAYS OF INNOCENTS	Lucy Golden	
EMMA'S SECRET DOMINATION	Hilary James	
EXPOSING LOUISA	Jean Aveline	
FAIRGROUND ATTRACTIONS	Lisette Ashton	
GISELLE	Jean Aveline	Oct
HEART OF DESIRE	Maria del Rey	
HOUSE RULES	G.C. Scott	Oct
IN FOR A PENNY	Penny Birch	Nov
JULIE AT THE REFORMATORY	Angela Elgar	
LINGERING LESSONS	Sarah Veitch	

Title	Author	Price	Date
THE MISTRESS OF STERNWOOD GRANGE	Arabella Knight		
ONE WEEK IN THE PRIVATE HOUSE	Esme Ombreux		
THE PALACE OF EROS	Delver Maddingley		
PENNY IN HARNESS	Penny Birch		
THE PLEASURE CHAMBER	Brigitte Markham		
THE RELUCTANT VIRGIN	Kendal Grahame		
RITES OF OBEDIENCE	Lindsay Gordon		
RUE MARQUIS DE SADE	Morgana Baron		
'S' – A JOURNEY INTO SERVITUDE	Philippa Masters		
SANDRA'S NEW SCHOOL	Yolanda Celbridge		Dec
THE SCHOOLING OF STELLA	Yolanda Celbridge		
THE SUBMISSION OF STELLA	Yolanda Celbridge		
THE SUBMISSION GALLERY	Lindsay Gordon		
SUSIE IN SERVITUDE	Arabella Knight		
TAKING PAINS TO PLEASE	Arabella Knight		
A TASTE OF AMBER	Penny Birch		
THE TEST	Nadine Somers		
THE TRAINING OF FALLEN ANGELS	Kendal Grahame		
VIRGINIA'S QUEST	Katrina Young	£4.99	

ANCIENT & FANTASY SETTINGS

Title	Author	Price	Date
THE CASTLE OF MALDONA	Yolanda Celbridge		
THE FOREST OF BONDAGE	Aran Ashe		
NYMPHS OF DIONYSUS	Susan Tinoff	£4.99	
TIGER, TIGER	Aishling Morgan		Dec
THE WARRIOR QUEEN	Kendal Grahame		

EDWARDIAN, VICTORIAN & OLDER EROTICA

Title	Author	Price	Date
ANNIE	Evelyn Culber		
ANNIE AND THE COUNTESS	Evelyn Culber		
BEATRICE	Anonymous		
CONFESSIONS OF AN ENGLISH SLAVE	Yolanda Celbridge		Sep
THE CORRECTION OF AN ESSEX MAID	Yolanda Celbridge		

THE GOVERNESS AT ST AGATHA'S	Yolanda Celbridge	
THE MASTER OF CASTLELEIGH	Jacqueline Bellevois	Aug
PRIVATE MEMOIRS OF A KENTISH HEADMISTRESS	Yolanda Celbridge	£4.99
THE RAKE	Aishling Morgan	Sep
THE TRAINING OF AN ENGLISH GENTLEMAN	Yolanda Celbridge	

SAMPLERS & COLLECTIONS

EROTICON 4	Various	
THE FIESTA LETTERS	ed. Chris Lloyd	£4.99
NEW EROTICA 3		
NEW EROTICA 4	Various	
A DOZEN STROKES	Various	Aug

NEXUS CLASSICS
A new imprint dedicated to putting the finest works of erotic fiction back in print

THE IMAGE	Jean de Berg	
CHOOSING LOVERS FOR JUSTINE	Aran Ashe	
THE INSTITUTE	Maria del Rey	
AGONY AUNT	G. C. Scott	
THE HANDMAIDENS	Aran Ashe	
OBSESSION	Maria del Rey	
HIS MASTER'S VOICE	G.C. Scott	Aug
CITADEL OF SERVITUDE	Aran Ashe	Sep
BOUND TO SERVE	Amanda Ware	Oct
BOUND TO SUBMIT	Amanda Ware	Nov
SISTERHOOD OF THE INSTITUTE	Maria del Rey	Dec

Please send me the books I have ticked above.

Name ....

Address ....

....

....

.... Post code..................

Send to: Cash Sales, Nexus Books, Thames Wharf Studios, Rainville Road, London W6 9HT

US customers: for prices and details of how to order books for delivery by mail, call 1-800-805-1083.

Please enclose a cheque or postal order, made payable to **Nexus Books**, to the value of the books you have ordered plus postage and packing costs as follows:

UK and BFPO – £1.00 for the first book, 50p for the second book and 30p for each subsequent book to a maximum of £3.00;

Overseas (including Republic of Ireland) – £2.00 for the first book, £1.00 for the second book and 50p for each subsequent book.

We accept all major credit cards, including VISA, ACCESS/MASTERCARD, AMEX, DINERS CLUB, SWITCH, SOLO, and DELTA. Please write your card number and expiry date here:

....

Please allow up to 28 days for delivery.

Signature ....